3000AD

3000AD

T.D. Presland

authorHOUSE®

AuthorHouse™
1663 Liberty Drive
Bloomington, IN 47403
www.authorhouse.com
Phone: 1-800-839-8640

First published by AuthorHouse   10/25/2011

ISBN: 978-1-4567-9383-8 (sc)
ISBN: 978-1-4567-9384-5 (ebk)

Printed in the United States of America

Any people depicted in stock imagery provided by Thinkstock are models, and such images are being used for illustrative purposes only.
Certain stock imagery © Thinkstock.

This book is printed on acid-free paper.

This book is dedicated to my parents, for their endless support, constructive criticism and encouragement. It has not gone unnoticed. Thank you.

PART ONE

The Town
2987-2996AD

My friends we are at the beginning of the end.

Our lands have been torn apart through war, famine, disease. Our children are uneducated; the sick are not cared for. Our natural world has almost been destroyed, leaving us with a waste ground; devoid of hope, devoid of love, devoid of God. But God has not forsaken you. I am the last hope, the last saviour of mankind. I say today, the same words I spoke three thousand years ago. I am the Way, the Truth and the Life. He who believes in me shall not die, but have everlasting life. There is a way out, a way forward, a way to redemption. That redemption lies with me . . .

1

That speech, twelve years ago, was the start of everything. The Messiah seemed to gaze directly at us through the screen. He could have been speaking to us, imploring us, calling us, almost begging us to save ourselves.

Back then I was a child, with no appreciation for the years of turmoil that would follow, but even then I felt some premonition; that somehow this man would be instrumental in our destinies, for better or worse.

The image was cut off and replaced by that of a man hanging lifeless on barbed wire. There was a caption:

"YOU WANT TO KNOW WHAT AWAITS YOU OUTSIDE?"

My father scoffed in his chair. 'Whoever believes in such stuff?' he retorted. '"I am the Way, the Truth and the Life". What is he going on about?'

'Sylvia says the Ministry is getting close to blocking these transmissions,' said my mother.

'Well it can't come soon enough,' said my father. 'These are dangerous times.'

This was an oft repeated phrase of my father's: 'these are dangerous times', but I couldn't quite understand why. As long as you played by the rules, everything was fine, everything was simple. This desolate world that the Messiah talked about did not seem real to me. It existed outside of our town. We saw it on the TV and were warned often of it in school.

The Outside was bad, the Outside was dangerous. There was nothing Outside which could possibly be of any interest to us whatsoever; at least that is what we were told. We had everything we could possibly need in our town. We had an education. We were taught mathematics, languages, history, science, nutrition, exercise, architecture and citizenship.

We had enough to eat; we had trees and plants. One of my friends at school even had a pineapple tree. The fruit was delicious and we used to go there to have pineapple parties. That was until his mother was found to have been engaging in subversive activity. She had been a secret musician. She had a long thin piece of wood which she had been blowing into and showing it to the rest of her family. Rumour has it they were caught right in the act, dancing around the living room. "Imbeciles", my mother had called them. The next day they had disappeared and were never heard of again. Mind you, everyone had always said there was something a bit strange about that family.

The next day I was walking to school with my younger brother, David and worrying about what we had seen on the screen the night before. What had worried me was the fact that David had watched the screen so closely and had been completely silent. In fact he was silent the rest of the night and that could be a dangerous sign. Silence suggested thinking and I knew how impressionable he could be. He was only nine years old at the time and I was twelve. Not much older, but old enough to be able to discern the truth from fiction, the reality from the fantasy. Childish fantasies were normally crushed out of us by the time we reached our teens. There was certainly a higher expectation for me then there was for him, but I wanted to nip this particular fantasy in the bud straight away. I could sense him mulling it over in his mind, the lie perpetuating itself over and over.

'David, you do know this Messiah is fake, don't you?' I asked him

David just shrugged his shoulders, his head still hanging down.

'David.' I put a hand on my shoulder to stop him and he looked up at me. 'It's very important you don't talk about this, to anyone. Do you understand?'

'But why not?' said David.

'It's dangerous.'

'But what if it is true?' he asked.

'It's not, David, trust me.' I struggled to find a way to explain this to him. He wasn't getting it at all.

'You know you used to have an imaginary friend,' I said.

'Yes.'

'And you know that this friend wasn't real, don't you?'

'I suppose so,' said David.

As I remembered Mother had locked him in the cellar whenever 'Thomas' was mentioned. David was petrified of the dark and while he was kicking and screaming in there, Mother would shout through the door that if Thomas was real, why didn't *he* let him out. David would then shout back that Thomas was locked in there with him. Eventually David learnt not to mention Thomas in front of our parents again but I still heard him talk to him in the middle of the night for a while after.

'Well God is no more real than Thomas. He's just a make believe friend who some people pretend to talk to. You understand now?'

David nodded and I breathed a sigh of relief. I thought that might just be the end of it.

Over lunch the Messiah's latest message had caused a ripple of excitement amongst my friends. We sat in the refectory at school and discussed it amongst ourselves. As much as we all dismissed him as a superstitious lunatic; there was something thrillingly dangerous about superstitious lunacy.

'I've heard these Christians were cannibals,' said Jackson, with a mischievous glint in his eye.

'What?' we all said in disbelief.

'This guy that they all go on about, Jesus. He told them to eat his flesh and drink his blood, and that's what they all did in their churches for centuries after.'

'Well whose blood and flesh would they eat then, Jackson?' I asked him.

'They'd pick on someone each week to sacrifice,' said Jackson. 'They'd nail him to a cross like they did with Jesus and then they'd carve him up and eat him.'

'That's disgusting!' said Vincent, a tall beanpole of a boy. 'You've got a sick mind, Jackson.'

The rest of us nodded in solemn agreement as Vincent was generally accepted as the leader, but Jackson was not to be deterred.

'Why do you think they all wore those crosses?' he continued. 'Cannibals the lot of them.'

This inspired a lot of joke retching amongst my friends until we were glared at by one of the teachers. We hushed up for a bit, then Vincent leaned forward and motioned for us to do the same. He gestured towards a small boy sitting on his own.

'Hargreaves,' he whispered. 'Has been writing *poetry*.'

. . . . and I felt a chill run down my spine.

Poetry and stories were my secret vice. Even though we had been warned of its dangers, I had grown attached to the power of the written word; its rhythm and rhyme, the way it could encapsulate a feeling or emotion. I loved reading, especially my astronomy books. It was my escape. Even though I could never know what existed on my own planet, at least I could read about the surface of Jupiter, or the dark side of the moon.

Once I had watched the sunset through my bedroom window and felt a sort of emotion. I couldn't understand why it had made me feel this way. I knew the sun was a giant star, which the planet was orbiting. I knew that it supported life even though some said it would end up killing us due to our depleting ozone layer. There was no reason to feel emotional about an inanimate ball of gas burning in space, but I did anyway. It was something about how it just carried on supporting us, continuously over billions of years. It seemed so perfectly symmetrical as it sunk down beneath the horizon, its reflection shimmering in the body of water that was forever the furthest thing I could see.

I used to fantasise about escaping the town with my family and going to that body of water. We could use a boat to get out onto the water. Then we could lie back and eat a picnic as the setting sun shone down on us. We could look at the stars and the moon and feel absolutely free. The boat could carry us off to a strange and magical land where anything was possible, where you could speak your mind and sing your heart. Where you could dance and sing and tell poetry and tell each other stories and play games.

I wrote this whole scenario down into my notebook. My first ever story which I called "The Secret Lands". I stuffed it under my mattress and went to bed. My mind was buzzing with this wonderful idea of escape, my whole body was tingling, thinking of this illicit document, hidden away underneath me. I longed to share this idea with someone. The question burned deep within: "What did lie beyond the boundaries of the town?"

Of course we were told in school, on TV, that the Outside world was a terrible, dangerous place. Not only that, but the people were nothing more than Neolithic creatures, engaging in all sorts of depraved, primitive behaviour. We were all told that we were very lucky to be in the best possible place and there was nothing Outside which would be of any interest at all. It couldn't escape my mind however that none of us had ever seen the Outside at all. How could anyone know these things about the Outside? Where did they get this information from?

The body of water in the horizon, stretched between two clumps of black trees, appearing no bigger than the length of my index finger; that, and the setting sun became the focal point for these curiosities. Someday, I thought, I will go to that water. I will be the first person ever, in the history of the town to break through the armed barricades and see the Outside. I longed to talk about this with someone, but who could I tell? David was forever being punished by our mother for his flights of fancy and I felt too much of a sense of responsibility to encourage his imagination any further. Obviously the same treatment would be meted out to me if I told Mother so I decided to confide in my father. My father never punished David when he pretended to be a space invader or even when "Thomas" made an unwelcome entry into our home. He would merely sigh and say 'not this nonsense again,' as my mother dragged David off to the cellar and berated my father for his lack of parental concern. Maybe, I thought if I caught my father at the right time I could share this idea with him.

I seized my moment when my mother had gone out to a meeting. My mother worked for the Public Information Agency and they were working on another campaign to avoid subversive behaviour. David was in bed asleep.

I was sitting there next to my father and we were watching a film about the gestation of whales. The question was burning inside me and I realised it was now or never.

'Father,' I asked him.

'Yes, Richard,' my father said stirring himself in his seat.

'Have you ever wondered what's Outside?'

'Outside where?' My father looked at me seriously and I began to feel quite afraid but I had gone too far to backtrack now.

'Outside the town,' I whispered. I held my breath and waited for his reaction. Would he shout at me, lock me in the cellar? After an awkward pause he did neither. I felt his hand gently rest on my shoulders and I breathed again.

'What made you think of this?' he said with a sigh.

'I've just wondered,' I started, then stopped to reconsider. Was this such a good idea after all?

'Go on,' my father coaxed.

'We see these things on the TV and are told about these things, but if we never see them for ourselves, how can we know?'

'Yes,' said my father, and for a second my heart leaped for joy. He understands, I thought. At last there is someone I can talk to, I'm not alone.

'It is natural to wonder about these things, but what you will learn as you get older is it is better just to shut it from your mind.'

'But how can you do that, Father. What if the Outside is a wonderful place?'

'We have to accept what we are told, Richard. Questioning it, will only lead to pain and this I do know. We live well here, why risk throwing it all away?'

Then I had an idea and ran upstairs to my room. Pulling the tattered notebook from under my mattress I ran back down and showed it to him. Surely this will make him understand. This was all I wanted to say, which I didn't have the courage to actually speak out loud. My father took the notebook off me and my heart glowed with anticipation. Then I saw his eyes change and turn hard. He looked up from the pages and glowered at me, his face like thunder. I don't think I had ever seen him look so angry before.

'What is this?' he roared. I looked down at the floor, unable to say or do anything.

He pressed his fingers into his forehead and sat down. He looked at me again, his eyes still hard.

'Do you know how hard your mother and I work for you and your brother?'

'Yes father,' I murmured.

'Then why—' he stopped and made an effort to compose himself. 'Why do you do this and threaten to ruin it all?'

'I'm sorry Father.'

He handed the book back to me. 'Rip it up!'

I looked down at it and cried.

'Rip it up!' he bellowed.

With my face burning and my eyes welling up I did as I was told.

'Your brother is young; I would expect such things from him. But you Richard.' He shook his head in disgust and I felt genuinely ashamed.

'I would have expected more from you.'

'I'm sorry Father.'

'No more of this now,' Father said. 'Don't speak of this to anyone, you hear? Not to your friends, not to your mother and certainly not to David.'

'Yes Father.'

'And I don't want to hear of it either. You are old enough to stop this childish way of thinking and focus on the real world.'

'Yes Father.'

Then he walked off muttering and the matter was never raised again.

2

That same evening we had to go to Vincent's house. Vincent's mother, Sylvia worked with my mother in the Public Information Agency. They would often have these meetings to discuss the latest catastrophe to hit our town. Vincent's father was an Enforcer. He had a very senior position in the Enforcers which gave him a huge amount of status; as did his huge physique and bushy moustache. He was a man of few words who always seemed to be a bit of an enigma. I often wondered what actually happened when someone disappeared and this man was the one that actually carried it out. Vincent himself idolised him. 'My father will sort them out,' was a phrase he used often, towards somebody who he suspected of some kind of subversion, or who had just displeased him in some way. This of course gave Vincent himself a huge amount of status, which he continuously lorded over everyone. When Sylvia opened the door to greet us, he was standing just behind her, leaning against the wall, eyeing us with a kind of smug contempt.

'Oh Francis, do come in,' said Sylvia to my mother. 'And how your boys have grown,' she said looking at me and David. I saw Vincent's lip curl as I walked past him. 'They'll both be assets to the town, I can tell,' continued Sylvia, oblivious.

'They're good boys,' said my mother. 'Richard came top in his class for astronomy.'

'Oh, how nice,' said Sylvia. 'Trevor never cottoned onto astronomy that much. A bit too otherworldly for him.'

Out the corner of my eye I saw Vincent pulling on David's ear lobe and David repressing a cry of pain.

'John,' Sylvia addressed my father. 'I'm sure Alfred would like to speak to you upstairs.' My father smiled as he trotted upstairs to see Vincent's father. My father worked for the Enforcers in an administrative capacity; although what he actually did was shrouded in mystery.

'And I'm sure you boys don't want to hear us women talk,' said Sylvia. 'Why not go into the garden? I'll bring out some drinks later. I'm sure you've lots to discuss.'

We went out into the sunshine and saw Jackson there, grinning as always.

'Hey Stirling,' he said. 'How's business?'

'The business is as it has always been,' answered Vincent for me. 'Sick and depraved. This town is being over run by perverts, Stirling. You know it and I know it.'

I sat down on the grass and David sat next to me.

'What do you know of Hargreaves, Stirling,' Vincent asked me.

'Not much,' I said with a shrug. 'His parents are merchants I think.'

'His parents are merchants of filth,' said Vincent. 'My father's onto them. He's been studying them for years; Hargreaves and his revolting family. They've been doing it all. Music, dancing, story telling. I've heard they've even been . . .' he leaned forward, speaking the next words as if they had a bitter taste on his tongue . . . 'worshipping religious idols.'

Jackson let out a hiss between his teeth and shook his head. He may have been my best friend, but he was an ingratiating little creep at times.

'What will they do to him?' asked David. I groaned inside. Only David would have asked such an obvious question; the question you never asked.

'Words cannot describe,' said Vincent as he leaned into David's face and swirled his hands around like a wizard. David looked a little stunned and then carried on picking at the grass.

12

'They're history!' squealed Jackson, breaking the silence.

'Good riddance,' said Vincent. ' . . . and what *are* you doing?'

Vincent was looking at my brother who had a chain of daisies lying across his lap. I went cold. Vincent glared at me and I turned to David and smacked him over the head. David looked at me in disbelief. I hit him again which made him cry.

I looked to see Vincent's look of approval, then a voice called out behind me.

'Drinks boys.' It was Sylvia arriving with a tray of drinks. I snatched the daisy chain off David and stuffed it under my leg. I grabbed hold of his arm and shook him to stop him crying.

'Must be thirsty work all this talking,' said Sylvia, putting the tray down.

I caught Vincent's look of disdain and that was when I realised, for the first time, that I actually hated him.

3

'They're really up in arms about the Messiah,' said Mother, when we returned home. She took a handful of books from her bag and placed them on the table. I looked at one of them. It was entitled CHRISTIANALITY: THE EVIL OF OUR TIMES. 'They—are—furious,' she emphasised.

'Really?' grunted my father.

'Well, the audacity of it,' said Mother. 'How dare he think he can warp our minds like this?'

'Haven't they found a way to block the signal yet,' said Father.

'Not yet,' said Mother. 'But they will do, I'm sure of that.'

'Mother, I'm tired,' said David. 'May I go to my room?'

'Yes, David, go on up.'

Mother continued on her tirade about the ominous threat of the Messiah whilst Father watched a film about the gestation of giraffes. After about forty minutes the screen went black and a message in bold white capitals announced a broadcast from the Public Information Agency.

'Francis,' I think this is one of yours,' said Father.

Mother returned to the living room clutching her hands together in nervous anticipation.

'I do hope they got the editing right,' she said. 'Bill does tend to be a little lax at times.'

An image of the Messiah came onto the screen. Then he began to speak. It was a version of his last broadcast spliced up.

'My friends. War lies with me. Famine lies with me. Disease lies with me. I am devoid of hope, devoid of love, devoid of God. I have forsaken you. He who believes in me shall die. He who believes in me shall die. He who believes in me shall die . . . .'

The last sentence repeated over and over. A caption appeared on the screen:

'THE TRUE MESSAGE OF THE MESSIAH.'

'Excellent!' said Mother, clapping her hands in joy. 'It's perfect, you'd never know.'

'It's not a bad job,' agreed Father.

'May I go to my room now Mother,' I said. 'I'm quite tired now.'

'Oh if you must,' said Mother without looking at me. 'But no messing around up there.'

I went up to the room I shared with my brother and found David there, lying on his bed, looking up at the ceiling.

'What are you doing,' I asked him.

'Nothing,' he replied, turning to face the wall.

'You're not still upset with me about earlier,' I said, shaking his arm. 'You know what Vincent's like. You brought that on yourself.'

I saw David's shoulder blades rise and heard a sniff.

'Do you want a story?' I asked.

'No.'

Stories used to be a secret thing between the two of us. I would think up of a wild tale of some scary make-believe creature. I would make wild gestures with my hands to scare him and he would sit there, goggle-eyed, soaking it all in. Then when I had finished I would tell him if he told anyone, the creature would come to get him in the middle of the night. This was sufficient enough threat to keep him quiet till the next story. David was always up for a secret scary story, but not now.

'This Messiah is an awful man,' I said. 'Mother always says so.'

'How does she know,' said David, turning round to look at me.

'Mother knows everything,' I said. 'She has connections and they know everything he's been up to.'

'What's that?'

'I've heard . . . 'I thought back to what Jackson had said earlier. 'I've heard he eats your flesh and drinks your blood.'

'Really!' said David, his eyes widening. I seized on the opportunity.

'He sneaks into your room in the middle of the night and—' I suddenly grabbed him under the arm and he let out a little scream and giggled. I hushed him up quickly and he looked at me quite concerned.

'Will you stop him, Richard?'

'Yes I can stop him,' I said with the authority that only a big brother could have. 'He's no match for me, but first I need you to promise me something.'

'What's that Richard?' He pulled himself up and sat cross legged on the bed. His eyes fixed me in that awe struck way that had always made me feel so important and so powerful. I knew I had him back now. I had pulled one back from the Messiah.

'Never tell anyone about this—ever,' I said fixing his eye.

'I won't, Richard.'

'Promise?'

'Promise.'

Later on when I was just getting off to sleep I heard a loud whisper from across the room.

'Richard.'

'What?'

'Should I not talk to "him" either?'

'Who?'

'You know HIM.'

'No.' I said. 'Definitely not.

4

Three years went by without us being overly concerned with the Messiah at all. There were a few more messages coming through on the TV network, but I was satisfied that David had got over that phase in his life. He had acquired an interest in chemistry, especially in how certain substances would react. He had taken great pleasure in relaying a story in how the teacher had created an explosion by sealing frozen carbon dioxide and water into a plastic container.

I meanwhile, had become top in my class at quantum mechanics and astronomy. I had certificates all over my bedroom wall praising my aptitude in this field.

For some reason nothing happened to Hargreaves and his idol worshipping, music loving, poetry writing family. I would see Hargreaves, picking his delicate way around the school, his glasses looking like they would fall off at any moment, books piled up in his arms. He would normally sit alone. Nobody would want to be associated with him.

One day however I was sitting at lunch with Vincent and his gang when we saw Hargreaves sitting with two other boys. One of them was called Killinger, a blond haired, blue eyed boy who was so effeminate everyone suspected him to be a homosexual. Not that that was a crime in itself but it was often thought that homosexuals had a tendency towards the artistic design of clothing and dancing to music. The other boy was called Roberts who was without doubt the most dim-witted boy in the town. Once in class he couldn't even explain Einstein's theory of basic relativity.

Vincent glowered at them all from across the room. 'Look at them all!' he muttered. 'Talking about their next prayer group, no doubt.'

The other boys, including me, nodded with an equal look of contempt. I couldn't afford anyone to suspect me and I was already playing with fire by writing little haikus in my room. I would destroy them all immediately but it was still a dangerous game. I was getting to the age now when it wouldn't be let go and I could risk myself and my family if I was caught.

Later, as I was walking down the corridor I saw Hargreaves, weaving his usual tentative way through the crowds and I suddenly felt quite angry. Why did people have to rock the status quo? Why couldn't they just be satisfied with the way things were? In that moment I wanted to kill everyone who had ridiculous spiritual or artistic notions. I despised myself for writing those stupid little poems in that book. Who did I think I was—jeopardising my family like that. I wouldn't let this idiot do the same thing.

I caught up with Hargreaves and shoved him into the toilets. He screamed like a little girl and shielded his face with his hands as I shoved him into the wall.

'Listen you idiot, they're onto you! They know all about what you and your stupid family are doing. Don't you realise?'

Hargreaves just cringed and blubbed and I slapped him around the face, knocking his glasses off.

'They're going to kill you, stupid!' I screamed in his face. 'I'm the one trying to help you here, don't you understand?'

Hargreaves was quiet now. He just stood there looking down at the floor, his face puckered up. I picked up his glasses and gave them back to him. He took them silently, but still wouldn't look at me.

'Just quit it, Hargreaves,' I said softly. 'You can't win. You can never win.'

On the way home I split from the others and saw David there leaning against a tree, looking up at the sky. The sun was setting and looking very symmetrical. It made me shudder every time I saw it now. David turned and smiled when he saw me.

'How was school?' I asked.

'It was ok,' he said.

'Did you learn much?'

'We learnt about molecular density,' he said.

'Oh, what did you learn about molecular density.' I would always try and test him, to make sure he had been paying attention.

'We learnt that water molecules are very small.'

'Oh, how small?'

'If you cup your hand with water, there are more molecules in your hand than there are grains of sand in the whole world.'

'Oh that's very good.' I saw him smile slightly, impressed with his own cleverness.

'And how many is that?' I continued.

David spread his arms and puffed his cheeks out.

'The answer is six, followed by twenty three zeros,' I informed him. 'And we learnt that by year three.'

'Oh—and what do you call the number six with twenty three zeros?'

'Don't cheek your big brother,' I said. 'And what else did you learn about molecular density.'

'There are seven types in the human body. Water, protein, lipid . . .' he paused and then shrugged.

'RNA, DNA and other organic and inorganic types,' I finished for him. 'And we learnt that by year five. Don't they teach you anything these days?'

We walked in silence for a while. I could sense David planning something. Then he suddenly tapped me on the arm and ran away.

'You're it!'

I groaned and looked around to make sure nobody was looking before I chased after him but he was hiding already. I was feeling slightly nervous about being caught but there was still a childish part of me that still enjoyed these stupid games and the adult part reasoned that it perhaps got it out of his system. I crept up to some bushes and peered round them when someone kicked me from behind. I whirled round to see David there laughing his head off. I chased after and grabbed him, grinding my fist into his scalp until he yelled out in mock pain.

'You're going to get us *killed* one day.'

'I'm sorry,' he said, still laughing.

'You *will* be,' I said.

As we walked back I could sense David simmering down and starting to worry.

'Do you think I'll really get us killed?' he asked in the end.

'No,' I said. 'But you do need to be careful.'

'Are you going to tell Mother and Father?'

'Don't be ridiculous, of course I won't.'

We carried on walking a bit further.

'Do you hate me, Richard?'

'Why would you ask such a stupid thing?' I said.

'It's just you're often telling me off, like Mother and Father.'

'And you think that means I hate you?'

David shrugged.

'It's because I'm your big brother and I have to look out for you. You understand?'

David nodded. 'Yes, I'm sorry Richard.'

'Well can you stop asking stupid questions now?'

'Ok.'

We walked for a bit in silence.

'Did you really not know I was there?'

'Of course I did, you're useless at that game.'

He tapped me again and ran. I chased him until we got home. Then we put our serious faces on.

5

The plan was set for after school the following day. We sat and discussed it over lunch.

'I don't want any quitters,' said Vincent. 'I could pull strings on any one of you remember. I've got connections, so *don't* let me down.'

I could see Jackson looking decidedly queasy at the whole idea. I for one had got better at disguising my emotions.

'But do we have to go *that* far?' he said.

Vincent turned on him, his eyes were like daggers.

'I haven't got any time for weaklings, Jackson. This town is full of weaklings. That's why it's being overturned with filth. As far as I'm concerned if you're not with us, you're against us.'

I could see Jackson's face turn a new shade of pale and I actually thought for a moment he might vomit right there and then over the desk. There was an uneasy silence as we waited for Jackson's answer. We all knew what would happen if it wasn't to Vincent's liking. Jackson swallowed and nodded and I could feel the collective sigh of relief. One of the boys, Frampton, slapped him on the back.

'It's the right thing to do, Jackson.'

'It's the *only* thing to do,' said Vincent. 'Remember this is a war and there are only two sides; the right side and the wrong side. And if anyone gets on the wrong side of me . . .' Vincent cocked his head to one side and glowered at us all. It was something no one planned to do.

That afternoon after school I met David for the walk home as usual. The conversation during lunchtime had plagued me so much I hadn't been able to concentrate during quantum mechanics which was my favourite lesson.

'David,' I told him. 'Tomorrow you can't meet me after school, ok?'

'Why not?' he asked.

'I can't say, just trust me will you. Go straight home.'

David looked puzzled but agreed anyway.

'Promise me David. Don't wait here. Go straight home.'

'Ok,' he said. 'What shall I tell Mother and Father?'

'What?'

'If I get back before you, they'll wonder why.'

'I don't know,' I said. 'Just tell them I'm doing some extra home work.'

'Is that what you're doing?'

'Yes.'

'No it's not.'

'David, can you just say it.'

'Ok,' he shrugged.

The conversation didn't arise again for the rest of the journey home. When we got there, my father was watching a programme about the gestation of crocodiles. 'Hello boys, how was school?'

'It was fine,' I said.

David didn't say anything but sat straight down at the table and pulled out his homework.

'The Enforcers have been busy today,' said my father without taking his eyes off the screen.

'Really?' I said, watching a male crocodile mount a female one. Crocodiles must have been very good at gestation as they only became extinct five hundred years ago.

'Music lovers,' said my father. 'Ten of them. At this rate there won't be anyone left in this town.'

I thought back to the body of water that lay on the horizon and felt a longing for it. I wondered if that's where all the people that disappeared went.

'Where's Mother?' I asked.

'She's at one of her meetings. Someone was found with subversive literature recently. A story book. They're trying to find out where it came from . . . oh here we go.'

The humping crocodiles had been phased out of the picture and were replaced with horizontal white lines. Then the screen cleared to show the face which had become equated with death in our town. The milky blue eyes, the raggedy beard, the long unkempt hair. He was wearing a white gown with a blue robe over it. I noticed a very slight scar down the side of his cheek and wondered how that had happened.

'Friends this is a war,' he began.

Where had I heard that before?

'A holy war of astronomical proportions. As I said, my brothers and sisters. As I said three thousand years ago I did not come to bring peace to the world I came to bring a sword. We are fighting for the souls of the world. Fighting for eternal life. The world is coming to an end, of that there is incontrovertible evidence. But this world is just the beginning. This world is just the training ground for eternity. The choice is simple. Eternal bliss or eternal damnation. Eternal sunshine or eternal darkness.

Heaven or hell. Life or death.'

I glanced over at David but he hadn't looked up from his work.

'The path to salvation is not an easy one. Some of you will have to take it alone. Some of you may have friends or family that will not see the light. That will not accept God's everlasting love. Brothers and sisters I urge you. Be faithful to the one true Father. Maker of Heaven and Earth. Place your head on his alter and pray for his forgiveness. Pledge allegiance to the one true Church. Pledge your allegiance to me.'

The screen went blank and shortly afterwards the crocodiles returned. I felt numb, I couldn't move. My father sat still next to me and didn't say a word. I looked round and saw David had gone. I left and went quietly up to mine and David's bedroom. I stood outside the door and heard whispering. I hoped it wasn't David praying.

6

The next morning we were called into the hall. A huge picture of the Messiah was on the back wall. The principal walked in and motioned for us to sit down. He was a man of about forty, bald and overweight. He began by taking off his glasses and picking up a large stick. Then he began to beat the cloth picture over and over; his bald head seemed to glow all the more redder through the exertion of it. Then he stopped and looked at us.

'Filth!' he screeched, his eyes bulging out their sockets. He pointed at the cloth picture of the Messiah which was shrouded in dust. It made the Messiah somehow look even the more mystical. 'Liar!' he shrieked again.

He turned to face us and put his glasses back on. He put the stick down in the corner, and paced up and down in front of us all. He reminded me of a huge caged beast which had gone mad.

'Many of you will have seen the disturbing images on the screen last night,' he said. 'This *charlatan* who claims to be the Son of *God*. Who claims that the world will soon end. Who claims that *he* is the saviour of mankind. What arrogant nonsense is this? Worse still I hear that he is attracting a following in this very town. This town that our forefathers built with their own hands. This town whose values are steeped in reason, not superstition. Fact, not fiction; science not so called spirituality.

'Let me assure you. There is no God, there is no heaven or hell, there is no Messiah. The world is not going to end for another five billion years and this hypocrite shall not cloud our reasoned mind with dangerous, subversive falsities.'

Some of the older boys let out a whoop of support which prompted everyone else to do the same. The principal looked stony faced and gestured for us all to be quiet.

'Be under no illusion,' he said. 'There are traitors in our midst. Those who would spit in the face of our forefathers to follow this dangerous lunatic. Those who would choose fantasy over reality and scourge this fine town with their lies. Let me tell you, if you are amongst us now, you have no place to hide. The fine people of this town will not tolerate you. You will be rooted out and pay the penalty for your perversion.'

This was followed by some more fervent cheering.

'I ask the rest of you to stay on your guard,' the principal continued as he quietened the din.

'The traitors could be anyone. It could be the student standing next to you, it could be your closest friend or a member of your family, but I implore you.' He raised a finger up to the sky.

'If you know—or even suspect *anyone* of subversive activity; do not shelter them. Do not be a party to their misdeeds. Come forward and speak. These miscreants must have no place to hide.'

This prompted some more prompted cheering and the principal took the stick and beat the picture a few more times before walking out the room. A crowd of students then gathered around the picture to take turns at having a swipe at the picture with the stick. In amongst the chaos I could sense Jackson standing next to me. I couldn't help noticing that he looked rather pale. At lunchtime, he came and sat opposite me. His hands were shaking as he bolted down his food. Not far from us sat Hargreaves and his two friends, Killinger and Roberts. They were huddled together and seemed to be talking rather earnestly. I could sense Jackson looking at them out the corner his eye.

'Get a grip on yourself, Jackson,' I muttered. 'Or they'll start suspecting you.'

'I can't help it, Stirling' he whimpered. 'I can't get it out of my head.'

I looked him in the eye and levelled with him. His eyes were shifting all around and his face was white. He looked dangerously close to floundering.

'If you don't watch it,' I said. 'You'll get the same as them.'

Jackson wiped his face with his hands and seemed to be getting control.

'You know what will happen if Vincent thinks you're cracking,' I said again.

'I know, I know. It's just . . . don't you sometimes feel there is something else out there?' Jackson looked at me earnestly, begging me to agree with him. It reminded me of the conversation I had had with my father all those years ago. Was he trying to find some solidarity like I was? It crossed my mind that this may be a trap. How did I know he wouldn't be reporting straight back to Vincent. This could have been all set up by Vincent as far as I knew. In fact, as I looked into his searching eyes this seemed to be the most likely explanation.

'Shut up, Jackson.'

'But think about it. What if the Messiah is right?'

'He's not. He's a false teacher, just like the principal said.'

'Don't you ever question what the principal says?'

'No.'

Jackson glanced around the room before leaning into me. 'I can hear him calling me sometimes, Stirling,' he said. 'I can hear it in my sleep.'

I stood up to walk away at that point and walked straight into Vincent. He eyed me coldly. 'Don't forget tonight,' he said.

'I won't,' I said.

7

What we were planning was deeply wrong, of that I had no doubt. Hargreaves, Killinger and Roberts and done nothing to me or to Vincent, or anyone for that matter. The simple truth was that Vincent didn't like them; and when Vincent didn't like someone, that person was for it. Unfortunately Vincent would never act alone but make sure all of his gang, of which I was a sorry member, complied with his plan. No one could go against Vincent's will; nobody. Not only did he have a mind which only went in one direction and the self possession of someone twice his age, but his father was the Chief of Enforcement. He was the son of Death itself and that commands the sort of authority that is both loathsome and insurmountable. That is why myself, Jackson and three others were there alongside Vincent when we cornered the three miscreants after school. Even Jackson seemed to have got over his previous misgivings.

Vincent glowered at the three unfortunates. I thought there was a slight smirk in the corner of his mouth.

'So, you want to worship God do you,' he said, spitting in the dirt.

Roberts shook his head, his eyes like a doe eyed cow.

'Don't try and lie to me,' said Vincent, shaking his head. 'I know what you are.'

Killinger spoke up, his voice quavering: 'I think there was some mistake—'

'There's no mistake!' Vincent exploded, his face turning red. 'You are all in it together. You're lucky I'm not getting my father involved in this. I'm letting you off lightly.'

Vincent looked at me and I realised this was my cue. I was standing directly behind Killinger and I wrapped my arm around his neck getting him in a choke hold. Frampton then stepped up and kneed him in the groin. Killinger groaned and sank to the floor. Frampton then punched him several times in the ribs. 'You like that, do you Killinger, you like that do you?'

Killinger moans were truncated with the blows. I could feel them reverberating through my body. I released the hold and he sunk to the ground. I tied his hands together as Frampton tied his feet. I then became aware of Roberts getting the most terrific beating I had ever seen. Two of the boys were holding him while the other was pummelling him like a punch bag. Roberts' eyes were half closed and his blood was splattered down his front and over the ground. Meanwhile Vincent was kneeling on top of a prostrate Hargreaves, pressing his face into the gravel. Vincent's back was to me so I couldn't see exactly what he was doing. I wondered if the others were feeling as sick as me, or if I was all alone in my revulsion of what was happening, but I was powerless. Killinger was blubbing on the ground next to me; his face contorted in agony.

'Enough!' shouted Vincent to the boys behind him. 'Just get them both tied up, we haven't got all day.'

The boys holding Roberts let him go and he slumped straight to the ground like a sack. It hardly seemed worth the bother tying him up.

'Now help me with him,' ordered Vincent, gesturing towards Hargreaves. Dutifully we all grabbed hold of one of Hargreaves limbs, pinning him spread-eagled to the ground. Vincent stood up and slowly walked over to his bag.

'I know how you Christians like to suffer,' he said. 'Well now you can know exactly what your Saviour went through.'

He pulled out four nails and a hammer. He held the nails in one hand and the hammer in the other and grinned.

'Just remember, through all the pain, that God *loves* you.'

He knelt down and forced Hargreaves' fingers open. Hargreaves didn't say anything. He looked deep into the distance in the other direction as if looking for inspiration. Vincent placed the sharp point of the nail against Hargreaves' palm. I felt nausea in the pit of my stomach. I felt certain I would actually vomit if I saw what was to take place so as Vincent raised the hammer I looked away.

'Stop!' called out a voice. 'Please don't do it.'

It *couldn't* be. I had told him not to hang around. David's slight frame was silhouetted against the setting sun, his arms outstretched in a pleading gesture.

'Well what have we here?' said Vincent with that amused look on his face. 'Another little believer?'

He looked at me and grinned showing the gap in his teeth, his eyes dancing with mischief.

'I never knew this about your brother, Stirling.'

'David, go home, please,' I called out to him without looking at him.

Vincent walked up to David and looked down on him. David was at least half a metre shorter than Vincent but seemed unperturbed. 'Please stop,' he said again.

'David, go away!' I screamed.

Vincent grabbed hold of David's collar with one hand.

'I suppose you're going to make me stop,' he said and slapped David round the face.

'Are you going to turn the other cheek?' he said as he slapped him again.

Automatically I stood up and took a step towards Vincent.

'Please, Vincent,' I found myself saying. 'He's my brother.'

Vincent eyed me as if weighing me up. 'Well then,' he said as he hurled David towards me. '*You* deal with him then.'

I held onto David as Vincent took out a switchblade and flicked it open. It was about ten centimetres long and razor sharp. He took a step towards us and I took a step back taking David with me, his body limp.

Then Vincent turned the knife around and offered me the handle. It was shaped like a human clavicle.

'Cut him!' he said with a glint in his eye. I heard one of the boys give a cry of delight.

'What?'

'Cut him, right now and you both live. Otherwise, you both die, right here, right now.'

My eyes flicked between the back of David's head and the knife. I was frozen. I could feel the eyes of the other boys on me, waiting for my response.

'I can't,' I choked.

'You can, you know,' said Vincent. 'It's easier than you think, inflicting pain. When you're used to it that is.'

I wrapped my arms tighter around my brother. I could feel myself shaking but David kept perfectly still.

'Cut him!' said Vincent more vehemently, his eyes almost bulging out his head.

My eyes fixed on the knife. I would have to take it. I realised I had no choice. What I was going to do with it was another matter. Suddenly, David broke away and grabbed the knife himself. Before I knew it he had the blade pressed against his forearm. I grabbed hold of his arm and felt someone grab my trouser leg. Looking down, I saw Frampton, and kicked him in the face. He sprawled backwards and I wrenched the knife out of David's hand just as I saw Vincent striding towards us. I realised what had to be done. I had to ram that blade right into Vincent's ribs and kill him; and I would have done if we hadn't have been interrupted.

A car screeched to a halt and a large man with a moustache got out. It was Vincent's father.

'Get in the car, Trevor!' he ordered his son.

'Father, these are traitors!' screamed Vincent.

'Get in the car!' the huge man roared.

Vincent turned to us, his eyes blood shot and full of tears.

'I'm going to get you,' he said to me. Then he pointed a finger at David. 'And you, you little traitor. You're both dead!'

'Get in the car now!' the man said even more vehemently than before. Vincent turned, kicking the dust and got in the car. The car sped off leaving me with one arm around my brother, the other holding the knife. I noticed Hargreaves had gone. Roberts and Killinger were still tied up on the ground. I used the knife to cut them free and they scrambled to their feet and were gone. I then flicked the knife closed and put it in my pocket and David and I went home.

8

David was quiet on the way to school the next day. We hadn't spoken of yesterday's occurrences at all last night. He walked with his head down, looking deep in thought. My own thoughts were mainly concerned with what Vincent would do to either of us in school. I still kept the knife in my pocket—just in case.

'David, why did you do that last night?' I asked in the end. There was an aggrieved tone in my voice which I hadn't intended but I did feel angry with him. His actions, however brave and heroic, had almost certainly landed us in all kinds of trouble. David just shrugged his shoulders. 'I couldn't let them hurt him,' he said.

'Why not?' I snapped. 'Who do you think you are; some kind of hero? You're a little kid; you shouldn't go messing with things you can't handle.'

David flashed me a wounded look. 'Because it's wrong,' he said. 'I may be a little kid, but I know what's right and what's wrong.'

'You don't know anything,' I said. 'You think everything's so simple, don't you. You think you know it all. Well you don't, let me tell you that. You have no idea.'

David suddenly turned and walked away. I watched his small frame assimilate into the crowd, his head down, hands shoved into his pockets like some wizened old man. He seemed a lot different somehow and it hurt. I had lost something the previous day that I couldn't reclaim.

Someone called my name and I spun round. To my relief it was only Jackson.

'What is it Jackson?'

'Sorry I didn't mean to scare you.'

'I wasn't scared.'

'Haven't you heard the news?' Jackson said, eyebrows raised.

'What news?'

'About Vincent.'

My mind went into overdrive. What was he planning this time? Whatever he wanted to do to me or David, I could be sure he would find people willing to help.

'He's gone, Stirling.' Jackson had a smile on his face which he couldn't repress. It was like hearing that a particularly nasty teacher had just died. You shouldn't find pleasure in it, although it did make your life a lot easier.

'What do you mean—gone?' I said.

'I mean gone—for good. *Disappeared.*'

'You're not serious,' I stammered. 'Why?'

'I heard his whole family were into witchcraft.'

'*Witchcraft!*'

'Yeah, you wouldn't believe it would you?' said Jackson. 'It just goes to show you never can tell. See you around.'

Jackson slapped me on the arm and walked off, leaving me stunned and relieved.

With the absence of the king pin, the rest of Vincent's group simply dispersed leaving me sitting alone at lunch. I could see Jackson chirping away to some other boys in the corner but I didn't want to join him. For one thing I didn't want to listen to him talking about Vincent's disappearance. I didn't want to think about Vincent at all, even if it was thinking about his absence. For another thing I just didn't want to listen to Jackson talking. I wanted to sit in the warm sun, in solitude and enjoy my new found space and freedom. More importantly I wanted to forget about everything that had happened the previous day; the nail going to

Hargreaves' palm, David's silhouette against the sun, the back of his head as Vincent was offering me the knife.

My new found solitude was broken by the most beautiful girl in the world opposite me. Miranda Erikson was the most talked about girl in the school, at least amongst the boys. Many had said what they would like to do to her—all in very clinical, scientific terms of course. She flicked her hair back and smiled at me. She had a folder in her hand.

'Hi,' she said, flashing her perfectly white teeth at me.

'Hi,' I said back. I imagined all the other boys looking at me and seething in envy.

'I wondered if you could help me,' she said.

'I could try.'

'I'm having trouble with my biology work,' she said. 'It's a two thousand word essay on the immune system. Would you look at it?'

'Yes of course,' I said. As I looked down to take the folder my eyes settled on her breasts and I shuddered. She brushed her hand against mine as she withdrew.

'That would be great,' she said and with that she was gone, leaving me with the folder.

I looked around and saw that nobody else was looking, before opening the folder. I scanned through the first page which was an adequate explanation of the human immune system. The next page however was almost completely blank apart from a short caption at the top of the page.

'Sometimes I wonder if we can ever be immune from love.'

I shut the folder fast.

9

Later I sat in my room and pored over that one sentence again and again. What could have been her motivation for giving me that note?

I wouldn't have even dreamed she would have taken an interest in me. She must have realised what a risk she was taking. Or maybe it was a trap? You could never be sure who you could trust. If that was so, why would she suspect me? I was pretty careful in those days. The only person who I had ever showed my poems to was my father on that one occasion and that had deterred me from showing them to anyone else again.

The only other person who I had shown a remotely imaginative or playful side was David, but he seemed preoccupied. He hadn't been the same since the incident with Vincent.

If I responded to this gesture then it would make Miranda Erikson the third person in my entire life I had revealed myself to. Still, I had a feeling that she was the real deal and besides which she had my hormones pumping. I looked out at the setting sun again and the far distant body of water. I imagined myself again on a boat on that body of water, although this time my family wasn't there. It was just me and her, underneath the stars, arm in arm. We could lie there together and express our admiration for the different constellations and perhaps even mate together, like those animals I had seen on television. That would be a fine thing. Feeling emboldened I came up with a response to her question.

'Only in our hearts can we ever truly be free.'

It was a bit lame really. It wasn't even an answer to the question although I had taken the question to be rhetorical. I had considered something like 'if love was a disease I would want to be infected by you,' or something similarly disgusting but I thought the response I settled for was a little more cautious. If she was setting a trap I didn't think it would be too incriminating. I slipped the paper back into the file and hid it in my desk. Then as I lay on the bed, I fantasised more about what I'd like to do to Miranda Erikson.

The next morning I could hardly think of anything else but Miranda and her smile and eyes and teeth and lips and breasts. David trotted along beside me talking about some chemistry experiment and how it had caused a huge explosion in the classroom and singed the teacher's eyebrows but I wasn't listening. Then before I knew it, he had gone and Miranda herself was standing there.

'Hi Stirling,' she greeted cheerfully.

'Hi there,' I said. 'I looked at your essay. It was fine.'

As I handed back the file she brushed my hand again.

'Really,' she said flashing me a smile.

'Really,' I said. 'I couldn't find anything wrong with it at all.'

'That's great!' she said. 'Well thanks for looking at it.'

'No problem,' I said and then she was gone again. I watched her figure as she walked down the corridor. It was enough to inspire a thousand poems.

Over lunch time I noticed Jackson trying to latch onto Frampton and his new gang. It looked like Frampton was trying to establish himself as the leader in Vincent's absence, but I didn't want to get involved. I did not want to sully my conscience any more. I had decided to just quietly get on with school, keeping my little indulgences to myself and staying out of trouble. Miranda and her little note had stirred the otherwise tranquil waters of my mind. I wanted to know more about her, but still wasn't sure if I could trust her. The niggling thought was in my mind that she might show my reply to the note to someone else. I had heard of it happening before. Wives would inform on husbands as husbands would on wives.

Children would report their parents and once I had heard of a father actually handing over his own son to the Enforcers himself. I suppose I was lucky my father hadn't done that with me.

The afternoon seemed to pass in a haze. I walked home with David but didn't even hear what he was talking about. Everything seemed to have the sound turned down. Later that evening Mother was going on about the Public Information Agency's latest film and Father was nodding and making approving noises and I wondered if they had ever been in love. Did Father ever feel the way I was feeling now? This man who I had known all my life and not really known at all? He who did nothing but sit back and make correct responses? The only time I had ever known him to become impassioned about anything was when I had shown him my story of escaping the town and going to the out of reach body of water. This was the only time I can recall, when I had genuinely tried to reach out to him in my loneliness and he had snatched his hand away. The man I should have been able to tell anything had forbidden me to share my feelings with him again. He had cut himself off and put himself back in his comfortable little cell again. *'It is better to shut it from your mind.'* Isn't that what he said to me? And then it occurred to me that I might end up the same as him. I found this thought terrifying. That maybe this was the most alive I would ever feel. Suppose I ended up in a joint union with Miranda and we ended up having children? Then in ten or fifteen years I could be sitting in a chair making the right noises while Miranda told me about how the Enforcers had caught twenty music lovers last night. Maybe my son would come to me asking what was on the Outside and I would tell him to put it out of his mind and not to trouble me with it again. All of a sudden I felt trapped by fate. There was no way out.

I lay in bed that night, looking out the open window at the stars. There was no breeze and the sheets clung to me like a shroud. A moth flew in through the window and clicked its way around the room before making its exit. I thought of how wonderful it would be to have that freedom. Just to be able to come and go as you please. To have no expectations to meet and no threats looming over your shoulder. To be yourself without anyone to tell you it was wrong. That was the kind of aloneness I wanted. I would be happy never to see another human being my whole life if that was what it took to be free. I could just live in peace and write my poetry without interference from anyone. I could even shout it up to the stars if I wanted. There would be no one there to care.

I realised I had got out of bed and was standing there gazing out the window. I pulled some clothes on and stepped outside my room. I passed my parents room and could hear the sounds of them sleeping. Whether their eyes were open or not, they were always sleeping. I for one was more aware, awake and alive then I had ever been. As I walked down the stairs I felt a real sense of peace; a serenity. It was like I was being guided by a force outside of myself as I opened the door and stepped outside. There was a full moon and the air smelt different. Was it the smell of promise? I slowly started walking, past the bushes where David and I used to secretly play hide and seek, past the stone well which we were told was the town's only water supply many thousands of years ago. I walked past the school and on through the village area. The Vincent's house stood empty and boarded up. One day, I thought, the Enforcers would come for me. If they came for their own Chief they would definitely come for me and my whole family. My mother's devotion and my father's acquiescence to the Cause would all be in vain because of me and my brother. It would be one of us that would ruin everything that was for sure. The job of the old is to control the young, just as the job of the young is to resist that control and overthrow the old. There is a natural order to it; the young will always bring down the old in the end.

Beyond where the village lay, there was a small wood. The last remaining trees in the world stood proud and firm. They were like an anchor stuck in the ever moving sea. It was pitch black as I made my way through. I realised I had gone out without any shoes and a twig stuck in the sole of my foot causing me to wince. I persevered however and suddenly I was thrust out the other side. The iron fence stood almost as tall as the trees and hummed as if issuing a warning. Flood lights stood the other side which cast a shadow of the huge vertical bars into the space between the fence and the trees. Keeping hidden amongst the trees I made my way along the side of the fence. There was the gate. There were two men armed with rifles standing either side. Here was my chance, possibly the only one I'd ever have. Either escape or die trying. I stood there transfixed by the gate. There it was the whole world the other side. Maybe I'd get to see just a little of it before they shot me down. Maybe that would make it worth it. I had almost summoned up the nerve to do it when a small hand grabbed my wrist. For a split second I thought I would die right there and then, before I realised who it was.

'David!' I hissed. 'What are you doing?'

'What are you doing, Richard?' he answered back.

'I'm getting out of here,' I said. 'You need to go home and not tell anyone what you've seen.'

'Richard, you can't go.'

'Why not?' I said. 'I'm sick of it here. One day you'll understand.'

'Please don't go,' David said. 'Please I need you here.'

'You don't need me here. You shouldn't have followed me. Just go home, please.'

'If you're going, I'm going with you,' said David.

'Don't be stupid you'll be killed.'

'I don't care,' said David. 'I'm not leaving you and you can't make me.'

I could tell by the look in his face that he would not back down. It was the same look he had when Vincent was about to crucify Hargreaves. I cursed and grabbed David by the arm pulling him back through the wood. When we'd cleared the wood I grabbed his other arm and shook him before launching him backwards into the ground.

'Why do you always have to interfere?' I shouted at him. 'Why do you always have to be so virtuous all the time? Can't you see nobody likes you for it? You—you . . .'

David just stared back at me, motionless. Unable to say anything else, I picked up a stick and raised it, expecting him to flinch. He remained still, his eyes impassive. Frustrated I tossed the stick into the woods and went home leaving David to follow.

10

The next morning I woke up to see that David had already left. I was quite pleased; I wouldn't have known what to say to him. There was dirt in the sheets from where I had got into bed without cleaning my feet. There was an impression on the sole of my right foot from where I had stepped on that twig. I sat on the bed and rubbed my eyes. I had hardly slept at all and I would have to be going to school before too long. I felt a desolation that I had not felt before. Almost certainly, if David had not followed me I would have charged for the gates and been shot dead. I owed him my life, although I couldn't feel grateful to him for that. It was the life that I had been prepared to throw away in the slight chance of a new one. Now I was condemned to the life I despised. I felt certain that I wouldn't try escaping again.

As I cleaned myself up and got dressed however, I began to feel better and as I walked to school, books in hand, I felt better than ever. It was a sunny day and the first lesson was quantum physics. Besides which I'd get to see Miranda Erikson again.

When I got to the gates I saw Hargreaves, Killinger and Roberts across the courtyard. Roberts was still swollen up from the beating he had endured at the hands of Vincent's posse. One of his eyes was like a slit and I thought for a moment that he had caught me looking at him. I looked away, ashamed. The other day I had switched the names on our respective chemistry exam papers. I was fairly sure I would have got a good mark and he would have got a pathetic one. It was my way of trying to make amends. In my naivety, I thought it was somehow noble; enduring the shame of a bad mark to help out one of life's victims. It seems now like a pathetic, cowardly gesture, born out of sheer inadequacy. I would have like to have spoken to them in person; to explain how I never wanted to be in Vincent's gang and couldn't bear what we had actually done to them and *would* have done if it weren't for my little brother. David was the one who had faced them down and saved Hargreaves from being nailed to the ground. David was the one who had come after me in the middle of the night and would have faced being shot down rather than let me run for the gates myself. Little David, who I used to carry over muddy puddles so he wouldn't get dirty. Who used to be so in awe of my stories. Who used to think that I knew everything and could do anything? Who would have looked to me for advice and protection. Who was I kidding that I still had the right to that role in our relationship?

My thoughts were soon interrupted by Miranda brushing my arm and that put everything else out of my head until I went to meet David after school. He wasn't where he normally was; I hadn't seen him since the foiled escape technique. I walked around the school grounds looking for him and ended up walking straight into Frampton and his new gang. Frampton had a mark near his eye from where I'd kicked him during the scuffle with the knife. He clamped an arm round my neck and squeezed.

'Ah Stirling, wondering when I'd get to see you again.'

I could feel the rest of his gang closing in on me.

'So how's that brother of yours? Still saying his prayers?'

'I think there's been a mistake,' I said.

'Oh I think the mistake is yours, Stirling. I suggest you take that brother of yours in hand a little.'

'David's not interested in religion,' I said. 'None of us are.'

'Well I hope your right,' said Frampton. 'Because I'll be watching you Stirling. The Cause isn't over. Not by a long chalk. There's still a lot of weeds to pull out the garden, if you get what I mean.'

One of the other boys pointed into the distance.

'Isn't that your brother there, Stirling?'

And there was David, books in hand, talking to who else but Hargreaves. Frampton laughed and called out:

'Hey! Jesus boy! Come on over and show us a miracle, why don't you?'

The rest of the boys all laughed. I saw Hargreaves look up and then sidle away.

'We haven't forgotten you either, Hargreaves. Your day will come.'

Then David did the very thing I was willing him not to do and came over. He gazed up at them all curiously. Frampton and his gang all laughed at the sight of him. One of the boys knocked the books out of his hand and another one shoved him.

'All out of miracles today are we, little man,' said Frampton.

'Just leave him alone,' I said.

'Oh, is that fighting talk,' said Frampton his tone suddenly changing as he squared up to me. He was bigger than me, stockier and taller but I stood my ground.

'You think you're really something round here, don't you Frampton; but you're not, you're nothing.'

I had already crossed the line and the boldness of having done so was exhilarating. Frampton curled his lip; I could smell his breath.

'You'd better watch out,' he muttered.

'You've got nothing on me, or David, or even Hargreaves. The only one who we do know something about is Vincent. A member of *your* gang, Frampton.'

'And yours,' said Frampton.

'Not any more,' I said. 'It's a great cover story, isn't it Frampton? Trying to pin blame on others to take attention from yourself? But it didn't work for Vincent, did it; or his father? So maybe *you're* the one who'd better watch out.'

'We'll see, won't we,' said Frampton backing away. 'We'll just see about that.'

'Yes we'll see,' I said as the group dispersed. One of them pushed David over. After they'd gone I reached out a hand to help David up and he took it, a huge beam on his face. He flung his arms round me and clung to me and I felt the way I had felt three years before when I told him I could protect him from the Messiah.

Later on I looked at the folder Miranda had given me. The message inside read: *'What is the meaning of life?'*

I wrote a note back: *'Only when we are prepared to lose everything, do we gain anything.'*

11

Jackson had a big house. It was even bigger than Vincent's had been. He had a palm tree in the back garden which was nice to sit under on a hot day. Jackson's father wasn't often there. He was an agricultural businessman and was often at the office. Jackson was very proud of his father who he hardly saw. It was on account of his father being at work so much that afforded them such a luxurious house. It was his mother that he really loved though. She was a huge woman, in spirit as well as size. Hers was the only house I had known where it was possible to play as a young child. As long as nobody else was there Jackson and I were free to play tag or hide and seek to our hearts content. Ironically we even used to play at being Enforcers. One of us would chase the other and 'arrest' him on a charge of music playing, or dancing, or story writing. Once, when I had been playing the role of Enforcer I was running at break neck speed. So eager was I to catch the teasing Jackson who would frequently stop to pretend to play a flute, that I ended up crashing face first into a chair and falling to the ground. I tentatively put my fingers to my nose and saw blood and I cried in shock and pain. Jackson's mother then picked me up and jiggled me about on her ample lap making reassuring gurgling noises, a huge smile on her face. My own mother scarcely touched me, let alone showed affection like that, so of course I lapped it up. I would find opportunities to deliberately fall over when she was around. Now when she opened the door she looked delighted to see me. She screamed in delight and threw her arms in the air. It was the first time I'd been to the house in years.

'Richard, how you've grown. You're almost a man!' she said.

'Hello Mrs Jackson,' I said with a smile. 'Is Frederick around?'

'He's in the garden waiting for you,' said Mrs Jackson. 'And how many times, you can call me Rosie.'

I walked into the huge garden and Jackson was there sitting under the palm tree. 'Hey Stirling, how goes it,' he greeted.

'I'll fetch you drinks,' said Rosie.

I went and sat down next to him.

'I hear you've been talking to Miranda Erikson,' he said, nudging me.

'Hardly,' I said.

'Everyone's seen it,' said Jackson. 'Passing files between you and everything.'

'She wanted help with homework,' I said, starting to feel worried. 'That's all, it's nothing.'

'So you haven't started mating yet?'

'No, I haven't.'

'I would if it was me. She's—' he indicated her shape with his hands.

'Is this all you wanted to talk about,' I said, annoyed.

'Alright!' he said with a laugh. 'It's just your luck's in Stirling. I've seen her give plenty the brush off and she's after you.'

'She's not after me,' I said. 'I've hardly spoken to her.'

This was true although lately her notes had become a lot more graphic.

'So have you seen Frampton and his gang lately?' said Jackson finally changing the subject.

'No.'

It was six months since the episode in the courtyard and Frampton seemed to have left both me and David alone.

'I don't want to be in his gang anymore,' said Jackson.

I thought back to the time when Jackson was ready to bail out on the attack on Hargreaves and his friends. *I can hear him calling me sometimes,*

Stirling. I can hear it in my sleep.' Isn't that what he had said? I had a bad premonition he was wanting to confide in me a deep dark secret that I didn't want to know.

'I don't want to be in his gang either,' I said. 'I've got far too much work to do.'

'What I mean is—' and at that point his mother appeared with a tray of drinks and a few apples. She smiled and left without saying anything, as if she knew what conversation we were having and didn't want to disrupt the flow.

'What I mean is I don't believe in their *Cause*, Stirling. And I don't believe you do either.'

'What makes you think that?' I said.

'I remember when we used to play here,' said Jackson. 'We used to get up to all sorts, didn't we?'

'We were children then,' I said. 'We didn't know any better.'

'Stirling, you're good, but you're not that good. Don't you trust me, this is me talking.'

I took a sip of drink and turned away.

'I've seen you when we were doing all those things with Vincent. You couldn't stand it any more than me. You might fool Frampton and his cronies but not me.'

'I didn't like it, no,' I admitted. 'But that doesn't mean I'm on the side of Hargreaves and his friends. They brought it on themselves.'

'If they were more careful you mean?' said Jackson. I shrugged and took another sip of my drink. It was lemonade, both bitter and sweet at the same time and delicious. Jackson's mother always used to make it from her own supply of lemons and give it to us as children.

'I'm not like you Stirling. I've had a different upbringing.' Jackson leant back and looked into the distance. 'My father was hardly ever here and it was just me and my mother. We used to do everything. Before I started school I didn't even know about these stupid rules. I used to play in the garden and my mother used to sing to me.'

I couldn't help but feel envious. It must be better to have everything from one parent than nothing from two.

'And then it all changed and I had to become someone else when I was outside. Someone I wasn't. You must know what I'm talking about Stirling.'

'We all have to grow up, Jackson. We need to focus on the real world.'

I really was turning into my father. The words felt flat and hollow and I despised myself for saying them. Of course I knew what he was talking about. I'd been thinking about nothing else my whole life.

'And what is the real world?' said Jackson. 'It's you who's not living in the real world. You just want to reduce everything to a series of numbers. It's not a real existence at all. It's a sham, a paper thin existence and you know it.'

I looked to see he had tears in his eyes which he furiously blinked away; I realised I had let him down. He had put his faith in me and risked himself and his beloved mother and I didn't even have the courage to reciprocate in the smallest degree.

'I'm sorry Jackson,' I said putting my hand on his shoulder. I leaned forward and whispered in his ear. I could hardly bring myself to say it.

'I know,' I said and I could feel the air between us change. For once in my life was I about to have an honest conversation? Jackson didn't look at me but continued looking down.

'But there's nothing you can do,' I continued. 'Don't you see? *Nothing!*

'I'm not saying we can change the whole system,' said Jackson his voice still croaky. 'Just have a small oasis of freedom, that's all. Just do something here.'

'They'll find out,' I said. 'They always find out.'

'They haven't yet,' said Jackson looking at me. There was a slight smirk on his face.

'What?' I said, meeting his eye. 'What are you talking about?'

'Look at these walls,' said Jackson pointing around. The walls stood a good five metres tall and encircled the whole garden. 'What happens within them, stays within them.'

'How long?' I asked.

'Three or four years,' said Jackson. 'Three and a half I think.'

Three and a half years! That was when Vincent had first targeted Hargreaves and Jackson had said that all Christians were cannibals. All the time I had never suspected.

'Who?' I asked. 'Not David?'

'No, no,' said Jackson holding his hands up. 'Not David, I promise. Just people in our year.'

'Who?'

'Howard, Nelson, Hargreaves . . .'

'Hargreaves!' I spluttered on my lemonade. No wonder Jackson had balked at our dastardly plan. How could he have been so two faced?

'That's why I had so much trouble with what we were about to do. But I've spoken to him since and he's fine with it.'

'This is madness,' I said finishing my drink. 'I suppose you think I'm going to get involved in this, well you've got no chance.'

I stood up to leave.

'We're meeting tomorrow,' said Jackson.

'Forget it,' I said.

'And Miranda Erikson will be there,' said Jackson, a grin appearing on his lips.

12

I once heard someone say that when you fully accept you are going to die; this is when you really start to live. I wasn't sure I was going to die, but I did feel my eventual arrest and disappearance by the Enforcers was inevitable. Moreover I felt that this was somehow appropriate and fitting. What was the alternative but to become the walking dead like my parents? Regardless of the wisdom of my actions, I felt that my fate was sealed in one way or another. Why waste time and energy trying to avoid it? Of course there was also Miranda Erikson, who was certainly an emboldening incentive. The day after my conversation with Jackson, she was in one of my classes and sat next to me. Then, when the teacher wasn't looking she stroked her finger along my forearm and told me that she was looking forward to meeting me later. It would have been impossible to have not gone after that.

It was quite a small group in Jackson's back garden. Hargreaves, Killinger and Roberts were there and it made me start. Jackson approached me.

'It's alright, Stirling,' he said. 'There're fine.'

I approached them and nodded apprehensively. They all nodded back; Hargreaves gave a little smile.

'As we said before, the whole incident with Vincent has been forgotten,' said Jackson, looking to the three for confirmation. They all gave it with another nod.

'We don't blame you,' said Roberts. 'Besides it was ages ago now.'

At the age of sixteen, six months does seem a long time, although I couldn't quite believe their attitude. I decided I would tread on the side of caution with them for a while. My awkwardness soon left me however when I saw Miranda sitting there, smiling up at me. She gestured for me to sit down next to her and she wrapped her little finger around mine.

'Doesn't your father work for the Enforcers?' said Killinger.

I thought for a moment if this was a hostile question but I saw just curiosity in his face.

'Only in admin,' I said. 'I've no idea what he does.'

'Some inside knowledge would be good,' said Hargreaves.

'Well I don't know what he does,' I said, beginning to feel threatened. 'And I don't know what this is all about.'

'Its ok,' said Jackson with a laugh. 'Keep your hair on, Stirling. It's just you could be useful to us. You're the closest to the Enforcers than anyone. If you could find out anything. Anything at all, it could all be useful for us.'

'Well I'm not spying on my own father,' I said.

There was an awkward pause; then I felt Miranda pulling on my hand.

'Could I speak to you, Stirling? Just for a minute.'

I stood up and allowed her to lead me off. I scanned the other's faces to see if they were smirking but they weren't.

She took me to the back of the garden, out of sight of anyone else. She held onto my hand and swung it nonchalantly.

'It's ok Stirling, you can relax.'

I smiled and looked down at her hand holding on to me.

'I think the notes you wrote for me were really good,' she said. 'What did the last one say?'

'Love is as eternal as the sun, as restless as the wind and as untouchable as the clouds.' I winced as I said it. It was corny and ridiculous.

'That's just beautiful,' she said moving her hands up my sides. She leaned into me, her mouth slightly open. I panicked.

'It's alright,' she said. 'All animals do it you know.'

And then our lips met for the first time and I had never felt so free in all my life.

We went back to the group but I hardly listened to what they were saying. I didn't know if you could call this love or not, but whatever it was I was in deep. It was still on my mind the next morning; the smell of her hair, the feel of her hand in mine, her chest pressing against mine.

'Not hungry today,' my father said, cutting through my stupor.

'No, I think I have stomach ache,' I said, pushing the barely nibbled at bran bread away from me.

My father sat down opposite me and I felt the sudden urge to get away. Surely he didn't want to have a heart to heart with me?

'I've been thinking,' he said. That was an ominous sign.

'It won't be long now until you leave school and have to make your way in the world.'

The usual school leaving age was eighteen and I had another two years left. It seemed to me to be an eternity, but I nodded anyway.

'Well have you thought about what you want to do?' he asked.

'No, not really,' I said. 'I thought maybe I could work in Hargreaves' shop.'

'Oh no no no,' said my father. 'That would be a very bad idea. I'm afraid that family are heading for trouble. I'd stay away from them if I were you.'

'Well I don't know then,' I said. 'I'm sure something will come up.'

'Well actually Richard, something has.'

I felt a momentary chill. I felt certain I wouldn't like what he was going to say.

'A position has opened up within the Enforcement Agency.'

I felt like I was going to sink through the floor. Alarm bells shrieked in my head. I couldn't think of anything worse.

'What kind of position?' I asked tentatively.

'An administrative position, like mine,' said my father. 'If you think about it, it would be ideal. I could show you—'

'I don't want it,' I said.

'But think of the advantages—'

'I don't care,' I said. 'I don't want it. I'm going to school now.'

'Well think about it,' called out my father as I slammed the door shut.

At first I felt revolted by the very idea. Then I thought that he may be right. Maybe I was never meant to be an anarchist but a grey, pen pushing non entity like my father. Then I recalled something Hargreaves and Jackson had said. Something about having inside information; so that evening I told my father I had changed my mind. I would be interested in a job with the Enforcers.

13

My father had a real look of pride on his face as he led me through the wrought iron gates that led to the dreaded Enforcement Office. I remembered the time I had shared my feelings with him at the age of nine and had imagined this many times. However my father was not gleefully handing me over for the crime of writing poetry. He was showing me his place of work so I may one day follow in his footsteps. I had finally become my father's son.

'The Enforcement Agency isn't all about arresting people,' he said as he led me up the winding pathway. It was aligned with oak trees, all trimmed to look exactly the same, standing with military precision around a metre apart. I wondered if they measured the gaps to make sure it was an exact metre.

'Isn't it?' I asked.

'Of course not. You remember the rally in the park?'

I certainly did remember it. The whole school had been forced to go there to see Victor Callahan, the Chief of Enforcement give a speech. There was a huge crowd closely monitored by armed guards who stood around the parameters in full armour, looking out for trouble makers through their tinted visors.

'It's about education,' he continued. 'Getting the message through.'

My father wasn't usually this animated. This was obviously something quite special for him. Perhaps he felt we might bond through this exercise.

He reached the huge oak door and inserted his pass key into the slot. With a clunk the door was ajar and we walked through. The foyer smelt musty, like old books and it was huge. Red and black tiles covered the walls and there was a staircase going up to the next floor. Underneath the staircase was a heavy wooden desk and sitting behind it a motionless fat man in uniform. He took us in as we approached. Behind him was a framed picture of Isaac Heffer. Heffer had founded the town way back in the year 2550. It was he that had set the rules which had prevailed for the following four hundred and forty one years. His expression almost matched that of the fat man; cold. He had a white wig on and glasses were perched on the end of his nose, like an old fashioned judge. Heffer was always hailed as a hero in our school but I had always despised him. If it weren't for him, we could all be free.

'I just came to show my son around,' said my father.

'Only in administrative quarters,' said the fat man.

'Of course,' said my father. 'Just my work station. He may well be joining us some day.'

The fat man raised his eyebrows slightly. It was the only expression he had shown and I couldn't work out if it was from approval or disbelief. He cocked his head to one side to gesture us to move on and my father led me up the wooden staircase. I was expecting to see more pictures, but it was just bare white walls. The paint was falling off. The whole place looked as if it hadn't changed at all since it was built.

At the top of the stairs was a door going through into a small room. A single computer was there at a small desk and a filing cabinet stood in the corner. My father touched the screen and it came on. He pressed his finger onto a sensor on the keypad and a whole list of names came up.

'Here we have the names of everyone in the town,' said my father. 'Together with addresses and dates of birth.'

'Are we on there?' I asked.

'Of course.' He typed in our surname; all four of us were there. I found it a bit disconcerting. I wanted to ask what happened to the names of people who had disappeared, but couldn't quite bring myself to. My father exited the screen and brought up another list.

'Here are all the names of the Enforcement Officers,' he said.

'So what is it you do then?' I asked. I was wondering exactly what use they had of my father. After all the mystery of what he did, it seemed a bit of a letdown.

'I manage the finances, order in equipment needed, organise rallies, keep profiles on suspects . . . '

'Suspects? Which suspects?'

'Oh I can't tell you which ones,' he said with a laugh. 'But it's a very thorough job. I'm sure you would be good at it though. They are looking for another administrator.'

The door then opened and it was who else but the Chief of Enforcement. Victor Callahan was a giant of a man. Not particularly stocky but very tall. His grey hair was swept across his head and his jaw jutted out. I guessed him to be in his fifties. He had been the Chief since Vincent's father had been disappeared.

'Ah Stirling,' he addressed my father. 'I take it this is Richard.'

'Yes sir,' said my father. 'He may be interested in a job here.'

Callahan looked at me down his nose. 'Well why not? It's about time we had some new blood round here.'

I felt a chill as he stood over me. This could be the last thing I ever see, this man's hard cold eyes staring down at me. I felt like he was weighing me up. Was I one of the team or one of the enemy? I wasn't even sure myself.

'So Richard,' he said with a cough. 'What is your opinion of the Messiah?'

'He's a menace,' I shot straight back. 'A scourge for the weak elements of the town. The sooner he's out of action the better.'

'Well that's right,' he said. 'And it is thanks to the good work of men like your father that we are ridding the town of these "weak elements".'

I could sense my father puffing up with pride next to me but my eyes were transfixed on this phantom of a man standing over me; the hard lines going from his nose to the corners of his mouth, his eyes burning into mine.

'And some day,' he continued, his mouth twitching. 'Some day we will destroy the scourge.'

He slapped me on the shoulder and the moment of tension passed as he turned to my father. 'Excellent, Stirling. I'm sure your boy will be a fine asset to the Agency.'

'Thank you sir,' said my father.

The dark shadow passed and I was there alone with my father.

'He's an extraordinary man,' he said in hushed awe as if he was afraid Callahan might be around to hear. 'You could learn a lot from him.'

14

Jackson's mother greeted me with a smile and showed me through to the garden; Jackson was there with about ten other people. Amongst them were Hargreaves, Killinger and Roberts and of course Miranda. I had a poem I had written for her burning a hole in my pocket. I had spent half the night working on it.

'How did it go?' Jackson blurted out. 'Did you see the inside?'

'Yes I did,' I replied. 'It gave me the creeps.'

I noticed the others all looking at me, slack-jawed. Could I now be trusted? Had I joined the other side?

'What was it like?' asked Hargreaves. 'Did you see any of them there?'

'I saw Callahan,' I said. 'But I didn't learn anything new.'

'You saw Callahan?' Killinger said, his eyes widening. 'What was he like?'

'The same as he always is.'

I was a little uneasy with my new status; that of being the one amongst their peers who had actually gone into that building and had come back to tell the tale. I realised I was playing a dangerous game. All my life I had been a private double agent but this was somehow all the more deceitful and provocative should the whole thing blow up in my face; which I felt certain it would some day. Nonetheless I told them the whole story while they stared at me goggle eyed. When I had finished Jackson put his hand on my shoulder: 'So Stirling; are you going to join them?'

'I don't want to,' I said. 'And I only went to look around for all of you, for us. Inside knowledge, yes?'

'That's right,' said Roberts putting his hand on my other shoulder. 'That was good work, Stirling.'

The others made noises of agreement and I actually felt quite special.

'I won't actually be joining *them*,' I said. 'I'll be working *with* them.'

'*For* them,' someone said. I gave him a dirty look.

'I'll just be keeping their paper work in order that's all. In fact I don't want to do it at all now.'

'No, no,' said Jackson. 'You have to go ahead with it now. This could be really vital Stirling. So you can see who their suspects are? Who they're planning to move on?'

'I could do yes. If I joined.'

'We trust you Stirling,' said Killinger. I was amazed at how easily he'd forgotten how I'd put him in a choke hold and tied him up while Frampton had pummelled him in the ribs.

'Yes we trust you, Stirling,' they all joined in. 'You'll always be one of us.'

Then Miranda, who had said nothing, suddenly put her arm round me and kissed me on the cheek, inciting lots of cheers from the boys.

'So that's settled,' said Jackson, standing up and puffing out his chest. 'Now enough talk. Let us hear sweet music. Let us dance until dawn or at least until we all fall down with exhaustion. Let the fun begin!'

'Jackson,' someone whispered. 'Not out here. We should go inside.'

'Quite right, quite right,' said Jackson. 'Inside we go.'

We all traipsed into Jackson's living room, feeling a mixture of anxiety and excitement. It would only take one person to blow the whole thing open and I had wished Jackson had been a little more selective with who he'd invited. Nevertheless it was one of those things, once the idea is put in motion it is impossible to resist, no matter how much your common sense screams against it.

Jackson begun with a song. It was a very old song that he said his mother had taught him. It must have dated from around a thousand years ago. He stood there, arms by his side like a statue and sang and it was with such conviction that it was unnerving.

'In Dublin's fair city, where the girls are so pretty
That's where I first met sweet Molly Malone
She wheeled her wheel barrow through streets wide and narrow
Singing cockles and muscles
Alive alive-o!'

He continued through the next two verses and half way through someone took out a drum to accompany him, tapping out the rhythm of the chorus.

As I listened I felt somehow moved, although I couldn't understand why. It was the first time I had ever heard music. I had heard the birds sing of course but this was different. This was coming from somewhere very deep, that couldn't be expressed in words. It was the desire for freedom. It was something inside that could never be crushed, no matter how hard the Enforcers tried. Miranda slipped her hand into mine and I lay back until the music finished.

'What's a cockle?' someone asked.

'And where's Dublin,' said another. 'I've never heard of it.'

'It's just a song,' said Jackson, looking at the floor. 'I don't know what it's going on about.' He sat down and everyone looked at each other in silence.

'So have you got something, Stirling?' said Roberts.

'Everyone's got to do something,' said another. 'Especially on the first night.'

I thought of the poem I had written. I hadn't intended to read it publicly but something told me that this was fate. I needed to show them I was genuine. I stood and took the piece of paper from my pocket. I cleared my throat and began:

'If love is but a chemical
An electric bolt to the brain
If love is a drug to the system
A disease that inflicts the insane
Then I'd be a fool for loving you
But I'd do it all the same
Love is an echo down the hall
Memories trapped inside
A precipice from which we're bound to fall
A bomb to explode all reason
But still I wait to hear you call
To make me feel alive once more'

I put the piece of paper in my pocket and sat down, my face burning when I discovered everyone clapping. I felt a lump in my throat as Miranda kissed me and people clapped my on the back.

'I never knew you had it in you,' said Jackson.

Then someone started the drum playing once again. It was fast and rhythmical and others joined in clicking fingers or slapping thighs. Then to our astonishment, Jackson's mother burst in through the door like a hurricane of flesh, swirling her hips, arms waving in the air.

'Come on, let's dance!' she called out. 'On your feet, boys!'

We started getting up one by one and moved to the rhythm of the beat. Miranda clung to me like a second skin. I rubbed my hands up and down her body as she kissed my neck and ears. I felt a knot in the pit of my stomach which almost became unbearable.

That was when I told her I needed to see her alone.

15

The next day I had a smile on my face as I walked to school. I couldn't help it. I had found an outlet for my creativity and finally, people who appreciated what I did. I had found a place where I could talk freely; an oasis as Jackson had called it. Most importantly I was in love. I had hardly exchanged ten words with Miranda but already we had a connection. From the first time she had handed me that note it had been building and it would surely erupt before too long.

I caught David looking at me out the corner of his eye and saw the grin appear on his lips. 'What?' I said.

'Nothing,' he replied.

'Don't think I can't see you.'

'Don't think I can't see *you*.' He put on a face, imitating mine and I gave him a playful shove.

'Who are you thinking about?' he said.

'It's none of your business,' I said. 'Not that I'm thinking of anyone in particular.'

'I know who you're thinking of,' he said. 'Jessica Althorp.'

Jessica Althorp was the most annoyingly pedantic girl in my year; everything was about proving herself correct. Besides which, she had a face like an erupted volcano. If anyone else had suggested it I would have assumed they were doing it to tease me but I knew David was always entirely literal.

'You imbecile!' I laughed. 'It's definitely not Jessica Althorp. Try again.'

For the duration of journey he continued coming up with guesses, naming just about every girl in my year apart from Miranda Erikson.

As we approached the school, I picked out several people who I had seen the previous evening and consciously avoided them. It was a whole conspiracy of silence and none of us acknowledged each other throughout the day. We all knew we were playing with fire, committing treason in the eyes of many and couldn't bear to play out the pretence with each other. At lunch I sat with two relative unknowns, Ferdinand and Harris, who were discussing the possible effects of gravity should a missile hit the earth. I was only half involved; Miranda was sitting with some other girls at the other end of the dining room. She was talking and laughing when I noticed her glancing in my direction.

'What do you think, Stirling?' Ferdinand said.

'Sorry?'

'Do you think we'd all be thrown into space?' he said. 'Harris thinks we all will, but I'm not so sure.'

I noticed Miranda standing up and looking in my direction again.

'Neither am I,' I said. 'Look if you'll excuse me, I have to go.'

Miranda made her way towards the door and I went after her, pushing my way through all the other students until I got in calling distance. She stopped and turned round. As bit down her lower lip, twitching into a smile. 'Hi Stirling.'

'I need to see you again,' I said.

'So do I,' she replied. 'Where?'

'In Cooper's yard there's a shed. It's always unlocked. Can you meet me there at midnight?'

'I'll see you then,' she said and then was gone.

Nothing else was on my mind for the rest of the day. During the evening, I hardly spoke to my parents or to David; I felt like I was in a bubble. When the time came to leave, I crept out the house and ran. When I got there she was waiting for me.

At the time I only knew one word for it: mating. But since then I have learnt a lot better terms; the one I like the best is making love. Whatever you call it; that is what we did. We didn't speak until it was done. She approached and we kissed, fumbling with each others clothes. She cried out as I penetrated her. I was afraid and almost withdrew, but she gripped onto me, digging her nails in my back. Afterwards we lay naked, wrapped in each others arms.

'I've waited for years to do that,' said Miranda.

'So have I.'

'Was it as good as you expected?'

I nodded. 'Was it your first time?'

'Yes. It always hurts the first time,' she said. 'But it gets better.'

I looked around at where we were, lying in a shed on a woollen blanket, farming equipment lying around. The Coopers had been agriculturalists before they had disappeared.

'You know I hardly know anything about you,' I said. 'What do your parents do?'

'They trade in automobiles. Father sells them and Mother—well she does the paperwork.'

'My mother makes the public information videos,' I said. 'It's all she has ever done. It's all she is interested in. And my father—well you know what he does.'

'He works for *them*,' she said.

'And so will I some day soon. Does that bother you?'

'It should do,' she said. 'But I can sense who you are. Inside, you're like me. Never satisfied, always trying to find that something else.'

'Sometimes I worry,' I said. 'That I'll end up like them. I don't worry about being caught; I worry about turning into them. Do you understand that?'

'I do,' she said. 'I feel the same.'

She turned my face so I was looking into her eyes. I held her closer, running my fingers through her hair.

'Once I tried to escape,' she said.

I was surprised by this, but not shocked. After all I had done the same.

'What happened?' I asked. She exhaled through her nose and turned onto her back, mirroring my posture.

'I was only thirteen,' she said. 'The guards caught me and took me home. They told my parents that the next time they would shoot me in the stomach and leave me to the rats.'

I winced at the thought. That could have happened to me, if it wasn't for David. 'What did your parents say?'

'They were furious. My father locked me in my room for three days. He only let me have water. He said he couldn't believe my ingratitude. How hard he'd worked for me and all the sacrifices. He said he would hand me over to the authorities himself next time.'

There was a tear on her cheek; I kissed it, tasting the saltiness. You'd try to keep your feelings covered, although they would often manifest in some small way. With me I think it was my eyes; with Miranda that solitary tear told a lifetime of pain.

'I despise my parents,' she said. 'I despise my sister. She's always been a despicable little sneak. Always getting me into trouble to make herself look good. Miranda's playing with dolls, Miranda's drawing pictures, Miranda's tying her hair up in knots. I hate them all.'

Whilst I had often resented my parents I would never have considered that I hated them. I certainly can't recall feeling much fondness towards them.

'I'm sorry,' I said.

'I don't care,' she said. 'I'm beyond caring. Some day I will escape the town for good. Would you come with me?'

'Escape the town?'

'Haven't you ever thought of what life could be like Outside?'

'All the time,' I said. I told her how I had written a story about escaping and my father's reaction; and how I nearly escaped but David stopped me.

'Your brother's very unusual,' said Miranda.

'You could say that.'

'I've seen you two together at the gates. He thinks the world of you, I can see it. It's something very special. Something I've never known.'

I looked at Miranda lying next to me; a wave of compassion, adventure and physical arousal overpowered me. I wanted to be that one person who she could relate to. I wanted to protect her; to be her comfort, her solace, her soul mate. Her body was cold; I held her close and kissed her. I could feel her give herself entirely to me and I to her. As we made love again I knew that our destinies were sealed. For however long we managed to stay alive, we would be together. I was sure of it.

16

The principal passed down the line shaking hands with each of us. I had hardly spoken a word to him since I had joined the school as a five year old. Now I was out; eighteen years old and destined to follow in my father's footsteps. I saw him talking to Frampton; they were smiling and laughing together. Frampton could turn the charm on when he wanted to, especially with authority figures.

The principal approached me, standing a little closer than was comfortable, pummelling my hand.

'So, Stirling, I hear you're joining the Enforcers,' he said.

'I'll be working in administration,' I corrected him. I was always keen to stress I was working *for* them, not joining them.

'All part of the same Cause, all part of the same Cause,' the bald man muttered. He adjusted the glasses on the end of his nose.

'Well good luck with that Stirling,' he said as he moved onto the next in line.

Looking out into the hall, amongst the lines of pupils watching our passing out ceremony, I caught my brother's eye. He had a smile on his face and it puzzled me. It could have been pride but there was something else there; a reluctant acceptance perhaps? Did he think that now I had joined the other side completely? That he had lost me for good? I could almost read his mind as it said goodbye to me and it stung a little.

Outside my mother hugged me and my father patted me on the shoulder. 'A grown man now, look at you,' he said.

'And going on to serve our community,' added my mother. 'You'll make us all so proud.'

I should have felt overwhelmed by this gushing of sentiment from my parents, in the way that a man dying of thirst is gratified by water. I should have been excited about being free from school and all the gangs and dogma attached; but somehow I felt nervous. I was on the edge of a precipice hanging on by my fingernails; my feet dangling over a void which couldn't be seen; only felt. Now I was an adult, I had no one to hide behind and I had to make my way in the world. One of my first steps was to move out of my parents' house and move into a one bedroom property with Miranda.

My position with the Enforcers gave me no further insight into the burning question that everyone wondered but no one voiced. What actually happened to the people that had disappeared? It was a question that would remain a mystery to me for a while to come. For two years I ordered their stationary and fetched their drinks. I had no access to the list of suspects although I kept details of all the births and deaths within the town. Whenever someone disappeared I was simply instructed to erase their name from the records.

I had learnt some things about the activities of the Enforcement Officers from Frampton, who had decided to pursue his victimisation by joining up. Thankfully, I didn't see him that often, although he would sometimes walk into my office to brag about an unnamed suspect he had beaten. What I had not known is that the Enforcers would not always take people the first time. Sometimes they would issue a 'warning'. This would normally involve humiliation, terror or pain and normally a combination of all three. Frampton had taken my involvement with the Enforcers as a token of support for the 'Cause'. He would relish in telling me stories of how he had stripped suspects naked and whipped them with belts; or tied them up and forced laxatives down their throats until they soiled themselves. Frampton told me once how he had raped a woman in front of her husband. He told me in such detail I felt sick, but I had little choice but to nod and wait for him to finish. Keeping the inside and the outside separate was second nature to me, although there was one incident in particular that made me question why I was having anything to do with them.

A few months after we had left school, Miranda and I had our joint union ceremony in the town hall. We both wore black as was customary for these occasions and we had around twenty guests including our families.

Jackson, Killinger, Hargreaves and Roberts were there; as was Frampton who I had little choice but to invite.

The Official Registrar spoke of the importance of joint unions within the community. How vital it was to provide a stable unit in which to have children and the importance of bringing them up within the traditions of the town; the traditions which had made the town great. Then we were invited to sign the register and everyone clapped.

Afterwards Frampton approached me while Miranda was busy talking to my mother about her dress.

'Nice to see you two together,' he said.

'Nice you could come,' I replied.

'I'm surprised your friend, Jackson came,' said Frampton.

I looked across the hall and found Jackson standing alone. He glanced round at me before diverting his eyes.

'Why's that?'

'It was a busy night for us last night,' said Frampton. 'And not a particularly good one for him. Still, maybe he'll learn yet. There's always hope. Don't you think, Stirling?' His eyes flashed a warning as if to challenge me to attack him.

'Let's hope so,' I replied.

Frampton sidled away and I saw Jackson go outside. Checking to see if Frampton was looking, I worked my way through the crowds to follow him out. He was standing there leaning against the wall. When he turned to look at me, I saw he had a black eye.

'So you two got it together then,' he said. 'I'm glad.'

'Thanks for coming, Jackson,' I said. 'It means a lot.'

'Hey,' he said. 'How could I not show up to the union of my oldest friend.'

He patted me on the arm and I gave him a hug. His body felt frail, as if it belonged to an old man. I squeezed him as if I could take away his pain. I wanted to reassure him that I was still the same person; that I wasn't one of them. It was a futile gesture. I had no idea what they had done to Jackson and his mother but it had taken everything from him. There was no reciprocation in his embrace. He probably thought of me as one of them. And maybe I was.

17

Miranda and I didn't go round to Jackson's house anymore. It was far too risky; although I often thought of him. I couldn't get the thought out of mind. I buried myself in my work and my head in the sand. I didn't think about what the Enforcers were, or what they stood for. I just wanted to do the best job I could and then go home and switch off. Every now and then I would hear raised voices from my office, but I tuned them out. As long as the records were in order and Callahan received his drinks the way he liked them; that was all I was concerned about. After all, what could I do? I was only one person; how could I overthrow the system that had prevailed for nearly half a millennia? Many must have tried and failed. To rebel was nothing but a suicide gesture. I had no desire to throw my life away and mercifully neither did Miranda.

Then, when Miranda became pregnant, there truly was no way back. I was going to be a father and through my excitement, I remembered my thoughts as an earnest fifteen year old; the thoughts that had caused me to try and escape. I was certain if my son or daughter were to approach me as I had approached my father with dangerous subversive ideas, I would react exactly the same way. My prophecy had come true and I had turned into my father; but this was a good thing, a necessary thing, a vital thing. I would do anything to protect the life that was in that womb. The denial of self was a small price to pay.

All my family were thrilled, especially David who seemed more excited than me. I have this abiding memory of him, standing in our kitchen with his hand placed against Miranda's belly. He was seventeen years old and on the cusp of manhood but he had the same look of awe on his face as he had when I used to tell him stories as a child.

'It's in there, it's really in there?' he kept saying. 'My little nephew or niece? It's in there?'

'It's in there,' I laughed.

'So now you're a big daddy as well as a big brother.' He flung his arms around me and Miranda and kissed us both on the cheek. 'I'm so happy for you both,' he said, tears in his eyes. 'No one deserves it more than you.'

Even then, I felt a twinge of guilt. Did I really deserve it? I who routinely listened to the sounds of torture and did nothing? However these thoughts were drowned out by the sentiment of the moment, just as my twinges of conscience were drowned out by my concern for my work. I found that the voices which used to bellow in my head were now just a minor rankling. This was until something happened which changed everything for ever.

I was taking a drink to Callahan one afternoon, when I heard voices coming from down the corridor. They were coming from the same restricted area that all the other voices had come from. The difference was that this time the door was open and I could hear what was going on. Callahan's door was also ajar and the room empty. I crept towards the voices with my heart pounding and my hands sweating. It wasn't just idle curiosity; I *recognised* one of the voices. It was a woman's voice. I didn't want to acknowledge it when I realised whose. It was the woman I had once wanted as a surrogate mother, Rosie Jackson.

'I don't care what you do to me,' she was saying. 'I will never tell you anything. You are pigs! Nothing but bully boys! Scum!'

I reached the door that the voices were coming from and peered through the window. Frampton standing in front of her with a hand on her throat. Two other officers were holding her arms. 'You will talk, believe me woman. You will talk,' he was saying.

Rosie responded by spitting in his face. Without hesitation, Frampton punched her in the jaw. It was a full force blow, but to my amazement it did nothing but cause her to stagger back a few paces. Then, like a coiled spring, she launched herself at Frampton, breaking free from the guards. She howled like an animal as she clawed his face, forcing him to the ground.

'Get her off! Get her off!' Frampton screamed, as the two guards tried to pull her away. Rosie was a force to be reckoned with, but she was no match for the two guards who eventually had her pinned to the floor out of my sightline. Frampton stood up, his hair dishevelled, his face ashen white. Claw marks ran down his cheeks and around his eyes. He looked down at Rosie, gurgling on the floor. Frampton stood tall, his shoulder blades tightened; I knew what to expect. He reeled his body back and forward and I heard a thud and a groan from below. Then again—and again, although this time there was no groan. I could feel the bile rising in my mouth and ran back through the door out of the restricted zone and into the rest room where I vomited in the toilet. My whole body was shaking and my eyes stung. I looked at myself in the mirror and could see my eyes were bloodshot and my face pale. I splashed myself with cold water and tried to slap the colour back into my cheeks before returning to the office. I sat down with my face straight; I had studied it in the mirror to make sure there was no trace of any emotion.

Frampton walked in wiping his face with a cloth and sat on the end of my desk.

'I tell you Stirling; some of these traitors have got some fight in them.'

I felt the urge to smash him in the nose. I stared into the computer, willing him to go away.

'Some people just don't know when they're defeated,' he continued.

'Frampton!' a voice bellowed out. I looked up to see Callahan standing in the doorway, his face like thunder. Frampton jumped up, his face almost as pale as mine had been. I had never seen Frampton afraid before.

'Yes sir?' he stammered.

'In my office! Stirling, you can go home.'

'Thank you sir,' I said.

As I packed my things away, I listened to the storm that was brewing in Callahan's office. 'What am I going to do now?' he was shouting. 'How am supposed to find out the names of the other subvertors?'

'She wasn't going to say anything—' Frampton started before Callahan steam-rolled over him.

'She's certainly not going to say anything now, is she? I ought to have you thrown out, Frampton. You're a disgrace.'

'But sir there's always—'

'I don't want to hear it. Get out!'

There was a pause, which I took to be Frampton, too stunned to speak.

'I said get out!' Callahan screamed.

I didn't want to have to see Frampton again so I slipped out then.

As I walked home I struggled to take in what I had witnessed; what I had learnt. Frampton had finally done it; perhaps not intentionally, but done it all the same. And why did it have to be Rosie? All that vitality, all that energy, all that love; stamped out by someone whose world revolved around self interest and hatred. I wondered if Frampton would actually feel bad about it. Would he ever actually realise the measure of what he had done? I doubted it.

I had to go to Jackson's house on the way back, just to confirm what I already knew. The door had been forced, crockery was smashed on the floor and furniture upturned. The house was empty.

When I got home I lay in the bath tub and wanted to cry. Rosie Jackson was dead and her son, my best friend was in the holding cells. Before too long he would probably be dead as well. I wanted to cry for them so I could feel human. So I could feel that at heart I was a decent, compassionate person and I hadn't been conditioned beyond all hope. But I couldn't cry. I couldn't release these feelings because pervading all of them was another which prevented such weaknesses. Stone cold hatred.

18

Hargreaves didn't want to see me but I pushed myself through the door anyway. He looked afraid and it reminded me of when I had pushed him up against the wall to try to and warn him about Vincent. Now it was a different enemy, but the same old war.

'I'm not with the Enforcers, Hargreaves calm down,' I said.

'I don't know anything,' said Hargreaves, his hands in the air. 'Please leave me alone.'

'Jackson's in gaol,' I told him. 'Did you know that?'

'No,' he said and I could see the thought processes flicker across his eyes. 'But there's nothing I can do.'

'What's more,' I said. 'They killed his mother. Frampton beat her to death.'

Hargreaves sat down and pressed his fingers into his temples.

'I'm sorry,' he said after a while. 'But there's still nothing I can do.'

'Don't you realise what's going to happen,' I said. 'They're onto *us*, they're onto our group. They were trying to get information out of Rosie, but she wouldn't give it. That's why she died, Hargreaves. She died for us.'

'But what *can* we do, Stirling?' said Hargreaves. 'We can never hope to get him out, and even if we did, what will we do then?'

'We get out of here, Hargreaves.'

'Out of where?'

'Out of the town.'

I fixed him with a stare as I said it. I wanted him to know I was deadly serious. Hargreaves looked at me as if I was insane. 'That's impossible,' he said. 'No one leaves, you know that Stirling.'

'All I know is that if we stay we are dead men. And you know that as well.'

Hargreaves shook his head in bewilderment.

'Jackson will talk in the end,' I said. 'I know him and he's not that strong. They'll break him down and he'll confess. All he has to do is give one name, and that person to give one more name.'

'But how?' said Hargreaves.

'I'll find a way—somehow, but we need to move fast. Can you get Killinger and Roberts round here tomorrow night?'

Hargreaves nodded.

'Good. We'll come up with an action plan then.'

'Stirling,' said Hargreaves and he had that frightened rabbit look on his face again. 'I'm not cut out for this you know.'

'Don't worry,' I said. 'We're going to make it Hargreaves. We're going to get out of here.'

I wished I could feel as confident as I was trying to sound. This was tantamount to suicide, but I couldn't see any other solution.

My opportunity came a week later when ten new rifles arrived at the office. The Enforcers usually only carried weapons during rallies and I wondered if they had anything planned. Callahan had me sent down to put them away in the weapons hold. This is a place which I never normally had access to, so one of the guards had to take me down, using his pass key to get through into the restricted area, past the interrogation room and down into the basement. We approached another door. The guard slid his key into the slot and it clunked ajar.

'Don't get too excited,' he said with a grin. 'Just put them neatly in the racks and make sure it's all tidy and clean in there. I'll see you in five minutes.' Then he left me to it and I stepped inside. The room was filled with dust and illuminated by a single bulb. As my eyes took in the contents of the room I began to realise why the guard had told me not to get too excited. Along the walls, standing in racks stood about twenty rifles, barrels pointed to the ceiling. There was a further ten machine guns next to them. In the corner was a case of hand grenades, tear gas and ammunition. On the opposite side the wall was adorned with hand guns, around forty of them hung on hooks. I saw some of the hooks were empty. After I had put the rifles in their racks I took one of the hand guns and weighed it in my hand. It was loaded with a magazine cartridge but was still seductively light. I slid it into my jacket pocket, then took another and slipped it in my other pocket.

When I got home I examined them carefully. I had never held a weapon before; it sent tremors up my arm just holding it. Miranda didn't even want to look at it but I was fascinated. I practised my aim in the garden, aiming the laser sight at a mound of earth. I squeezed the trigger, enjoying the sensation of the round shooting out the barrel. It pounded into the ground, sending showers of stones and dirt scattering over the grass. It gave me more than a little satisfaction to have all that power at the twitch of a finger. I imagined shooting Frampton. I imagined the look in his eyes as the round passed through his heart. I didn't want to kill anyone, but the idea was so alluring I couldn't get it out of my head.

A few days later we met at Hargreaves' house. Killinger and Roberts were there as was Miranda. I had gone through the plan in my head and discussed it with Miranda many times. This was our only chance and it had to be done correctly, with military precision.

'As we know, Jackson is being held at the Enforcement Office,' I said.

'Are we sure about that,' said Killinger. 'How do you know he hasn't already been killed?'

'I don't,' I admitted. 'But unless we know for sure, we're not giving up on him. His mother died for us and that means something to me even if it doesn't to you.'

'It's ok, Stirling,' said Roberts. 'We're with you.'

I looked at Killinger who wasn't putting up any argument.

'Hargreaves, I want you to get my brother and go with him and Miranda to the meeting place,' I continued.

I had decided early on that Hargreaves could be a liability in a conflict and wanted him out the way. Hargreaves readily agreed and I expected the others to protest but to my relief they were obviously of the same mind.

'These are the two most important people in the world to me,' I said to Hargreaves. 'David knows nothing of this yet, but he will come. Just tell him I sent you.'

'I will,' said Hargreaves.

'Killinger and Roberts, I'd like you to come in with me, if you're willing.'

'I'm willing,' said Roberts.

I could see Killinger was thinking about it.

'Killinger?' I prompted. I wasn't going to take anyone in who wasn't willing but we had a better chance together. We would already be outnumbered by around twenty to three.

'Yes,' said Killinger eventually. 'I'm willing.'

'Thank you,' I said. 'Like I said, they don't carry weapons on them. As long as they don't get to the artillery we'll be fine.'

'But what's going to stop them?' asked Killinger.

'Don't worry,' I replied. 'I have a plan.'

I kept that plan in mind when I went into work as normal the next day and pointed a gun in the guards face.

19

It was the same guard that was there when I had first entered the building with my father four years prior. He had the same expression on his face. He didn't even seem surprised at seeing Killinger and Roberts there with me, let alone be staring down the barrel of a gun.

'You're going to take these two to the weapon artillery and he will take a gun,' I said gesturing to Roberts who was the only one not armed. Then you will take Killinger to the cells and release Jackson. Is that understood?'

The guard looked me in the eye and his hand crept under the desk.

'Don't!' I said, raising the gun.

The guard didn't take his eyes off me or the expression off his face. I heard a click shortly followed by a shrieking alarm.

'Upstairs, quick!' I shouted, running up the stairs. Killinger and Roberts followed. I stormed straight into Callahan's office. He barely had time to look up before I had got behind him and locked my arm around his neck. I held the nuzzle of the gun against his temple. The guards stood and started creeping forwards.

'Everyone back!' I yelled. 'Killinger, cover them.'

Killinger stood in front of me his gun outstretched. Roberts who was still unarmed, looked completely bewildered.

'Foolish boy!' said Callahan. 'Did you think you could get away with this?'

'Tell them to get Jackson!' I said.

'I will do no such thing!' Callahan retorted. 'You don't stand a chance, look.'

A barrage of armed guards suddenly burst through the doors. I forced Callahan to his feet using him as a shield whilst still keeping the gun on him. Killinger's aim started to lower as his arms started shaking.

'Keep your gun up, Killinger!' I shouted. 'Stand firm!'

'Give it up, Stirling,' said Callahan. 'What are you going to do? Shoot me?'

'If I have to,' I said. 'Tell them to lower their weapons.'

Callahan started laughing and I tightened the grip on his neck until he stopped.

'Lower your weapons!' I shouted. 'Do it!'

The guards remained in their crouching position. They had rifles all aimed at me. I lowered the gun and shot Callahan in the leg. He cried out and started to slump, but I held him up.

'I'll take you out a piece at a time if I have to,' I said. 'Tell them to lower their weapons.'

'Stand down, stand down,' he called out and the guards started to lower their arms. 'Let's sort this out like gentlemen, shall we?'

'Give one of the guns to Roberts,' I called out to one of the guards. He looked at Callahan for confirmation, who gave it with a nod. Roberts seemed a lot more comfortable with a rifle in his hands. He cocked it and faced outwards with Killinger. I dropped Callahan in his chair and sat opposite him, the gun aimed at his face.

'You're making a big mistake, Stirling,' he told me. He was perspiring and grimacing from the pain. I threw a cloth towards him.

'Wrap that around it,' I said.

Callahan stooped down.

'Don't try anything,' I warned as he tied the cloth around his shin. He sat up and wiped his face with his sleeve.

'What is it you want?'

'I'm getting out of here,' I said.

'Why would you want to do such a foolish thing?' said Callahan. 'There's nothing out there. Just desert and rocks. Don't you watch the TV boy?'

'Its all lies,' I said. 'I should know; my mother works for them.'

'Ah yes, your mother—and your father. What would they think of this?'

'They don't know the truth,' I said. 'They've been here too long.'

'The arrogance of youth,' laughed Callahan. 'You're not the first who thinks they can buck the system, Stirling.'

'I know what happens to people that buck the system,' I said. 'And that's why I am getting out of here and so is Jackson. Bring him up here.'

Callahan just looked at me as if he was trying to read my mind.

'Bring him up here!'

'Are you sure you know what you are doing?' said Callahan.

'I saw what you did to his mother,' I said. 'Do you think I'd leave him here to the same fate?'

'You're going out on a limb for him,' said Callahan. 'It's a brave move. A foolhardy one if you ask me. You'd have been better off just trying to skip the fence.'

'Well I'm not like you Callahan. I'll never be like you.'

'I disgust you don't I Stirling?' he said.

The question surprised me a bit and it took me a while to answer.

'You're all bullies and cowards,' I said. 'I'm disgusted with myself for having anything to do with you.'

'Ah yes. The self loathing, the inner conflict. I've always sensed that about you, Stirling. I sensed it when I first met you. Your father; he had the same thing, but he buried it deep inside. With you, it's always so on the surface. It's your weakness.'

'I've no self conflict now,' I said. 'I am leaving this town. We all are, and taking Jackson with us.'

'And your brother?' said Callahan.

I saw a twinkle of amusement in his eyes and it shook me to the core.

'Yes.'

'And what makes you think he is still alive?'

I was freefalling; my mind blinkered. 'What do you mean?'

Killinger spoke up: 'Stirling, he's playing with you. We need to get out of here.'

Callahan laughed as if someone had told him a delightfully witty joke. 'Foolish boy! You put your life on the line to save someone who gave up your own brother.' Callahan pressed the intercom button. 'Bring him in,' he spoke into the machine.

The doors opened and Jackson was slung onto the floor. He knelt there his face gaunt, his body rake thin. Without taking my gun or eye off Callahan I stooped and lifted Jackson's shirt. Laceration marks were scored across his back. I lifted his head but he wouldn't look at me.

'You see, he can't bear to look at you!' said Callahan. 'Isn't it obvious, boy? Use your head. I know about your quaint little meetings at his house. I know about your charming little poem to your lovely wife. How would I know these things if he hadn't told me?'

'What about David?' I asked. 'What have you done with him? Where is he?'

'Stirling, don't!' called out Killinger.

'Where is he?' I screamed. It was like a demon had possessed me. The rational part of me was telling me to get a grip but the demon wasn't listening. It was after vengeance.

'Alright boy, I will tell you the truth,' said Callahan. 'You have not attended these pathetic little meetings for a while, granted. Commendable, I believe. I was actually going to overlook your past transgressions in the hope of fully reforming you, Stirling, but alas, it seems it is too late now.'

'Where is David?'

'David is dead,' said Callahan. 'I shot him through the head.'

My brain couldn't compute what he was saying. 'What do you mean?'

Callahan laughed.

'Stirling, he's lying!' shouted Roberts.

'After you had finished attending these illicit meetings, I'm afraid your brother started. Your friend here was most helpful—'

'Callahan, you're a liar and I'm going to shoot *you* through the head.'

I stood up and aimed the gun right between his eyes. Callahan just stared back as if he was a cow that didn't know he was to be slaughtered. It would be so easy, I thought. Just one squeeze.

'Stirling, don't,' said Killinger touching my arm. 'If you do, all of this will mean nothing. It's what he wants you to do.'

'We'll find your brother, Stirling,' said Roberts.

'Get up!' I said to Callahan. I pulled him up onto his feet. 'Cover me,' I told Killinger and Roberts as I started moving Callahan towards the door of his office. One hand was on the scruff of his neck and the other held the gun against the back of his head.

'We're going to search the cells,' I said. 'Keep Jackson with you.'

I could sense Roberts help Jackson to his feet and we shuffled through the main office. The guards kept their distance, their arms ready but not aimed. Killinger and Roberts kept either side of me. At Callahan's direction the guards let us through the doors into the restricted area. Then we shuffled down the stairs towards the cells.

'If I were you I would shoot him,' Callahan said. 'If it wasn't for him your brother would still be breathing.'

'If I were you I would keep quiet.' I refused to let him play with my head anymore. 'You've always got another leg I could shoot you in.'

'Here are the cells, they are empty,' said Callahan.

We looked into every one and they were all empty.

'Your brother is not here, Stirling. His body has been incinerated. There are no traces.'

I spun Callahan around and pressed the nuzzle of the gun under his chin.

'Callahan I don't believe you,' I said. 'I will never believe he is dead until I see his body and I will never stop looking.'

'You'll be looking a long time boy,' he said. 'He is nothing but a few particles of carbon. I told you.'

'And if I do find out he is dead I will come back and kill you, I swear it.'

'I am not afraid of you,' said Callahan. 'Take your best shot boy. I have no fear of death.'

'We are going,' I said.

'Going where?' Callahan's eyes sparkled again. 'You will never get out of here boy. They will cut you down like flowers.'

'Not if we leave in a tank, they won't.'

Callahan's eyes changed. He had realised we could do it after all. We weren't just kids with a crazy idea. We knew what we were doing. We had a plan.

'Let us out through the outside door,' I told one of the guards. I knew the tank would be outside from where they had transferred the last prisoners.

The guard let us out and we blinked the sunlight away as our eyes adjusted.

'Open the tank and let us in,' I said. 'Callahan will stay with us until we're safely away from the border.'

'You can't do this, Stirling,' said Callahan. 'I am wounded. How will I make it back?'

'Not my problem,' I said. I was now feeling buoyant for the first time. We had nearly completed our mission. We were getting out, finally, after all these years of dreaming about it, the dream had become reality. What is more I was convinced we would meet David at the meeting point as arranged with Miranda and Hargreaves. I could sense Callahan's desperation as he realised we were winning. His ploy to mess with my mind had failed. We would all be free.

The tank was now open and Roberts and Killinger were already in and calling me up.

'Up the steps!' I instructed Callahan, hauling him up. Roberts reached down and pulled him in; I quickly jumped in after him and slammed the lid down. Roberts had already got into the drivers seat.

'You know how to drive this thing?' I called out.

'Aye aye captain,' called back Roberts as the engine roared into life. We all cheered as the great beast of a machine lurched forward.

'You see Callahan. Now we will see what a liar you are,' I said. 'You have lost. Your regime has failed. You cannot defeat the people for ever.'

'We will see boy, we will see,' said Callahan.

We smashed through the wire railing that surrounded the compound and continued on through the town.

'It's alright Jackson,' I said to my friend who was starting to whimper next to me. 'We are free. We are out of this for ever.'

'He knows the truth,' said Callahan. 'See how he cannot look you in the eye. He is ashamed.'

'He is broken,' I said. 'Because of what you have done to him he is broken. But he will be healed.'

'Your mother would be proud,' I said to him rubbing his shoulder. 'This is her dream come true.'

Callahan scoffed and I turned to him with a smile. 'You know what Callahan. I'm debating whether to let you go once we pass the border or just kill you. Either way it's better than you deserve.'

'This is it,' called out Roberts. 'This is the meeting place.'

The engine stopped and I held my breath. This was the moment of truth. The lid opened and Hargreaves climbed in. Miranda followed straight after and fell into my arms. I clung onto her, my heart about to burst.

Then the lid slammed shut.

'What are you doing?' I called out. 'What about David?'

'David's gone Stirling,' said Hargreaves.

'What?'

'I'm so sorry Richard,' sobbed Miranda. 'When we got there, the house had been broken into. No one was there.'

'What?'

The tank lurched forward again.

'What are you doing?' I yelled. 'What are you doing? We can't leave without David! Stop! Stop!'

'We can't hang around,' said Hargreaves. 'David's not here, Stirling. We searched everywhere. He's gone.'

'He's not gone, he's here!'

I lurched forwards towards the driver's seat. Killinger and Hargreaves grabbed hold of me and pinned me to the floor. I started screaming for them to stop, to let me go, to find David. I slammed my head against the floor; Miranda grabbed hold of my hair, trying to comfort me. Eventually she screamed at me to stop and all the fight in me evaporated. I curled up and sobbed like a baby as she soothed me. I could sense Jackson and Callahan sitting there like twin accomplices. I could feel waves of remorse and despair from Jackson and cold satisfaction from Callahan. I could feel his eyes burning into my back as I lay there in tears. All shame had left me, I just wanted to give up.

The tank stopped and I heard Roberts say that we were a safe distance. The lid opened and I felt the presence of evil leave. Then the lid slammed shut again.

PART TWO

The City
2995-2996AD

. . . and so I urge you my brothers and sisters. Take up arms! The holy war is upon us. Show no mercy! Remember the Devil appears in many forms. It is only through our common resolve that we shall emerge triumphant. Show no fear! We are an army for the Lord. We will be relentless! We will be unstoppable! We will be victorious!

1

We travelled for five hours before the tank broke down.

Roberts had had to stop to be sick. He had become dizzy, having looked at nothing but the never ending sands passing underneath us. It would seem that Callahan was right. There really was nothing but desert lands outside the town. What is more we had no water and no supplies and the heat was getting unbearable.

After Roberts had finished emptying his guts onto the baking sands he couldn't get the tank going again.

'Come on!' he cursed as the engine did nothing but make feeble choking noises. 'I thought these things were solar powered.'

'Mains powered,' Hargreaves pointed out. 'Probably in case someone tried what we're doing now. We're stuck here. We're sitting ducks. What if they come looking for us?'

'Well we can't leave the tank, we won't last two minutes,' said Killinger. 'It's hot in here, but at least we're out the sun.'

'Didn't you see anywhere, Roberts?' said Miranda. 'Some settlement somewhere or at least somewhere where we can shelter?'

'Nothing but sand,' said Roberts. 'And the odd rock. We'll be vulture food out there.'

There was a collective sigh as we pondered what to do, before Killinger broke the silence.

'Hey is he alright,' he said gesturing to Jackson who was lying with his back to us, motionless.

Miranda left my side to check on him. She gently shook him. 'Jackson, Jackson are you alright?'

'Who cares?' I said.

'Richard, can't you see what they've done to him?' said Miranda.

'Better than he deserves,' I responded. 'At least he's still alive.'

'David's alive,' said Roberts. 'We'll find him—and your parents.'

'And you know that, do you?' I snapped back. 'Being so intelligent and informed? Well if you're such a genius how come you land us here in the middle of nowhere to die like rats? Why couldn't you have found somewhere by now?'

Roberts turned and looked into the distance. 'There wasn't anywhere,' he muttered.

Jackson made a gargling sound; I kicked him in the rear, causing him to groan.

'Richard!' Miranda hissed. 'Why can't you just leave it?'

'It's not your brother that's dead, is it?' I said. 'Dead because of him!'

'Hey just cool it, both of you!' Killinger butted in.

I slumped back against the wall of the tank. I didn't have the energy to fight.

'What's happened has happened,' said Killinger. 'Like it or not we're in this together. If we turn on each other, we're finished.' He put a hand on my shoulder. 'We'll find your brother, Stirling,' he said quietly. 'Somehow we will find him.'

I took a breath and put my head in my hands.

'But right now we've got to find a way out of here. Stirling, I'm sorry about what's happened to your brother but we can't blame Jackson. He's been beaten and tortured and he's lost his mother. You know what she meant to him Stirling.'

I nodded; in my head I knew he was right. Jackson had just gone through the worst experience of his life. I wanted to support him, but my mind kept replaying Callahan's words: *David is dead. I shot him through the head.'* Was he bluffing or had he really murdered David in cold blood? I kept imagining Callahan holding the gun to my brother's head; David accepting his fate, just as he had done with Vincent; the gun exploding.

'I should have killed him,' I said out loud.

'What do you mean?' said Hargreaves. I noticed everyone had turned to look at me.

'Callahan I mean. I should have killed him when I had the chance.'

I was surrounded by people making soothing noises.

'No, no,' said Roberts. 'We're better than that, we're not murderers.'

'He's right,' said Miranda next to me. 'You did everything right, I'm so proud of you.'

'I had him right here,' I continued. 'I should have shot him through the head.'

'What would it have achieved?' said Miranda. 'It would have made us no better than them.'

'It's just—I don't know—'

I had been determined not to break down but I couldn't help it. Miranda cradled me in her arms, rocking me.

'Callahan was bluffing,' said Killinger. 'I don't know what happened to him, but I'm sure he's alive.'

'Of course he is,' said Miranda.

'And another thing I'm sure of is we owe him a debt,' said Killinger.

I could sense the others trying to work out what he meant.

'Don't you remember?' said Killinger. 'All those years ago—with Vincent and—'. He stopped in his tracks. Of course everyone knew who the others were.

'Anyway, us three,' he gestured to himself, Hargreaves and Roberts. 'We all owe him big style. He put himself on the line for us.'

Roberts grunted in affirmation and Hargreaves nodded.

'And I for one will not stop until we find him,' Killinger continued.

'None of us will,' confirmed Roberts, laying a hand on my shoulder.

'But first we have to get out of here,' said Hargreaves. 'We've seen nothing but sand.'

Killinger looked annoyed at Hargreaves for bringing the conversation back to practicalities; but he had a point.

'It's baking out there,' Killinger said. 'But the sun will go down and it will get cooler.'

'And darker,' said Hargreaves. 'I say we should start now. We won't find anything in the pitch black.'

'It's the middle of the afternoon,' said Killinger. 'If we just wait a few hours, the temperature will go down and we can start looking for somewhere.'

'I don't know,' said Hargreaves. 'How do we know they haven't followed us?'

'They'd have done something by now surely,' said Miranda. 'Besides we would have seen them wouldn't we?'

'I haven't seen anyone about,' said Roberts. 'And we must be kilometres away from the town now.'

'How far?' asked Hargreaves. 'What speed were you doing?'

'Around sixty,' said Roberts.

'And we've been travelling for nearly five hours. That's around three hundred kilometres.'

'A good distance,' said Killinger.

'Unless we were going round in circles,' said Hargreaves.

'A straight line the whole way,' said Roberts. 'I should know.'

'Regardless,' said Killinger, stepping in before another argument started. 'I still think we're better waiting until it gets cooler. It will serve no purpose to collapse through heat stroke.'

'I agree,' said Miranda. She put a hand to her stomach and I put an arm round her. I had actually forgotten about the sixth person in the group.

'Are you ok,' said Killinger. 'How are you feeling?'

'I'm fine,' she said.

I kissed her on the cheek. 'I can't believe we actually did it,' I whispered.

'Neither can I,' she whispered back.

I think not long after that we all fell asleep.

2

I awoke to the sound of a scratching noise outside the tank. It was pitch black and Miranda was sleeping next to me. I felt for the gun, prodding Killinger in the process.

'What is it?' he whispered.

'A noise,' I said. 'Outside.'

'Where?'

'Just listen.'

More scratching.

'Hargreaves, wake up!' Killinger said.

'What—oh how long have we slept?'

'Never mind that, there's something outside,' said Killinger. 'Roberts!'

No sound.

'Stirling, wake up Roberts will you?'

I stirred to prod Roberts as Miranda stirred next to me.

'What is it?' she groaned.

'Don't worry,' I said. 'Probably just some animal.'

'It's night time.'

'I know. We've all slept too long.' I prodded Roberts again. 'Roberts wake up, will you!'

Roberts moved and yawned.

'Roberts,' snapped Killinger. 'Wake up and grab the rifle.'

More scratching.

'What was that?' said Roberts, jumping up.

'Just keep quiet and grab the rifle,' said Killinger. 'Use the laser sight so we can see what we're doing.'

I could hear Roberts stumbling about.

'I got it,' said Roberts. 'But I can't find the laser switch.'

'Oh give it here,' snapped Hargreaves, putting his elbow into my stomach as he clambered over me.

'Hang on, I've got it,' said Roberts. Suddenly the whole tank was illuminated in pale red.

'Take that gun off me!' said Killinger sharply. 'There's something outside. We don't know what it is.'

'We should have got out of here by now,' said Hargreaves. 'And now we're about to be eaten by some primitive wild animal.'

I reached for my hand gun and put the laser sight on.

'We've got guns,' I said. 'I think we can handle it.' I climbed up the ladder to the lid. 'Pop the lid, Roberts.'

There was a clunk as the lid popped ajar. I pushed it open and levered myself out. The sun was just under the horizon, throwing shadows across the sands and silhouetting the palm trees. Before my imagination could get the better of me I looked down. A dog was standing on its hind legs, its front paws up against the tank. We learnt about dogs and their usefulness and companionship to humans although no one in our town ever kept any themselves. I believe this one was a Samoyed dog; it was panting and looking straight at me, its tongue lolling out.

'It's just a dog,' I said.

'Can't they be dangerous?' said Roberts.

'It doesn't look dangerous,' I replied.

'Shoot it,' said Hargreaves. 'We could do with the meat.'

Miranda came up to join me and smiled. 'Oh don't shoot it,' she said. 'It seems friendly.'

Killinger then put his head out on the other side of me.

'It does seem friendly. But do we risk it? Maybe you should shoot it Stirling.'

I handed the gun to Killinger. 'Cover me,' I told him as I climbed over the top. Miranda grabbed me and told me to be careful.

'Don't worry,' I said. 'I've heard dogs and humans used to work together long ago.'

As I stepped down from the tank the dog left its post and stood underneath the ladder to watch me. I paused for a moment.

'He's watching you,' said Killinger. 'But don't worry I've got him covered.'

I stepped down onto the sand and the dog approached and started sniffing me. I stepped away and the dog followed me.

'This is what dogs do,' said Roberts who had come up to see the spectacle alongside Hargreaves. 'I learnt about it in natural history. It's just familiarizing itself with you.'

'Well it's getting a little too familiar for my liking,' I said, cringing as it sniffed around my groin.

'It's showing no signs of aggression,' said Miranda. 'When dogs are going to attack they normally growl and show their teeth.'

'I think it just likes you,' said Killinger.

'Well it's liking me too much at the moment,' I said. 'I'm coming back up.' As I lifted my head, I saw a figure about ten metres away. 'Killinger, look! Over there!'

I pointed towards the figure and Killinger snapped the gun on him. 'Stay where you are!' he ordered.

The figure stayed motionless.

'Is it human?' said Hargreaves.

'I think so,' I said. I started stepping towards the figure. It flinched away.

'I think it's just a kid,' I said. 'Hang on there!'

'Take it easy, Stirling,' said Killinger. 'We don't know if it's friendly. You've heard about the people on the Outside.'

'And you believe that?' said Miranda. 'I'm coming down as well Richard.'

I tried to protest but she was already down and at my side.

'We mean you no harm,' she called out. 'Killinger, take the gun off him.'

'No way!' called out Killinger. 'Not until we're sure about him.'

I stepped forward further and the figure came into focus. It was a boy, possibly about ten years old, with brown skin. He was wearing white trousers but was bare above the waist. His face was screwed up in a look of puzzled anxiety.

'Can you speak?' I asked.

He didn't move or change his expression. He just stared at us. The dog returned to us and stood next to the boy who put a hand on its coat. Miranda knelt down and held her arms out. 'Can you help us?'

The boy stepped up to her and stroked her face, his brow furrowed in concentration. Miranda smiled, placing her hands on his forearms.

'Everything alright,' called out Killinger.

'I think so,' I said, bewildered.

'You look sick,' the boy said. 'But my father can help you.'

3

'I don't know about this,' said Hargreaves as we trudged behind the boy and the dog. 'What if they're cannibals?'

'Then hopefully at least we'll get a quick death,' I said. 'What would you rather, die of thirst and exposure out here?'

It had been almost twenty four hours since we had last had anything to eat or drink. My head was pounding and my throat felt like it had thistles shoved down it. The sun was only just beginning to emerge from behind the horizon and we were all thankful for the cool air. I walked hand in hand with Miranda as Hargreaves tottered along beside us. Behind us Killinger and Roberts walked either side of Jackson, holding him up; he was almost completely out of it, his feet dragging through the sand behind him.

Ahead of us lay a small copse which the boy led us through. To suddenly be amongst trees felt disorientating; it was a struggle to keep focused in the minimal light that broke through the branches. There was a clear path through the bushes, trees and undergrowth and we trudged forward until we came to a little clearing. In it stood a small stone built house, the roof was made of branches.

'Please wait here,' said the boy. 'I will get my father.'

The boy ran into the house and we stood there shuffling our feet. Miranda squeezed my hand as we stared at the door waiting for someone to arrive; then a man stepped out.

He seemed to be virtually covered with hair and I thought back to when we were told the Outsiders were Neanderthals. His skin was also brown, like the boy's and he wore khaki coloured trousers and a sleeveless small jacket which seemed to be made out of an animal's skin.

'Maria, help the young lady,' he called out as he ran up to Jackson, taking him off Killinger and Roberts and hauling him into the house. 'Jacob, get some water from the well.'

The boy ran behind the house and a woman came through the door and approached us. Her broad smile and sparkling eyes more than compensated for her brown teeth and withered skin.

'We can help you,' she said. 'Won't you come into the house?'

The remaining five of us stepped through the door into a large clearing with wood panelled flooring. A gas lamp hung from the ceiling, illuminating the room with a warm red glow.

'Please sit,' said the woman. She propped up some cushions against the rough stones which held up the house. It wasn't the most comfortable looking arrangement, but we were too exhausted to care.

In the corner was a staircase which the man walked down, stroking his beard. 'You're friend has been beaten badly,' he said. 'What happened? Where do you come from?'

There was a silence as we thought about where to start. Then the boy came in with a tray full of wooden mugs. Each one was filled with water and we forgot about the question as we guzzled them down.

'Get some more water Jacob,' said the woman. 'Joseph, let them recover first; questions later.'

We took the second helping of water and thanked the woman, who nodded and smiled in return.

'My name is Maria and this is Joseph,' she said gesturing to the bearded man who was walking up the stairs with a mug of water. 'And this is our son Jacob. We have an older daughter too, but she is not with us at the moment.'

'Thank you for helping us,' said Miranda. 'We don't know what we would have done if we hadn't have seen your son.'

'You're most welcome,' said Maria. 'And you must stay until you are fully recovered.'

She glanced at Miranda's belly.

'You are with child at the moment?'

'Yes,' said Miranda with a smile. 'Two months now.'

'Oh!' said the woman. Her face glowed with pleasure as she bustled over to Miranda and started mopping her brow with a damp cloth. 'We must look after you then. You must take our bed.'

'Oh I couldn't—' began Miranda but the woman raised her hand to silence her.

'It is not just yourself you should think of,' she said. 'You must have our bed and the injured boy must have Jacob's.'

Jacob smiled and nodded earnestly.

'We don't want to trouble you,' I said.

'It is no trouble,' Maria said. 'You are the father?'

'Yes.'

'We will take good care of your beautiful wife,' Maria said. 'The rest of us must sleep down here.'

I wasn't about to argue and gave her a little smile and a nod in acknowledgement.

With heavy footsteps, Joseph returned, tutting under his breath.

'He has taken a little water,' he said. 'He is very weak but he will live.'

'I will prepare some tea,' said Maria getting up. 'And some food. Come along Jacob. Leave these people in peace for a while.'

Our hosts all disappeared into a back room, leaving us looking at each other in bewilderment.

'I sure am hungry,' said Roberts. 'I wonder what they eat here.'

'These people are savages,' hissed Hargreaves at us. 'How do we know they won't cook *us*?'

'You go if you want Hargreaves,' said Killinger. 'Maybe you can find a cactus to eat. Me, I'm taking my chances here. Besides which we still have weapons.' Killinger then looked around. 'Roberts what did you do with that rifle?'

'Oh, that man took it off me.'

'What?' spluttered Hargreaves and Killinger together.

'When he took Jackson from us, he took the gun as well.'

'You flaming idiot, Roberts!' hissed Killinger, punching him in the shoulder. 'You shouldn't be trusted with a blasted slingshot!'

'I didn't think he would do us any harm,' said Roberts, rubbing his shoulder.

'Well let's hope not!' said Killinger. 'Or I'll see to it you're first on the roasting spit.'

'I don't think they do mean us any harm,' whispered Miranda.

'I don't either,' I added. 'They seem good people.'

'Well this doesn't seem right to me,' said Hargreaves. 'I'm getting out of here.'

Hargreaves began to get up when Joseph suddenly appeared in the doorway at the back, the rifle slung over his arm.

'What kind of weapon is this?' he asked as he opened it and studied the ammunition inside. He snapped it shut again and cocked it. 'I've never seen anything like this before.'

'It's a standard rifle from the Enforcers,' I said. My eyes darted around at the nervous faces of my friends as we wondered what he would do.

Joseph snapped the laser aim on and raised the gun. We all gasped. It was primed at the front door behind us.

Joseph nodded with professional appreciation. 'Could be useful for hunting,' he said as he walked out the back.

4

The bowls of curried rice and bread we were given went down quickly; Maria frequently topped us up as we gorged ourselves.

When we had finally finished we sat back, contented against the cushions. Roberts let out a belch. 'That was delicious,' he said. 'Thank you.'

'You're welcome,' said Maria, smiling as always. 'You have not eaten in a while?'

'No,' I said. 'Not since yesterday morning. You were very kind to take us in.'

'It's a pleasure,' said Maria. 'Have you come far?'

We exchanged glances.

'Quite far,' said Miranda.

'What happened to your friend?' asked Joseph.

There was an awkward silence as we tried to think of how to explain where we had come from and what we had done.

'We're escaping persecution from our home town,' said Miranda.

'You are refugees?' asked Joseph.

'Yes,' replied Miranda. 'Our friend Jackson was being held and tortured by the authorities. We broke in and rescued him and then we fled.'

'Why was he being held?' asked Maria. 'He seems such a nice boy. What had he done?'

We explained the laws that we had been governed by and what happened to those who disobeyed them. We explained how we had been part of a group which engaged in subversive acts and how Jackson and his mother had been caught and how Rosie had been killed. We left out the part of how my brother was missing. I was waiting for someone to mention it and was grateful that nobody did. Maria, Joseph and their son Jacob sat and listened in astonishment.

'I have never heard of such a place,' said Joseph. 'You say this is just three hundred kilometres away?'

'We think so,' said Hargreaves. 'At least that's what Roberts told us.'

'And what is the name of this place?' asked Maria.

That was the first time we realised that the town didn't have a name; at least not one that we were told. Its namelessness implied its totality. It was everything, the air that we breathed, the Universe.

'You say there's no music?' said Joseph.

'No music, no games, no religion,' said Hargreaves.

'Just stone cold facts,' added Killinger.

'So if I played my flute I would—*disappear*, as you call it?' said Joseph.

Killinger nodded.

'Or if I played ball?' asked Jacob.

'I'm afraid so,' said Miranda.

'This rule applied to children also?' asked Maria, raising her hands in horror.

'Before the age of thirteen it is normally tolerated to a degree,' said Hargreaves. 'But it's not condoned.'

I remembered the secret games David and I would play. How our mother used to keep dragging him into the cellar. Seeing Jacob there, who seemed so much like David in his simplistic outlook, but so different in background was a painful contrast.

'Well you must never go back!' said Maria. 'Especially you, my dear,' she said to Miranda. 'That is no place to bring up a little one.' She put an arm around her son and tousled his hair.

'You should stay until you recover,' said Joseph. 'Then, there is a city you can go to.'

'A city!' burst out Killinger, his eyes widening. 'How far?'

'It is not too far,' said Joseph. 'About one hundred kilometres away. I can take you there in my hovercraft.'

'Please take us there now!' said Roberts. 'We have never seen any other place.'

Hargreaves looked wary, but then he always did. I myself was excited by the idea, but I was tired; both physically and emotionally as well as being concerned for Miranda. I didn't want to do anything that would jeopardise her or our unborn child. At least here we would be safe and able to recover some strength.

I was also highly reluctant to have to face Jackson again. Whilst he was upstairs recuperating, he was out the way and I didn't have to pay him much mind. It would be entirely different when he was recovered and back to his old self.

The trouble was I could not disassociate him from David's disappearance. I couldn't hear Jackson's name without thinking of his betrayal to me, to my family.

I realised this was unfair, but I just couldn't help it and resolved that myself and Miranda should break away from the group as soon as possible.

*

I am looking for David amongst the gorse bushes but I can't find him. He always likes to play this game. I call his name over and over but there is no response. I think this is all a part of the game initially. He always likes to tease me and jump out to give me a shock. After a while though, I start to panic and call out more frantically. Then I hear his voice coming from behind me. 'I am here Richard,' he says and as I look round he is standing there, looking at me, a huge hole through the middle of his forehead.

'David, what happened to you?' I ask.

'Your friend let me down, Richard,' says David. Then he gestures over to Jackson standing near by, who is staring at the ground, shame faced.

'He betrayed me to save himself and his mother.'

'Is this true?' I ask Jackson who sorrowfully nods in reply. Then I look down at my hand and see that it is holding a gun.

'You must take revenge, Richard,' said David. 'Do it for me, Richard.'

Then Rosie Jackson appears standing next to her son. She has bruises all over her face, her nose has crumpled, her eyes are puffed and swollen.

'Pull the trigger, Richard,' she tells me. 'He makes me ashamed to be his mother. I am disgusted this creature came from my womb. Destroy him now!'

Then Callahan appears behind David.

'Perhaps you don't have the guts,' he says, his cold eyes on me. 'You are weak, just like your father. 'Weak, weak, weak.'

I level the gun at Jackson's head. I can't do it. Callahan is right. Then Jackson raises his head, his eyes look directly into mine.

'Just do it!' he says.

I wake up in a cold sweat; the gun is in my hand.

5

Our time with Joseph and Maria was essential for our recovery. We grew stronger and fatter and revelled in our new found freedom. Their young son, Jacob taught us how to play baseball which myself, Miranda and Roberts enjoyed but Hargreaves and Killinger did not. Neither of them had any hand to eye co-ordination and seemed frightened of the ball. Killinger much preferred helping Maria in the home and became very artistic with some flowers which he had found in the copse. Miranda became more friendly with him and the two of them and Maria would often complete chores together and laugh together. Hargreaves spent a lot of time writing in a journal. He was very closed off and secretive about his journal and interacted little with the rest of us.

Whilst the rest of us positively glowed with health, Roberts appeared to be suffering with acute bouts of diarrhoea. Every now and then he would clutch his belly and groan, rocking back and forth before he would dash off to the latrine Joseph had built in the shed out the back. The rest of us found this quite amusing but Roberts became very embarrassed about it especially when their daughter Rachel appeared on the scene. At sixteen years old she was a fair bit younger than Roberts, although this didn't quell his infatuation.

'She's nice,' he whispered to me once.

'She's out of bounds,' I told him. 'I don't think Joseph and Maria would appreciate you slobbering over her.'

Rachel certainly was attractive and she was also surly and independent. She had been living in this mysterious city that our hosts would mention every now and then. Joseph and Maria seemed to hate the place. They had described it as a den of decadence and vice. They had left when Jacob was just five years old to live a simple life in the outback. Joseph had built the house himself using materials from the wood where possible, or from the city where it was not. He would hunt for food, just as the cavemen used to do in Neanderthal times. There was not much that could live in the desert conditions but he would find birds and lizards. Jacob was also a skilled hunter and would usually accompany his father. He seemed to have no problems living in this environment, but with Rachel it was a different story. They had had to let her move back to the city a year ago to stay with relatives after it was clear she would run away if they did not comply. She would often complain of the dirt and squalor of the house and how primitive everything was. In fact all of us grew to be quite irritated by her, except for Roberts who would often be caught gazing at her, doe-eyed. She made it clear that the feeling wasn't neutral, addressing him with a mild disdain as she got him to do favours for her as if she was an Empress addressing a dim witted servant. Roberts would of course gleefully run to do her every bidding, although we all told him it wouldn't make her interested in him.

Jackson recovered and kept a discreet distance from me. Every now and then I would catch him and Miranda exchange a smile. It would rile me so much I had to leave the room at times, but I kept my feelings to myself. In general he remained quiet and withdrawn; completely the opposite to his usual self. He didn't even respond to Rachel's obvious liking for him.

Even aside from the issues Jackson and I had at the time, the house was beginning to feel increasingly claustrophobic. We were fit and well and eager to explore these strange new lands that the family would talk about.

'Rachel works in the hotel industry,' said Maria over dinner once. 'They are looking for new staff, aren't they, my dear?'

'They're always looking for new talent,' said Rachel, chewing on a chicken leg as she spoke. 'But maybe not for you two,' she said gesturing to myself and Miranda.

'Why's that?' asked Miranda, bewildered.

'It just wouldn't work, trust me,' she said. 'Not in your condition, but I do know of somewhere else you could go. A friend is looking for some help to run his bar.'

'What's a bar,' I asked.

'You never heard of alcohol?' laughed Rachel.

It was true, we had never heard of alcohol or any type of drug. They just didn't exist in the town.

'You've got a lot to learn,' she said shaking her head. As annoying as she was, she was right. I began to realise just how unequipped for the real world we were. Nevertheless, we couldn't put it off forever and the next morning we said our goodbyes. Maria embraced us all warmly with tears in her eyes. It had been perhaps ten days since we arrived there, starving and thirsty, although it may as well have been ten years.

'You will always be like a son to me,' she said as she hugged me. The emotion took me aback a bit. I'd known she was very fond of Miranda and concerned over our unborn baby, but didn't think this extended to me.

'When your little one has arrived, maybe you will visit,' she said.

Jacob reached out and put something in my hand. It was the ball with which we'd all played baseball with; the game he had introduced to us.

'Thank you,' I said with a smile and ruffling his hair. 'I will teach it to my son one day.'

As Joseph smiled back, his eyes gleaming I thought of how I would be proud to have a son like him. A daughter like Rachel would be another thing altogether though. She sat in the hovercraft, arms crossed as Maria wished us well.

We climbed onto Joseph's hovercraft. As we watched Maria and Jacob's figures recede into the distance, waving to us side by side, I felt a touch of sadness as we left the first real family I had ever known.

6

The first part of the journey was much the same as what we had already seen; just desert and rocks. It was cramped on the hovercraft, Joseph and Rachel sat in the front and the six of us crammed into the back which was only meant to seat four. The craft sliced through the air, about a half metre above the ground. It had no roof so that at least alleviated the heat and we were content just to sit and let the sands fly by underneath us. Suddenly, Killinger sprang out his seat. 'What's that!' he exclaimed, finger pointed in the distance. A black speck was there in the horizon, getting bigger by the second.

'That's the city,' replied Joseph.

The speck began to transform into a concrete forest. I could sense the nervous excitement amongst us all, as we approached it. It was like a monstrous creature, waiting to devour us whole. As we actually entered the jaws of this huge beast, Miranda clung onto me tightly.

We were in it.

Huge towers and a cacophony of electronic noise overwhelmed us. Giant screens were everywhere, the voices from them competing for attention. Ahead of us a huge disembodied head of a woman started speaking and Miranda screamed and clung even tighter to me.

'What is that!' she squealed.

'It's a hologram,' sneered Rachel. 'Haven't you ever seen one before?'

We were heading right for the woman's face and we all buried our heads in our hands. Rachel burst out into hysterical laughter and we looked up to see the woman had gone.

'It's only light, that's all,' she said. 'Look behind us.'

Sure enough we looked behind to see the woman's face getting further into the distance, talking once more as if nothing had happened.

'It's double faced,' said Rachel. 'Whichever side you approach she's always facing you.'

'What's she talking about?' asked Roberts.

'She's advertising face transplants.'

'What!' several of us blurted out together.

'If you don't like your face, you can have it changed for a new one,' she said before turning to Roberts. 'Maybe you should try it.'

Roberts sniffed and looked away, I felt a little sorry for him and was glad no one else laughed at that.

'So where are we going?' asked Miranda.

'You can meet my boss, he's well nice,' said Rachel. 'Then I can show you all the best places.'

'But not for us two?' I asked, referring to myself and Miranda.

'Oh no,' she said. I can show you someplace else. It's not for you at all.'

I wondered what kind of a place would be for everyone apart from us. Was it because Miranda was the only female in our group; or that she was pregnant? I couldn't be bothered asking any more though, preferring just to sit back and take in the scenery.

And there was such scenery to take in.

Aside from the vast amount of hovercrafts zooming past us there was a lot of people on the streets. Some people had jackets displaying images of human faces or animals. These images would move, as if the wearer had a transparent, flexible screen plastered onto their clothes. Some people were on foot and some travelled on boards which would move suspended in the air like a mini hovercraft.

Some women stood on the corners wearing very little as if prostituting themselves and some wore nothing at all.

Amongst the affluent looking people, I saw a few in rags, mostly children who loitered in the shadows as much as they could, as if trying to avoid being seen. I saw one of them being beaten across the head by a man in a blue uniform.

'Who's that?' I exclaimed.

'One of the street beggars,' replied Joseph.

'That man's beating him, we should stop him,' I said. I felt ashamed of the way we had just passed by as if it wasn't happening. It reminded me of the Enforcers, Vincent slapping David across the face after he'd come to the rescue of Hargreaves. I shook my head as if I could shake the image out my mind.

'That man's a street cleaner,' said Joseph.

'He cleans streets?' asked Roberts, causing Rachel to turn away and roll her eyes.

'Street cleaners are employed to keep order on the streets, said Joseph. 'That boy would have been a pick pocket or something of the like.'

'They just beat them?' I said, incredulous. At least in our town a veneer of civility was kept.

'Street justice,' said Joseph. 'It's the way it is here. Dog eat dog. This is why we left. We told you the sort of place this was.'

I slumped back in the seat, depressed. Is this what we escaped the town for? We had such high hopes for the outside. All my life I had dreamed it would be a wonderful place.

'Don't waste your time feeling sorry for the underclass,' said Rachel. 'They're nothing but thieves and rapists.'

In an instant, my casual dislike to Rachel turned to intense hatred. Couldn't she see these people had nothing? How could she condone a grown man beating a boy no older than her brother?

'They are poor people?' asked Miranda. 'They don't have homes?'

'They get by anyway they can,' said Joseph. 'Some of them sell on their stolen goods. Others prostitute themselves or do favours for the rich classes.'

'Vermin,' muttered Rachel under her breath and with that every one was silent for a while.

'We're here,' said Joseph after a while.

We had stopped at a huge skyscraper. We stepped out, our legs buckling after being cramped for so long.

'I must leave you now,' said Joseph.

'Thank you for your kindness,' said Miranda as she took his hand. We all thanked him one by one before he left, leaving us on the pavement, disorientated and confused. 'This way,' said Rachel, as she led us into the building.

7

The foyer was huge and almost bare. The floor was made of a transparent hard white surface and the walls brilliant white. At the far end of the room sat a man at a desk who paid us no attention as we walked across the empty floor to an elevator. The sides of the elevator were transparent so we could see the city as we ascended the building. The buildings went as far as the eye could see and the air traffic was on several different levels. They ranged from being just a half metre above the ground to being as high as the top floor of some of the skyscrapers. Some of the air craft picked people up or dropped them off from the upper floors of the buildings, landing and taking off from a designated platform.

The elevator door opened and we were led out into a dimly lit corridor. The walls were black with lines of pink and yellow making a haphazard course across them. The clear white floor felt sticky to walk on and the whole place smelt of stale sweat.

'What is this place?' asked Hargreaves, wrinkling his face.

'This is where you'll be working,' said Rachel.

She took us down the corridor to a door which had a sign on reading BIG BOSS. As she knocked on it her expression changed in an instant from her usual surly demeanour to that of an excited child. The door was opened by an overweight, balding man wearing a string vest and shorts. She flung herself at him and he kissed her on the mouth. He then stood there with an arm slung around her shoulder and a pick between his yellow teeth, eyeing us all with a look of distaste. We must have been all looking back at him in amazement and disgust at how a young attractive girl like Rachel, however unlikeable she may be, could be involved with such an unkempt, seedy man obviously more than twice her age.

'These the new uns?' he grunted.

'That's right baby,' replied Rachel nestling her head into his hairy chest as she looked at us with smug satisfaction.

The man's face broke into a lurid leer as if something deliciously disgusting had just entered his mind. 'Why don't you go and fix me a drink honey,' he said to Rachel without looking at her. As she walked off he gave her a resounding slap on the behind and I could feel Roberts seething next to me.

'So you want to work for me, do you?' he said his eyes scanning from one of us to the other.

'We were sent here,' said Hargreaves.

The fat man's eyes then flashed onto Hargreaves like a flash light. Then, without warning he marched right up to him, shoving him against the wall with his elbow. His free hand travelled up between Hargreaves' legs and grabbed his crotch. Hargreaves yelped in shock and the rest of us were too stunned to do anything.

'Not as bad as I thought,' said the fat man. 'Got potential.'

He withdrew from Hargreaves who looked like he wanted to disappear through the wall, scanning us with his suspicious little eyes. He settled on Miranda and for a moment I thought he was going to do the same to her. I was just getting ready to hit him when his lip curled.

'Lady friend, huh,' he said. 'You must be the couple, I can tell by the look in your eye.'

I nodded slowly and put a hand on Miranda's arm.

'Ok,' the man said. 'My name's Bill and as the sign says on the door I'm the boss around here. I play fair but I play hard. I don't want no thieving, no back talk and no double crossing. You think you can manage that?'

To be honest I don't think any of us knew what he was going on about but we nodded anyway.

'Good. You two can work in the bar,' he said, pointing at Miranda and myself. 'The other four are up here with me.'

Rachel returned with a glass of some green substance and handed it to Bill.

'Take the couple down will you honey,' he said to Rachel, downing the noxious looking substance and handing back the glass. 'I've got some prep talk to do with these fellas.'

We followed Rachel back to the escalator leaving the other four looking bewildered and terrified.

'He's a really good man,' said Rachel as we descended in the lift. 'Once you get to know him that is.'

The elevator doors opened to reveal a long hall with a raised surface running a few metres from the wall. There were a number of empty tables and chairs dotted around. On one side of the raised surface was a number of high stools and on the other side a number of glasses and bottles with curious looking liquids in.

'This is the bar,' said Rachel. 'It gets pretty busy here at times. Your job is just to serve drinks and keep the customers happy. Frank will explain it all to you tomorrow.'

The sun had gone down and we walked over to the huge windows to look out at the city at night. It was an impressive sight. A collage of multi-coloured lights patterned the sky. Other lights darted across the scene like fireflies, presumably the lights of the hovercrafts, dashing from one side of the city to the other.

'This place is amazing,' said Rachel. 'It's the city that never sleeps. I can't understand why mother and father wanted to leave.'

'Maybe they wanted the quiet life,' I suggested.

'They're just losers,' said Rachel. 'They can't hack the pace. But this is all I've ever wanted. This city, this job, Bill.'

'You love him?' asked Miranda.

'Like no woman has ever loved a man before,' said Rachel, the same gushing look on her face as she had before.

I could have argued this point a bit more but I didn't have the energy or the will at the time. For a moment the three of us shared a certain serene moment as we stood looking out over the city that had become our home. That was before Rachel ran off on hearing Bill call her name. Miranda and I looked at each other and kissed. We stood hand in hand, looking out at the muted bustle happening below us. I felt an overwhelming sense of freedom. We were young, we were in love, we had the world at our feet. Anything was possible.

Our room at the hotel had a mirrored ceiling so we could see each other as we lay on the bed. It was certainly a luxury to have a bed to sleep in again, but the real prize was to have some time alone. The six of us who had broken out the compound had been stuck with each other for almost two weeks, in cramped conditions and at least to start with in fear of our lives. We had avoided being shot down during the escape and survived the heat of the desert with no food or water and had somehow ended up here, by complete accident. Wasn't this what I'd always dreamed of? Since I was a small child yearning for the body of water in the distance I had wanted nothing more but to escape and I was here, safely lost in the city with my wife beside me. It was a hollow triumph though, having lost my family and best friend in the process.

'What are you thinking about?' asked Miranda next to me.

'Just stuff,' I replied, not really wanting to go there.

'I can hear your brain ticking away,' she whispered in my ear.

'Well actually I was thinking that if I end up like Bill I want you to kill me.'

'Oh he's disgusting isn't he?' said Miranda. 'But you won't end up like him.'

'How do we know what we'll end up like?' I said. 'Maybe this is what this city does to people.'

'They'll be good people here, just like there were in the town.'

'Yeah, there were real good people there, weren't there?' I replied, the barb in my voice betraying more than I intended.

Miranda cuddled up next to me and I turned my head away, not wanting her to see the tear in my eye.

'We'll find him,' she said softly putting her head on my chest.

'He must be dead,' I said swallowing the words down like a bitter pill.

'We'll find him,' she said once more. 'You don't have to be brave any more. You don't have to hide yourself.'

'Old habits die hard,' I said, the tears streaming fully down my face. I kissed her gently on the head.

Miranda rolled onto her side and I placed my hand on her belly. I could sense the life there underneath my palm. It made my skin tingle.

'It's our future,' I said. 'We've got to look forward to our future. We've got to put the past behind us.'

'You really want to do that?' asked Miranda.

'What else can we do?' I asked in reply.

'Then forgive Jackson,' she said, caressing my fingers.

'I can't.'

'It's what you need to do, you know that. You'll never be able to move on until you do.'

'That's the point, he just brings everything back. I can't look at him without remembering.'

'That's because it's still unresolved,' Miranda said. 'Once you sort it out with him you'll just feel such a release I know it. We can start to look forward to the future again.'

'Maybe some day,' I conceded. 'But not yet.'

I knew she was right and part of me really wanted to, but it would have felt like a betrayal of David to do that, dead or alive. Maybe I didn't want to move on at all.

'I think you're lucky,' she said, looking up at the ceiling. 'I don't miss my family at all.'

8

It didn't feel any time at all before we were awoken by a furious knocking on the door. I opened it to see Rachel standing there, her hair standing on end and what looked like the beginning of a bruise on her left eye. She carried her usual look of disdain on her face. 'It's time to start work,' she snapped. 'Be at the bar in ten minutes.'

Our trainer in the art of running a bar was named Brad who was perhaps just a few years older than us. 'You might get some who start freaking out and getting agro,' he said. 'If that happens, you just press the button and security will get rid of 'em.'

'Sorry, what does this stuff do?' I asked, pointing to the bottles of liquid behind the bar.

Brad looked at the bottles and then back at me with a look of astonishment on his bleary face.

'You kidding right?' he said. 'You mean to say you've never heard of alcohol before?'

We shook our heads in bewilderment.

'Man, do you guys come from outer space?' laughed Brad.

At that point two other young men entered the bar. One of them was bald except for a green tuft of hair on his crown and had a nail going through his nose. The other had longer hair and a moving image of a dancing naked woman on his black jacket.

'These the new guys?' asked the man with the dancing woman on his jacket.

'We've got to show them the bright lights of the city,' said Brad with a mischievous grin.

'Awesome!' exclaimed the green haired man.

Throughout the day there was not much to do. A middle aged man entered and Brad taught me how to pour a brown bubbly liquid which was apparently called beer. My first attempt resulted in the glass being half filled with white froth, which the middle aged man seemed to find quite amusing. He then glanced over at Miranda who was polishing glasses.

'Care to polish something else, baby?' he said with a lascivious leer.

Miranda turned away and he leaned over the bar as if to slap her on the behind. I shot him a look which stopped him in his tracks.

'Easy there partner,' he said with a chuckle, raising his hands. 'Didn't realise the two of you were together.'

Brad threw me a disapproving look. Maybe it was part of the culture to treat women in this way, but it was something I would find hard to get used to.

As the hours wore on I became more and more aware of Brad and his two friends, huddled up in the corner, throwing us the odd glance and chuckling to each other.

'I don't trust those guys,' said Miranda to me quietly.

'I don't trust any of their hormones,' I said. 'They all want to mate with you, you realise that, don't you.'

'Will you not use that term,' hissed Miranda. 'We're not in the town any more. Just try to talk a bit like them.'

'Well what do they call it then? Copulating?'

'They call it making out,' corrected Miranda.

'How the hell do you know that?'

'Just stop it, will you!' she snapped. 'I can look after myself, unless you don't trust me.'

'I'm sorry,' I said, putting my hands on her shoulders. 'It's not easy for me, that's all.'

'I know,' she said. 'It's not easy for me either, but the thing I'm saying is we should be careful that's all.'

'Do you think we should go out at all?'

'Well,' she said with a smile, her eyes flashing with excitement. 'I think we should try. Aren't you curious?'

'I am,' I said latching onto her enthusiasm. 'Just stick with me, ok? I don't want anything to happen to you or the baby.'

'Me neither,' she said and we stole a quick kiss before Brad coughed to indicate a customer, gawping at us, open-mouthed.

Throughout the day I could feel the evening approaching like an arriving storm, making its presence felt the closer it got. Brad and his friends would continue to mutter and giggle in their little huddle and I couldn't be sure if I felt nervous or excited about what was to come.

When the hour finally arrived, Jackson, Hargreaves, Killinger and Roberts arrived in the bar accompanied by one of Brad's friends—the one with the green tuft of hair and the nail through his nose. I was a little reassured to see that they were all looking as nervous and unsure as me. Miranda seemed the most confident one amongst us; she leaned over the bar and greeted them with a smile. The green haired man winked at her.

'You all ready for the night of your lives?' asked the long haired man with the dancing woman on his lapels.

'You bet,' croaked Jackson.

'Take one of these,' said Brad handing round cylindrical capsules.

'What is it?' asked Hargreaves.

'Uppers,' said the long haired man. 'You'll never get through the night without them.'

To my surprise Hargreaves took it without another hesitation as did Jackson, Roberts and Killinger.

'I'm not too sure,' I whispered to Miranda. 'Think of the baby.'

'No, we'll be ok, thank you,' said Miranda to the long haired man as she handed the pill back. 'You can if you want,' she said to me.

'No. I'll be fine too,' I said.

'Suit yourself,' said the long haired man. 'My name's Jake by the way and this is Nath,' he said referring to the green tufted man who nodded in reply.

'Frederick Jackson,' greeted Jackson, appearing to try and drum up some of his old confidence by extending a hand.

The three city dwellers all collapsed in hysterical giggling.

'What kind of a name is that?' spluttered Jake.

'First names are fine,' said Brad. 'We'll call you Fred.'

We then established our new abbreviated names. Hargreaves became Rupe, Killinger became Stan and Roberts became Daz. I became Rich and Miranda became Randy which everyone thought was very funny apart from me.

'Let's go then,' said Jake and we followed him out into the wildness of the night.

9

Wildness was the only word I could think of to describe a place as savage and untamed as the city. The street was filled with the sound of shouting and the whirr of hovercrafts. A man was blowing fire from a lit torch, the flames billowing up into the night sky; another man was juggling daggers. The people were crisscrossing all over the street and as we got deeper in, the forest of bodies seemed to get thicker and thicker. I held on tightly to Miranda's hand. A little beggar boy seemed to emerge from no where and blocked our path, gazing up at Miranda with his hand cupped.

'Can't you spare a little money, ma'am,' he said. 'My family are starving. The cleaners shot my father and burned my house. Please ma'am.'

We didn't have anything and Miranda apologised.

'Please ma'am!' the boy said, his voice rising in even more earnest. 'We will all die, if you can't help us.'

'Beat it kid!' snapped Jake, raising his hand in warning.

The boy cowered for a moment and then disappeared.

'Don't trust them for a moment,' said Jake. 'They send the kids out to try and tug at the heartstrings but they'll stick a knife in you without a moments thought. I should know.'

He pulled down his sleeve to reveal a thin, red line going vertically down his forearm.

'That was done by a kid his age,' he said. 'So don't be taken in.'

Miranda sniffed next to me and blinked as she tried to recover herself. I squeezed her hand to try and reassure her.

'We'll be there soon,' said Brad. 'Just stick together.'

The crowd seemed to get denser and more violent the further we went in.

'The street down there,' said Jake, pointing a ringed finger towards a darkened alleyway off the main street. 'Don't ever go down there. It's full of pimps and lowlifes. Not even the cleaners go down there.'

As if to further emphasise his point he nodded towards a so called cleaner in front of us, clubbing a man about the shoulders. The man was stooping and cradling his head, as he tried to forge a path through the crowd to evade the blows.

'Down here!' said Brad pointing to some steps on our right.

We were herded down to some burly looking men in dark uniforms at the door; they nodded us through without a word.

Inside the air was thick with the smell of pine and the sound of pulsating music. A swirl of activity was all around us; a friendly, ambient vibe. Everyone seemed to be happy.

A blonde haired, naked woman carrying a tray approached Brad and grabbed his crotch. 'Hey Brad, nice to see you again,' she said with a smile.

'Hey baby,' said Brad returning the smile and playing with a ring through her nipple. 'Can you show us to a good table? We've got some outatowners.'

The blonde haired woman cast her eyes over us with a look of surprise.

'Sure!' she said turning back to Brad.

As she turned I noticed a little tattoo of a viper on her lower back. I sensed Miranda sighing next to me and I turned away. The woman led us to a table in front of a platform with a pole running from the floor to the ceiling.

'Drinks?' she asked Brad.

'The same as usual,' said Brad.

The woman turned and walked away and Nath, the green haired guy clapped an arm around a stunned looking Roberts.

'Is she getting your freak on or what buddy?' he said with a leer.

'Urr!' grunted Roberts, still looking in the distance.

'You like Natasha?' clarified Brad.

'I like Rachel,' replied Roberts.

'Oh forget her, she's a bitch!' said Nath.

'She's not!' snapped Roberts, turning on the green tufted man.

'Look buddy,' Jake said leaning over the table so the dancing naked woman on his lapel reflected in the table surface. 'I'm saying this 'cause I think you're a nice guy and I like you. You'll get nowhere with her. She's obsessed with Bill. She thinks he's the "one" or something. I don't know but she's messed up in the head if you ask me. The guy's pond life.'

'They make a good couple then,' said Nath.

'Hey easy dude,' said Brad to Nath as Roberts flashed him a look of contempt. 'The guy's in love with the girl. The thing is . . . thanks baby,' he broke off to take a glass of green liquid off the naked woman. She then handed the same concoction to everyone in the group. As she leaned over the table her breasts dangled just centimetres from Jackson's face, who goggled them in fascination. She strode off; her hips swaying from side to side in an easy rhythmical fashion. Those hips must have had some experience in their time.

'The thing is,' continued Brad to Roberts. 'She's a young girl and doesn't know what she wants; and you could do better. Tasha will sort you out.'

Roberts looked down, apparently hurt by the very suggestion.

'What about you Fred?' said Jake to Jackson. 'You look like you could do with some loving.'

'You should have seen his face just now!' laughed Nath. 'He's got a freak on for Tash alright.'

'We'll arrange something for later,' said Brad with a nod.

'What about you two?' said Jake, looking directly at Hargreaves and Killinger.

'Rupe and Stan,' said Nath, rolling the names in his mouth as if evaluating their taste.

'You want us to fix you up with some fellas?'

Killinger nearly choked on his drink and Hargreaves turned a curious shade of pale.

'We're not into that kind of thing,' stammered Hargreaves.

'Bullshit!' exploded Nath in what was either outrage or mirth. 'I've never seen such a pair of fags in all my life.'

'But that's okay,' interjected Brad. 'It's all okay here. Whatever gets your freak on is okay. Guys, gals. You could even get one of those little beggar kids to do something for a few coins.'

'Yeah, mind they don't bite down though,' added Jake which caused them all to wince in merriment. Killinger and Roberts looked like they wanted to disappear through the floor and I felt sorry for them. Of course we all knew their preferences, but it had never been a discussion point until now. Regardless of their sexuality they had been our comrades since the break out and I felt bad they were being ridiculed in this way. Mercifully for them however, the shift of focus soon turned to the stage. Natasha was standing there right in front of us, shimmying herself up and down the pole as if making love to it. More specifically she was right in front of me. I didn't know where to look with Miranda sitting right next to me. I tried to tactfully look down, but she put a foot underneath my chin and lifted my head so I was looking right up between her legs, her tasselled breasts jiggling underneath dispassionate eyes.

I could sense Miranda just shrinking next to me and reached out a hand to reassure her. As I took her hand she didn't respond and I had to think of a way out. In a flash I thought of it. 'Jackson!' I called out. 'I mean Fred. Get him up here!'

To my relief this was given vocal support by Nath, Brad and Jake who half man handled Jackson on to the stage. Natasha was joined on stage by three other girls who began stripping Jackson off piece by piece to the raucous cheers of the audience. I couldn't help joining in myself and feel a little satisfaction in Jackson's discomfort. All of a sudden I felt a tap on my shoulder. It was Brad.

'Maybe you'd better go after her,' he said.

'Who?' I asked as I noticed the empty space next to me. Brad pointed towards a door with his thumb and I quickly got up and walked out of it.

Miranda was there in the foyer outside the restrooms, leaning against the wall.

'What are you doing?' I snapped at her. 'I told you not to leave my side, it's too dangerous.'

She sniffed, tears glistening on her cheeks; my anger melted.

'I'm sorry,' I said. I tried to take her in my arms but she pushed me away.

'It's you I want, you know that,' I said. 'You and the baby.'

'You haven't got a clue have you Richard?' she said.

'What—what have I done?'

'How can you stand this place?' she said. 'It's such a horrible city. I hate it!'

'It's ok,' I said. 'It just takes a bit of getting used to.'

'You were loving it, weren't you?'

She glared at me through her tears; I felt irritated by the insinuation. I hadn't done anything to deserve it as far as I was concerned. 'I wasn't, Miranda. It's you I love. It's only ever been you I love. How many times do I have to say it?'

'I'm not talking about that.'

'Well what then?' I said, trying to muffle the frustration in my voice. Everything I had said was true and genuine. In fact apart from David, Miranda could have been the only person I'd ever loved in the world.

'Jackson,' she spluttered.

'Jackson!' I exclaimed. 'What about him. He's having the time of his life.'

'He's not Richard and you know it. That's why you sent him up there.'

'What's all this about Jackson?' I said. 'He killed my brother; you should be on my side not his.'

'That's not true!' she snapped back. 'That's not true and you know it.'

I realised this was unfair and felt a little ashamed. I couldn't bring myself to say so though and remained silent.

'I just can't stand this vindictive side of yours Richard. You used to be such a principled person. I really used to admire you and—I just don't know who you are anymore.'

She left to go back into the bar and I let her go. I went to wash my face in the bathroom and pull myself together. I could hear the distant raucousness coming from the bar as I looked at my bleary face in the mirror. Everything she had said was right. What kind of a person was I now? What had I left the town for? Everything in this city felt sordid and cheap and soulless. Was this all there was? Was this as good as it got?

The doors behind me opened and a group of young men walked in.

'Oh he's getting it good out there,' said one.

'Three at once. Such a lucky bastard!'

'I'd take the one with the tattoo myself,' said the first one. 'Right up the arse. Slam!'

The two men came and stood either side of me at the sinks.

'Such a lucky bastard!' repeated the other.

'Hey buddy, you okay?' said the other to me.

'Yeah,' I muttered.

'You're missing all the action, dude. You should get out there.'

And then they were gone. I took another look in the mirror and then walked out myself.

Miranda was sitting on her own, not far from the group. Roberts came up to me. 'Stirling, are you okay?' he said.

'Yeah I'm fine,' I replied.

'Oh, Jackson. You should have seen it.'

'I can only imagine,' I said, looking past him at Miranda.

I became aware of Jackson, now fully clothed, being congratulated by the others in the group. He stood there, in the middle of them all, looking flushed but proud as they all slapped him on the back. I thought I caught his eye for a brief second and saw perhaps a tinge of regret followed by defiance as he looked away. It was as if he was saying "you can go to hell Stirling! I'm not feeling bad for you anymore".

I went up to Miranda and put a hand on her shoulder which she cupped with her hand.

'I'm sorry,' I said as I sat next to her.

'Don't worry about it,' she replied. She gave me a smile of reassurance; a weary smile. It belonged to someone twice her age.

'One day we'll leave this place,' I said. 'You and me and the kid. We'll start a new life somewhere in a better place, a decent place. Like a proper family. The one we've always wanted.'

'Of course,' she said, rubbing my hand. Then we sat together, slightly away from the rest of the group and let the night wash over us as we sipped our drinks. And then strange things started to happen . . .

10

It seemed to creep up on us without us realizing it. We sat there watching the sea of naked flesh on the stage; young women, dancing to the music, doing things to each other and the occasional young man.

Miranda and I sat in quiet companionship, my hand on her back, sipping our drinks almost unconsciously. I don't know if someone kept topping the glass up but we didn't seem to get to the end of them. The music seemed to have a pervading consciousness of its own; it filled the room as if it was the air we were breathing. Everything was a part of the music, from the dancers to the people milling around.

The images became pixilated as though they were being viewed on a screen. The dots of light became separated and random, whizzing to and fro like fireflies.

I turned to look at Miranda to see she was looking straight back at me. Her eyes composed of millions of fiery dots, swirling around like sand in a storm. She said something I couldn't understand. I put my face next to hers and inhaled her aroma; like flowers in spring.

'I'm feeling strange,' she said, her voice amplified.

'So am I,' I said. 'But it will be okay. We'll take care of each other.'

Looking over at the group I saw Jackson dancing to the music as if his life depended on it. Hargreaves and Killinger were sitting next to each other, their arms around each other, deep in conversation. Roberts was sitting alone, head in hands. The three city dwellers were watching Jackson and the dancers on the stage, enjoying the show.

'Let's dance!' I said to Miranda, pulling her arm like an excited child.

'I don't want to,' she whined, resisting me.

'Come on, it will be fun,' I said, pulling at her with both arms.

In the end she allowed me to lead her to the dance floor. The music took control of my body: the bass resonated through my bones. It didn't take long for Miranda to join in and for a while, we became one and the same. There was no separation between me and her. We were together, man and wife, two sides of the sky.

Across our sky soared Jackson, his arms flailing like pirouettes. He sailed back and forth across my line of vision like an eagle in flight. Then I felt his hand on my back and his face next to me. His eyes looked huge and earnest.

'You know Stirling,' he said. 'I never meant any harm to come to your brother.'

Overtaken by a sudden feeling of warmth, I took him in my arms and held him close.

'It's okay Jackson,' I said. 'It's not your fault.'

I held him at arms length and could see his eyes searching me, looking for further reassurance.

'David's not dead,' I continued. 'I can still sense him. He's always here.'

Jackson nodded. 'My mother's not dead,' he said. 'She's in here.' He held a fist to his chest. 'I can feel her all around me.'

For a moment I broke off. My mind floated back to the old days in the town. To David's face looking at me in awe. At me, Richard; the great story teller. I snapped myself out of it. I was back in the club, staring at naked women.

'Great party Jackson,' I said vacantly. 'You always did good parties.'

Jackson didn't seem to be listening; he was back into the music again, pumping his arms as if dancing was the most serious business in the world. Then suddenly he was next to me again, glancing over at Hargreaves and

Killinger. They were deep into each other, their lips together, hands on each others thighs.

'You see them two?'

I nodded in mild surprise.

'I think it's great you know,' said Jackson. 'Why shouldn't they show some love.'

'What's wrong with him?' I asked, gesturing to Roberts who was still slumped on the table.

'Oh, I don't know,' said Jackson. He marched over to Roberts and started shaking him, bellowing in his ear. 'Hey Roberts! No time for sleeping now. Get up and dance!'

Roberts lifted his head and threw up over the table. The green vomit spread over the surface and dripped onto the floor. Roberts looked up at us, his eyes blurred and vacant, before he was hoisted onto his feet by Brad and Jake.

'Think it's time to go,' said Brad as he and Jake half carried Roberts towards the door.

'Come along, lover boys,' said Nath to Hargreaves and Killinger, who were still exploring each others tonsils.

We stumbled outside and the noise and darkness threw me into a panic. We were out into the danger zone again. Time to focus and move quickly.

All around us we could hear angry raised voices and explosions. I called out to Miranda and held her close as we paced through the streets. Everything felt like it was closing in on us. The noise, the heat, the light, the leering faces in the dark.

'Just keep going,' called out Brad in the distance. I looked round to see Hargreaves and Killinger behind us, their faces warped like a distorted mirror image.

'Keep going Stirling,' said Killinger, his voice sounding like it was travelling through water. I looked ahead and everything was blurred, almost beyond distinction until I felt the bile rising and collapsed to the side. I felt a moment of clarity as I looked down at my own vomit, listening to the sound of my own retching. It was almost like a focal point. I heard Miranda's voice soothing me and felt her hand rubbing my back.

'You okay dude,' said a voice which I think belonged to Nath. Then strong hands hoisted me to my feet and we were moving again, through the maze of bodies and discarded automobile parts to the serenity and blankness of the hotel foyer.

As we ascended above the city in the elevator, I held Miranda close, stroking her hair as she wept into my chest. There was an air of stunned silence in the unforgiving glare of the elevator lighting. Jake whistled softly.

'What a night,' he muttered to himself, leaning against the wall.

The doors opened and we staggered into our rooms for the night. There was no escaping the visions though as the darkness of sleep closed in.

I woke up several times during the night. The first was during a nightmare that haunts me to this day. David's face as a nine year old, centimetres from my own, smiling. His eyes are blank and his hair is swept across his forehead revealing a huge hole. Through the hole I can see Callahan grinning, whilst I am pinned, paralysed to the bed.

I woke up gasping for breath from that one.

The second time was Miranda groaning and thrashing around in bed. As I turned round, her face was distorted as if in pain. I gently took her arms and she resisted me for a moment before suddenly stopping. Her face relaxed and sank back into the pillow, sighing as if all the worries and tension were being exhaled from her body. She looked so beautiful in that moment, more so than I had ever seen her before. I wanted to capture that beauty for ever. I kissed her on the forehead and held her as I drifted back to sleep.

The third time I woke up was to the sound of muffled voices coming across the hall. I couldn't recognise the voices but they seemed to swell in volume before climaxing with an audible thump. I took no notice and returned to sleep once more.

When I awoke the next time it was to a furious knocking at the door. When I opened it, Rachel was standing there, in her nightclothes, her eyes haunted.

'Please come quick,' she croaked.

I followed her down the corridor and into another room where I saw Killinger, Hargreaves, and Brad standing together looking at the floor. Jackson sat with his head in his hands at the side of the room. Ahead of me was Roberts, his face ghostly white. Lying in front of him was a man with a fixed, horrified look of surprise on his face and a knife rammed into his rib cage. Around the knife a circle of red gradually expanded over a white cotton vest.

It was Bill.

11

'I never meant to do it!' were the first words that came out of Roberts' mouth.

'What happened?' I asked.

The question was met by a blank awkward silence. Hargreaves eventually spoke. 'It was a heavy night,' he said. 'We were all in here, laughing and joking . . .'

'And then he came and started getting agro,' said Killinger. 'Pushing and shouting.'

'He had a go at us all because we'd gone out instead of working,' said Hargreaves. 'Then he attacked Rachel.'

'Slapped her and called her a whore,' added Killinger.

'Your friend here was getting a bit hot and heavy,' said Jake referring to Roberts. 'The two were looking pretty cosy.'

Rachel made a sound of disgust and looked away.

'Don't try and wriggle out of it sweetheart!' snapped Jake. 'You were loving it just as much.'

'Disgusting!' muttered Rachel under her breath.

This seemed to provoke a wail from Roberts who sank to a crouching position, his head in his hands.

'Just chill it guys,' said Brad. 'This isn't helping anyone.'

'So—?' I started, not daring to ask it.

'Your pal did him,' said Nath. 'Stuck a knife in him and did him.'

'I didn't mean to,' sobbed Roberts again.

'Hey it's alright,' said Brad, walking over to Roberts and putting a hand on his heaving shoulder. I thought what a pathetic sight Roberts looked; blubbing like an overgrown two year old.

'I for one am not going to weep buckets for this guy,' continued Brad.

'He's had it coming,' said Jake with a grimace. 'He's had it coming a long time.'

Rachel then ran from the room and Brad looked at Jake and Nath.

'Go and get her!' he snapped, pointing towards the door. 'Go and get her now!'

Jake and Nath both ran out the room and soon returned hauling a resistant Rachel with them.

'Put her down there,' said Brad.

They flung her onto the couch and she spat in their direction, eyes blazing. 'You won't get away with this,' she said. 'He won't get away with this. I'll get the cleaners onto him!'

Jake stepped towards her but was held off by Brad. 'No, don't worry, she's not going to say anything,' he said.

'Oh yeah!' challenged Rachel.

'Yeah baby or I'll start recalling some favours.'

Rachel's eyes looked down and I could tell she was beaten, although I had no idea what he was talking about.

'You wouldn't dare,' she croaked through her hair.

'You wanna bet? You know I've got swing around here so don't push me, baby. You'll be selling your little ass down East Avenue before the day's out, I swear it.'

Rachel said no more but sat there on the brink of tears. It was the first time I had felt anything close to pity for her. What kind of life was this for a sixteen year old? Now the only figure in her life that she anchored herself to, however contemptible that figure was, had gone and she was alone and powerless. It was obvious Brad had her in the palm of her his hand and while it made things easier for us I couldn't help but empathise with that helplessness. I used to feel it all the time.

'Now this can all be sorted as long as everyone pulls it together and gets on with it,' said Brad gesturing to Roberts who was still weeping on the floor. Jackson walked over to him and spoke softly to him and the two went and sat on a sofa. Roberts snorted and took deep breaths.

'Good,' said Brad. 'First we need plastic.'

Jake found some clear white plastic sheets and we wrapped the cadaver up in it like a mummy. His eyes stared through the plastic with a look of alarm. For a moment they seemed to look straight at me and it made my stomach tingle to see it. We bundled Bill's lifeless body into Jake's hovercraft around the back entrance.

'This is no good, we can't hide this,' said Killinger. 'Everyone will see.'

'Ah, ye of little faith,' chided Jake as he pulled the plastic off the face and torso of the corpse and pulled it up in the back seat. Bill's body sat slumped with eyes still wide open as if transfixed by something on the floor. Jake closed the corpse's eyes and propped an elbow against the shoulder. 'Just taking a nap,' he grinned.

I looked to see Rachel turned away from the body, tears rolling down her face as she allowed Miranda to comfort her.

'You don't have to come,' said Brad.

'No. I want to,' she sighed.

We cruised through the streets just as the sun was rising, illuminating the carnage of the previous night. We left the city area and arrived at barren ground strewn with garbage, ranging from cans, used diapers, syringes, broken down automobiles and televisions. We were looking over a precipice. Some fifty metres or so below was a mosaic of multicoloured plastic bags. A stale stench wafted up on the dawn breeze. I remember wondering if anyone really deserved this as a final resting place; even Bill.

'Well I guess this is it,' said Jake. 'Give me a hand with this, fellas.'

Jake and Killinger hauled the semi wrapped corpse out the hovercraft and sidestepped towards the edge of the precipice.

'Wait!' called out Rachel.

Jake looked wearily at Killinger and they put the body down on the rubble for a moment. Rachel knelt down and stroked the stubble on Bill's face. I thought for a moment I saw a smile of warmth on her face, as if fighting the grief for one last fond farewell before she turned away.

Killinger and Jake quickly picked up the body and flung it over the edge. It floated through the air with an artless grace before landing in the plastic bags below with a soft thump. Looking down I could just see the top of Bills arm, poking out through the blue and green bags and couldn't help but feel a little satisfied at a job well done.

'Well we'd better head back,' said Nath.

'Not me,' came a voice. It was Roberts.

'What do you mean,' said Hargreaves.

'I'm staying here.'

Looking into Roberts' face I could tell he had made up his mind. He had obviously been thinking about this.

'What, you're staying here at a landfill,' said Nath. 'Bad call dude.'

'I'll find somewhere, somewhere alone,' said Roberts. 'It's what I want to do. It's for the best.'

'What do you mean it's for the best,' spluttered Jackson. 'You're not thinking straight. Let's just go back and talk about this.'

'Look you don't need to go,' said Brad. 'We can sort something out, you'll be fine.'

'No, it's not that,' said Roberts. 'It's just I've been following people all my life and I just mess up all the time.'

'I hope you don't think we feel that,' said Killinger. 'We couldn't have done this without you Roberts.'

'Who else could have driven the tank,' said Hargreaves, which provoked a laugh throughout the group.

'I love you guys, I do,' said Roberts. 'But I need to take control. Please, just let's say goodbye before I start crying again.'

We all stood there, feeling stunned for a moment. Eventually I stepped forward and embraced him. 'Take care, Roberts,' I said. 'And stay in touch. Don't let this be the last time you mess up for us.'

I could understand why he wanted to leave. It reminded me of my aborted escape attempt all those years ago. Now had we just exchanged one prison for another?

Each of us embraced Roberts and said our goodbyes. He tentatively reached out to Rachel, touching her arm. She flinched but didn't move it away.

'I really am sorry Rachel,' he said. 'I hope some day you can forgive me.'

Rachel nodded, tears in her eyes as she looked into the horizon. Roberts plodded into the horizon without looking back. We never saw him again.

12

For reasons I don't know of, Rachel continued working at the hotel, sometimes behind the bar and sometimes in other contexts which I preferred not to think of. I couldn't think why she stayed and faced such hostility when she could have returned to her parents, who would have welcomed her with open arms. It was clear she did have a lot of resentment coming from all sides. Killinger and Hargreaves didn't trust her after the way she had treated Roberts. Roberts had in fact been, in all likelihood, the only man to ever treat her with any respect at all. I doubted many would have stuck up for her in such an extreme way that Roberts had done that night. Whilst the likes of Brad, Nath and Jake openly despised her, they still used her for sex. I would hear them talking about it and they would try to get me to join in on these discussions, but it sickened me.

Even Miranda, who was initially perhaps the most sympathetic, seemed to have turned on her.

'She's got no respect for anyone,' she once told me whilst we were changing the barrels.

I suggested that maybe Rachel had gone through a lot of turmoil and maybe we shouldn't leap to judge but Miranda just muttered something about it been of her own making.

With the birth of our child becoming ever the more imminent, myself and Miranda were drifting apart. The connection between us was nowhere near as strong and unshakable as it was in our home town. We talked less and less and when we did it was usually in a disconnected, perfunctory manner. Her friendship with Jackson, on the other hand, seemed to be blossoming. He would often come into the bar whilst we were there and almost completely ignore me whilst he huddled up with my wife, whispering and laughing. I don't think Miranda had any idea how much this deeply disturbed me and how isolated and alone I felt. I would lie awake at night, watching the kaleidoscope of lights from the outside flash across the white walls and wish I was back in the town. Wish I was back with my brother, secretly playing hide and seek in the gorse bushes outside our home, secretly telling him stories which would make his eyes widen in suspense.

I even missed my parents for the first time and wondered what had become of them. I felt guilty over the fact that I had scarcely thought about their well being since our break out. Had Callahan or Frampton got their revenge on them for my actions? My father was a gentle soul and didn't deserve to suffer just because *I* wanted to leave. Just because *I* couldn't cope any more and wanted out.

As for my mother—well at least she had a cause, some values. I remembered how she had always had high hopes for me. How proud she had been when I had passed out of high school. I had yet to find anyone in this city who had any values whatsoever. No one had any cause, or purpose. Nothing was sacred, nothing was respected. Whenever I had to walk through the streets it felt like wading through filth.

It disgusted me the way they looked at Miranda, the way they would make insidious comments *in front of me*; but at least I could tell myself that perhaps they didn't know any better; perhaps they just didn't understand why a man would cherish his wife and expect other men to respect that. Jackson, on the other hand was a different matter. Of all people he should know better. He *did* know better and that was what really stung. Friends since infancy and he had sold out my brother and was now lording it about in front of me with my wife. No one would recognise it but me, but I knew what he was doing. It was like when we were five and whenever he won a game he would strut around and show off to taunt me. Now the game had changed but the way he played it was still the same. He had completed what he felt was an adequate penance for killing my brother and was now letting me know in no uncertain terms.

I didn't think anyone would understand how I was feeling; except perhaps for Rachel. Every now and then I would catch her glancing at me and then when our eyes met, she would turn away. When we were checking the sales figures on the screen, she would lean into me so I could feel her breasts pushing into my arm and smell her perfume. She would smile and repeatedly touch her face and hair in front of me. Her whole demeanour and body language suggested vulnerability, openness and suggestiveness.

I can't say I wasn't tempted.

Miranda and I hadn't made love since the breakout and were generally not getting on anyway. If things had been better maybe things would have turned out differently on one particular night I would live to regret.

The night in question, Miranda had gone to visit Killinger and Hargreaves over something and I was on my own in the apartment when there was a knock on the door. Rachel virtually fell through the door when I opened it.

'Richard,' she gasped. 'Thank God, you're here.'

'What's the matter?' I asked. She appeared quite shocked and panicked over something.

'Some guy was after me' she said.

'After you?'

'In the bar,' she said. 'And then I left and he started following me. I hope you don't mind, Richard but I didn't know where else to go.'

'That's fine,' I said. 'Just tell me who it is and I'll get security on him.'

'Oh, don't bother about them,' she said with a wave of her hand. 'They won't do anything.'

'Well—do you want *me* to do something,' I said; although I wasn't really sure what.

'Oh Richard, you're such a hero,' she said. 'But no, he's not worth bothering with.' She started simpering again, her eyes welling up.

'I'm just scared, Richard. Will you hold me for a while?'

'Why don't you sit down,' I said, gesturing to a chaise longue.

Rachel sat and started adjusting her hair. I could see right through the game; not that it was that subtle, but I played along anyway.

'Some guys get a bit much,' I said.

'You're the only one who understands me, Richard,' she said through her sobs. 'Everyone else hates me.'

'They don't hate you,' I said. 'Like you said; they just don't understand you.'

'All the guys, they only want one thing, but you're different Richard.'

'Am I?'

'You are,' she said. 'And I wonder at times, if Miranda really appreciates you.'

I stood up and walked towards the door. 'Maybe you'd better go.'

'Oh Richard, don't be like that.'

'I mean it Rachel. I'm not interested,' I said as she stroked a hand down my arm. I shook it off. 'Just leave it, ok.'

'It's not ok,' she said putting her hands on my chest. 'Maybe you'd better throw me out, Richard. Put your hands on me, Richard. Dominate me!'

I walked away. She called me but I ignored it. 'Richard!' she called again I felt a breeze at the back of my neck. Turning, I found the balcony doors open and Rachel standing on top of the ledge.

'Rachel!' I started forward and then held back, unsure.

'I'm sick of this life, Richard. I want to end it all.'

'Don't be ridiculous!'

'Do you think there is a heaven, Richard?' she said. 'Even if I end up in hell, it's bound to be better than this place.'

I walked towards her. There was a sheer drop of fifty stories underneath that ledge; it made my stomach turn to think of it. I couldn't believe she was doing this as a game. Did she really intend to throw herself off just to spite me?

'Come on, we can talk about this,'

I winced as she lifted one foot off the ledge and hovered there like a crane, arms in the air.

'Stop it!' I shrieked.

'They won't even know who it is when they find me,' she said. 'They won't even care when they find out from my DNA, Richard. Oh Richard.'

She looked at me, her eyes blank and somehow plaintive. As if in a trance, she started to tilt forward.

My stomach lurched at the same time as the rest of me. I grabbed her and pulled her off the ledge just in time. We collapsed onto the floor of the balcony, limbs entwined and I held her as she sobbed into my chest. Now it was real pain she was releasing. Years of abuse and indifference pouring out through her tears.

'Take me in Richard,' she said.

And so I did; and one thing led to another.

13

Not long after my liaison with Rachel, I accompanied Miranda to the clinic to have a scan. Our unborn child was a girl and my feelings of pride and excitement were tinged with guilt—and a morbid fear that Rachel would ruin everything.

I had played right into her hands and I was determined that there would not be a repeat of that night. Rachel hadn't said anything to me since, although she had given me looks in the bar which I had tried to ignore. She knew the sword she had over our heads and was wielding it with relish, just waiting for the opportunity to crash it down on us. The only option was to get away; to up and leave, just like we had done before; but of course that was out of the question.

'We don't want to bring her up here,' I said to Miranda once. 'Why don't we just get away and find a decent place. There must be somewhere that's not as rotten as this.'

'And bring her up on what?' said Rachel. 'We're in a good place here. We're earning enough to bring her up; we have a place to stay. We have to be practical.'

There was no persuading her otherwise and I had to admit she had a point. Leaving would be a gamble unless I could find a job elsewhere. I trawled the streets, asking in shops and bars but to no avail. The places that did have anything offered a pittance and no accommodation. Besides which Miranda was happy at the hotel. It offered some sort of security and we had got to know people there. I considered just being honest with her and telling her the truth, but I couldn't bring myself to. How could I crush her like that when she was perhaps the happiest I had ever seen?

Seeing the image on the screen was a revelation for both of us; the tiny little hands and feet, eyes closed and body curled as if in blissful sleep. It finally looked like a human being in there; a fresh soul, innocent to the world.

'I want her never to have the life we did,' said Miranda. 'I want her to be free, to be able to sing and dance and play and be whatever she wants. I want to name her Rosie.'

'After Jackson's mother?'

'She's the only woman I knew in that cursed place who was a free spirit.'

'And look what happened to her.' I could still remember her groans as Frampton kicked her on the ground and it made me shudder.

'Well she'll live on through our daughter. Oh come on Richard. You've got to admit it. It's apt.'

'I suppose so,' I said. I felt a bit reluctant to name our child after a relative of Jackson's, which in turn made me feel quite petty and small.

Rosie II became the only subject of conversation in our flat. We would talk about how we were so glad she wouldn't experience the oppression we had and how it was a fresh start for both of us. Jackson was thrilled about the fact that we had used his mother's name. He gave Miranda a big hug and I looked away, biting my tongue.

Killinger presented us with a set of baby clothes he had managed to secure on the black market. Clothes, like a lot of things were heavily taxed and there was a thriving underground trade in "luxury goods".

Hargreaves bought a doll which he awkwardly presented us with. He could barely conceal his desire to get back out the door as Miranda hugged and kissed him.

I was excited as well. It would be a new start for all of us as long as Rachel kept quiet. I would have to consider ways to pacify her, which didn't involve sleeping with her again.

I also felt a faint tinge of sadness. I remembered when David had put his hand on her stomach and been so excited. That was almost nine months ago but it may as well have been nine years. I'm sure he would have made such a good uncle.

A couple of nights later we all went out to celebrate the imminent arrival of Rosie. All of us that were left from the old town were there: Miranda and I, Killinger, Hargreaves and Jackson.

We chose a quiet bar in Western Street. It was strewn with artefacts from the 20th and 21st Centuries. An old bicycle hung on the ceiling which must have been a thousand years old at least. There were pictures of what used to be known as policemen on the walls. They did a similar job as the cleaners did in this city and the Enforcers did in our town, except they wore blue helmets and didn't carry tasars.

The front of an old automobile was hung above the bar, attended to by an old man who was thrilled to have the opportunity to show others his collection.

We sat at a big round table which had the pattern of bicycle spokes on it. Old forms of transport seemed to be the old man's particular interest.

Killinger started by proposing a toast.

'To the second generation, born in the free world,' he said.

'To Rosie,' added Jackson, prompting everyone to raise their glass.

'You must be proud,' Hargreaves whispered to me and I smiled back at him.

We sat for a while in silence, not really knowing what to say. We could never have guessed that one day we would be sitting here.

'When is it due?' asked Killinger.

'In the next week or so,' said Miranda. 'Richard's been getting so excited. He's even been writing poetry again.'

'Oh have you,' asked Killinger, looking impressed.

'Yeah,' I said, feeling awkward. 'Just to keep in practice.' Ever since I had shown that story to my father, I had always felt like doing anything creative or showing feeling was wrong. It was hard to break the habit of a lifetime.

'They've been wonderful,' continued Miranda, apparently oblivious to my discomfort. I hadn't shown her my other slightly darker ones, directed at Jackson and my own feelings of guilt and inadequacy.

'You know they have poetry readings,' said Jackson as if reading my mind. He had always had that knack. 'Down in the market square.'

'They sometimes cause riots,' said Hargreaves. 'If the crowd doesn't like them.'

It was true. I had witnessed rocks been thrown at orators before and one young man had even been stabbed when he made a reference to the Cleaners in his poem. The Cleaners denied that it had anything to do with them.

'Well we should try it anyway, don't you think Stirling,' said Jackson. I could swear he was playing with me. 'We didn't escape that town, just to hide away.'

'Well things change when you have responsibilities, Jackson,' I said. 'When it's not just yourself you have to think about.'

I saw Jackson look away and knew I had hit a nerve. It was a cheap shot but no worse than what he was doing.

There was an awkward silence before Miranda started talking again. I went to the rest room just for the sake of getting away for a moment. I washed my face and stood looking at myself for a moment. What kind of man was I? Cheating on my pregnant wife; did it get much lower than that? I became aware of the door opening behind me and saw Killinger there.

'Hey Stirling, you're missing your party.'

'I'm sorry,' I said. 'It's just—'

'-Jackson,' Killinger finished for me.

'I know I should let it go,' I said. 'I just can't.'

'He did feel pretty bad about that for a while,' said Killinger. 'I don't know if you realise just how much.'

'He doesn't care now,' I said. 'I know him, Killinger, I know him well. Everything he does is like a statement.'

Killinger leant against the sink next to me and sighed as he looked down at the floor.

'I don't think you know it all, Stirling. Not as well as you think.'

'What do you mean?'

'When we were at Rachel's parent's house, I went outside in the middle of the night and saw him there, sitting on a rock just looking ahead.'

'So?' I said. 'What does that mean?'

'He had one of the guns in his hand,' said Killinger. I looked at him and met his eye. He was being serious.

'You mean—'

'He was thinking of suicide, Stirling.'

'What happened then?' I struggled to take this new revelation in. I had been so wrapped up in myself at the time, I wouldn't have noticed.

'Nothing,' said Killinger. 'He heard me and stood up and looked at me. But his eyes were all blank, Stirling. I can't really explain it; it was like he was already dead inside. Then he just walked in the house. We haven't even spoken about it since.'

Then I remembered the dream I had in that house. The one where I had the gun pointed at Jackson and he lifted his head and told me to do it. Could it have been that night?

'What he's doing now is running away from the guilt. He can't bear the tension between you and him and he's reacting against it by going on the defensive.'

'I didn't think about it like that,' I admitted. 'And I really wish I could let it go, Killinger but I just can't. It would be like, like—'

'Letting down David,' Killinger finished for me once more.

I hadn't spoken to anyone like this before apart from Miranda. It felt strange standing in a rest room with a homosexual talking about it, but I felt I could trust Killinger. Behind those blinkered, short sighted eyes lay an intelligence which encouraged openness. We used to joke that he should save up to get laser surgery on those eyes, which sometimes appeared to be looking in different directions.

'What do you think David would do?' said Killinger.

'He'd be forgiving,' I said. 'I don't know. He had a quality about him, which I never had. Everything was so simple for him.'

The memory of the attack organised by Vincent came flooding back. Myself and Jackson had both been involved in that. Killinger, Hargreaves and Roberts had been the victims and David had been the hero—naturally.

'Killinger, you know when Vincent came after you,' I started.

'Vincent?' said Killinger looking baffled.

'Yes you know, me and Jackson—'

'Oh that!' said Killinger, rolling his eyes.

'I never apologised about that,' I said.

'Oh forget it,' said Killinger.

'No really. I'm sorry Killinger. I truly am. I'll say the same to Hargreaves as well.'

'You don't have to.'

'I want to,' I said. 'It was wrong and I really regret it.'

'Stirling, it's all in the past,' he said. 'Do yourself a favour and move on with the future. You have it all in front of you. We escaped the town. You've got a wife and family. You're secure. Just let the past go and lighten up.'

'You're right,' I smiled. 'I am a bit of a case.'

'That's one word for it,' said Killinger. 'Now let's go in before they start talking about us. Hargreaves will be getting worried.'

We laughed and turned to go back into the bar.

It was at that moment that the ceiling came crashing down.

14

What happened next was all confusion, a blur. I could hear Miranda scream as part of the ceiling landed on the table. Jackson chivvied her out of the building. The old man who was running the bar came up, his face ashen white. 'They're rioting!' he said. 'They're rioting! You have to get out of here.'

We navigated through the pile of rubble on the floor. The air was thick with dust. Just then there was a whistle and a whir of orange which crashed into the corner of the bar, engulfing it in flames. I could feel the heat burning the side of my face and my back.

'Get out of here!' said the old man again as the bottles of alcohol began exploding above the bar. He went to grab a club and ran out the door.

'Stirling! Killinger!' came a desperate voice from the corner of the room.

I looked round to see Hargreaves lying there, his legs buried under a heap of metal and wood. He was staring down at them as if he couldn't believe what was happening.

Killinger and I ran to him and started clearing it off. Hargreaves screamed as we uncovered his legs. Protruding just below the knee was dust covered bone.

'Come on Hargreaves,' said Killinger as we helped him to his feet. 'Just go Stirling, I can look after him.'

'I can't!' I said. 'I can't let him down.'

'Think about Miranda. Think about the baby, Stirling.'

'Jackson's with her,' I said. 'We need to get out of here.'

As we dragged Hargreaves to the door we were met with a seething, violent, mayhem outside. Bodies ran around, criss-crossing each other as they tried to escape the inescapable. Flaming missiles flew through the air and exploded onto the ground. One of them set a man's trouser leg on fire. As he danced around in panic it did nothing but fan the flames. I was getting so transfixed by this awful sight of a man burning to death in front of me, I failed to notice a man running straight at us, wielding a metal pole above his head.

I side stepped out the way, bowling over Killinger and Hargreaves in the process and launched him into the rubble with my foot. As we navigated our way through the madness I saw the Cleaners in their blue uniforms, beating random rioters with clubs. As we made our way towards the hotel we realised that the crowd was starting to clear. Just as I began to feel we were out of the worse of it, I realised why the crowd were running in the opposite way.

'Turn back!' shouted Killinger. 'Turn back, they're going to kill us!'

In front of us lay an impenetrable line of blue and white. It was the Cleaners, in armour, with weapons primed at us.

For a moment I heard nothing but my own pounding heart beat as we turned and ran for freedom. I focused my sights on a burst fire hydrant at the end of the street. I allowed myself to think of nothing else. Everything would be alright if I could get to that fire hydrant. My mind drifted away from the scene. I was back in the town, playing with David. I could see him running in front of me. I was chasing him. I had almost caught him when I heard a whistle and thud and felt myself falling forward.

'Stirling!' shouted Killinger. I looked up to see him hovering over me. I saw the shock and concern in his eyes. There was another whistle and thud; he rolled his eyes upwards before falling next to me.

Then the noise returned, the chaos returned and I was back in reality. There was a searing, burning pain in my right shoulder and Killinger was lying next to me with a bullet through his head.

I heard an awful wail of hopelessness and despair and then realised it had come from me. I became aware of Hargreaves next to me and realised he was screaming. I grabbed hold of him and edged towards the side of the road. I heard myself making noises of reassurance, saying everything would be alright. I don't know if I was persuading myself or Hargreaves. Then I realised Hargreaves was reaching out for Killinger, who lay there on his back, his eyes wide open at the sky he would never see again.

'You can't Hargreaves,' I said. 'He's gone, Hargreaves, you have to leave him.'

We shuffled on our backs into the side. A few people leaped over us as they attempted to flee from the whistling bullets over head. A young woman was shot in the back as she was in mid flight over us and the force of the bullet sent her on a further half metre. In the end we were backed up into the side of a building and couldn't go any further. We could do nothing but lie there and wait for it to end. In front of us Killinger's body lay in the road, trampled over by the crowd. I cradled Hargreaves in my arms as he sobbed, too distraught to know or care that he had lost control of his bladder. I wondered if we would die there, lying in the dirt, cowering for our lives. I wondered where Miranda and Jackson were and if they were still alive and in the end I passed out.

15

When I opened my eyes, all I could see was white. There was no longer concrete under me but rough cotton sheets. I felt my shoulder throbbing and looked down to see it had a dressing on.

'Only a flesh wound, you'll live.'

I looked up to see a portly, middle aged man in front of me. He had a shock of white hair and glasses hanging round his neck on a string.

'Don't worry, I'm a doctor,' he said. 'Not that that means much any more, and you're in my house. No point in taking you to the hospital. They've got their hands full at the moment.'

I tried to speak but my throat felt like it had needles stuck in it. The man held a glass to my lips and I gulped down the cold water.

'Not too fast, easy,' the doctor said. 'My name is Atkins and you are—'

'Stirling,' I croaked. 'Richard Stirling.'

'Ah Richard, yes. You're friend was muttering your name earlier.'

'Hargreaves?' I asked.

'Rupert, yes. He came in for it nastier than you. I was worried for a moment I'd have to take his leg off, but a good old cast I think will do the trick.'

'Where is he?'

'He's in the next room, but he's sleeping. I only have a limited amount of anaesthetic and he went through quite a lot. He was in a lot of pain and saying something about Stanley.'

'Killinger.' The image of his lifeless body being trampled over in the stampede has haunted me ever since.

Atkins pulled a pained face. 'Friend of yours was he?'

I nodded.

'His lover?'

'Yes,' I said my throat hurting again.

'I thought as much,' said Atkins. 'They really are bastards those Cleaners. When the riots start they'll just take pot shots at anyone. Women, children, homosexuals; they just don't care.'

'Why do the riots start?'

'No one knows,' said Atkins. 'They just do. It's as if a switch is flicked and everyone loses their heads. You get to recognise when it's about to start, in time. You can feel it in the air and when you get that whiff; that second sense that something is about to blow, you get out the way quick. Too late for your friend, shame to say.'

Atkins walked away tutting under his breath as I tried to get myself together. Feeling stiff and sore and with sickening shooting pains in my shoulder, I eased out of bed. I slipped on my shirt which was lying on a chair. It had been ripped open, probably by Atkins and a bloodstained hole covered each side of my wound. I stepped out through the door and along the hall. In the next room Hargreaves lay in bed; his leg in plaster and elevated on a pulley system. He was asleep, as Atkins had said. I stepped in and walked up to the bed. I touched his arm and his eyes opened and looked at me with relief. 'Oh Stirling, you're ok,' he said, phlegm rattling in the back of his throat.

'Yes, I'm fine. You don't look so good yourself.'

Hargreaves managed a thin lipped smile. 'I'm not too bad.' His eyes flickered and he raised his head off the pillow. I gestured for him to relax, but I knew what was in his mind.

'Where's Stanley? Did he make it?'

His face carried such childlike hopefulness I couldn't bear to look at him. Surely he couldn't have forgotten.

'Don't you remember?' I said, looking out the window.

'He made it, didn't he?'

I turned to him and shook my head. 'I'm sorry. He's dead.'

Hargreaves took a breath and held it. 'It can't be true.'

'I'm sorry Rupert,' I said. 'I wish it wasn't—' I cut myself off. I couldn't get involved in this any more. 'I'm sorry to do this Hargreaves, but I have to go.'

Hargreaves exhaled, sinking back into the pillow. He turned to the wall and nodded.

'I have to find Miranda. I have to make sure her and the baby are safe.'

Hargreaves nodded again.

'You'll be safe here. I think this guy's alright, he'll look after you.'

'You should go Stirling,' he said. 'I knew all the time. I just didn't want to believe it.'

'I'll be back,' I said grabbing his arm. 'I promise you Hargreaves. As soon as I find the others I'll be back for you.'

'It's ok,' whispered Hargreaves. 'Just go.'

I left the room and walked down the stairs and out the front door. I had no idea where I was or where I was going. I just started walking though the mess and the carnage and the bodies left behind.

16

I don't know how long I was walking for but it felt the longest journey of my life. A few of the underclass lay groaning on the ground; some had been beaten, some with bullet wounds, some with burns. The dead were beginning to be cleared. Funerals were rare in this city and reserved almost exclusively for the rich. Most would just be incinerated with no plaque to honour their memories. When you were gone here, you really were gone and no one entertained notions of any afterlife. When the streets eventually became familiar and I was nearing the hotel, I wondered what I was going to face and wondered for the first time if I wanted to. Why didn't I just walk away and start again somewhere? I didn't even know if I'd have anything to return to. There were security staff at the entrance and they gave me a double take before they let me in. I went up to the front desk. 'Is Miranda here?'

The gangly looking man looked like he'd not had a night's sleep at all. He just looked at me and my blood ran cold. What did that look mean?

'Don't just look at me, man!' I snapped. 'Is she alive or not?'

'Yes, she's alive,' he said with a sigh. 'You'd better go on up.'

I entered the elevator and took it up to my floor. I didn't know what to feel as I opened the door of my apartment. The first thing I was confronted with was Jackson. I pushed past him and went to the bedroom.

'Stirling, there's something you should know,' Jackson was saying, but I took no notice of him. Miranda was lying there, curled up with her back next to me. I called her but she didn't answer.

'Stirling!' repeated Jackson in a harsh whisper. He was standing next to me his eyes burrowing into mine. 'She lost the baby, Stirling.'

There was a delayed reaction while the words sunk in. I turned to face Jackson; it was then the truth hit home and it sent me reeling. I leaned against the wall, head in arms, trying to steady myself. I could feel Jackson's hand on my back.

'How?'

'A man hit her in the stomach with a piece of wood.'

'He did what?' I whirled round, fists clenched. 'Who would do such a thing?'

'It was all mayhem Stirling. I'm sorry, I did the best I could.'

I turned and slammed my fist into the wall. Some of the plaster flaked off. I studied my grazed fist, my eyes clouding over.

'We've been to the hospital, and it—' Jackson stopped to gulp before continuing. 'They removed it from her womb. I'm sorry.'

'You mean *her*. They removed her, Rosie; not *it*.'

'I'm sorry, yes.'

I turned to face him, my hands raised. 'Look Jackson, I appreciate the fact you've brought her back here safely, but could you give us some space, now.'

Jackson nodded and I walked to Miranda, kneeling beside her and taking her hand. She didn't respond; her eyes were blank and empty. I leaned forward and kissed her on the forehead.

What are we going to do?' I whispered, a tear rolling off my cheek and onto the bed sheet. 'We can get through this.'

Miranda did nothing but sigh.

'Nothing can shake us,' I said. 'We still have each other.'

'That's not the case, Richard.' Her voice was so calm and controlled it shook me.

'What do you mean?'

'You weren't there,' she said to the wall. 'You'd left me.'

'I'm sorry,' I said, my voice breaking. 'I couldn't leave Hargreaves he'd been hurt, and Jackson was with you.'

'Yes, Jackson was with me,' she said. 'He was with me when there was people fighting and dying all around me. He was with me when I was terrified for my life and the life of our daughter. He was with me when our dead daughter was taken from my womb. Where were you, Richard?'

'I told you,' I said between clenched teeth. 'I was with Killinger and Hargreaves. Hargreaves was hurt—'

'And how was Rachel?' Miranda looked into my eyes for the first time. I couldn't meet them.

'What do you mean?'

'Oh stop it Richard!' she snapped. 'I know you've been sleeping with her; I found a brassier down the side of the bed.'

The bottom fell out my world. I felt for sure I had nothing left. 'It was only once.' I said clinging to the bed cover. 'She manipulated the whole situation—'

'Oh and you were powerless to do anything about it.'

I turned to look at her but she averted her eyes.

'You men are all the same. I don't want to hear about it.'

'Miranda please!'

'Just go Richard.'

Miranda resumed her position, facing the wall. I opened my mouth to say more and realised I couldn't. I left the room to see Jackson standing there, studying his shoes. I walked past him and out the room. As I took the elevator down to the street level I wondered what I would do and where I would go. As I walked out onto the streets, I realised I no longer cared. In the absence of any better idea I decided to return to Hargreaves. I looked around; trying to remember the route I had taken. Wherever Atkins' house was, it was kilometres away from where we had ended up on the street. I started wandering, hoping I would find some landmark in all the debris, when I heard someone call my name. I turned to see Brad, standing there with his oafish grin. 'Hey Rich, hold up.'

157

'I can't,' I said, plodding on regardless. 'I've got to find Hargreaves.'

'Just stop,' he said, catching my arm. I winced from the pain in my shoulder and he held back, apologetically, a look of pity in his eyes. 'You're in a hell of a state, man. Look at you.'

I looked down at the ground not knowing what to say.

'Come on, he said. 'You need a drink.'

We went to the same bar we went to the first time, although it was quieter now and with no naked women. Brad ordered a couple of beers which we drank in silence. I felt the pain of the last twelve hours subside a little. I could see why people became addicted to the stuff and we ordered a couple more.

'Killinger's dead,' I told him breaking the silence.

Brad hissed through his teeth. 'That's too bad,' he said. 'He was a good guy. In the riots was it?'

I nodded. 'He was shot in the head in front of me. I was shot in the shoulder,' I said giving a nod towards my wound.

'Shit man, that's nasty,' said Brad. 'What about your other friend, Rupert?'

'He's somewhere. We got rescued by a guy called Atkins. He said he was a doctor.'

'I know about the baby,' said Brad. 'I'm real sorry about that.'

'She won't let me near her,' I said. 'All I want to do is be near her.'

'Just give her some time.' Brad took a drink and then put the glass down shaking his head. 'I mean why did you have to go with Rachel, dude. I've told you about her.'

'I know,' I said, circling my hand in the air. 'She—'

'Suicide trick was it,' said Brad. 'Yeah, she's tried that one before.'

'Really?' I spluttered.

"Really!' said Brad in a semi-laugh. 'I mean I've gone with her, but I've got nothing to lose. She's got no hold over me. You should have heard her bragging about it.'

'You mean she told Miranda,' I said.

'I don't know,' said Brad. 'But she told just about everyone else.'

'Christ!' I rubbed my face to stop the tears. 'I've lost everything!'

Brad put a hand on my shoulder and gently shook it.

'It's ok man,' he said. 'She'll come round.'

'How could I have been so stupid?'

'Look, you and her are meant to be together. No one can interfere in that.'

'Well,' I said, returning my hands to the table. 'It's a good job Jackson was there to save the day, isn't it?'

'What's going on with you two?' said Brad.

And then I told him. I told him all about where we had come from, all about our break out and David's disappearance. It was the first time I had ever told anyone the whole story and it felt good to purge myself of it. Brad just sat and listened until I mentioned the Messiah when his eyes lit up.

'The Messiah?' he asked. 'You mean that guy?'

I followed to where Brad was nodding to see the familiar bearded face on the screen. I gazed at his muted lips and felt that somehow he was speaking to me. His eyes were fixed on mine and seemed to reflect my pain and my longing. They seemed to say that he knew it too; he had been down the same path and he alone could lead me to safety, to security, to salvation. I thought in that instance that he really could have been sent to save me.

17

A few drinks later we went our separate ways. Brad asked if I was coming back to the hotel with him to make up with Miranda, but I declined. I couldn't trust myself to be in control of my actions if I saw her there with Jackson, who like a snake had slithered his way into Miranda's favour using the death of our child as a launch pad. Yes, I'd slept with Rachel as a one off but at least I had the grace to be ashamed of it. They seemed to think that they were vindicated in what they were doing, with what I was sure they had been doing for weeks.

I wandered back to Atkins' house. He answered the door looking vaguely surprised to see me. 'Ah, Richard, do come in. I was just drawing up a few lines.'

As I came through the door I saw Hargreaves sitting up at a table, his plastered leg propped up on a chair. His face was a healthy red which I took to be at least in part down to the lines of cocaine Atkins was slicing up on the table. Hargreaves smiled when he saw me.

'Stirling!' he greeted with a sniff. 'Great to see you! You should try some of this, it's great!'

'Do sit down,' said Atkins as he meticulously divided up the white powder into perfect lines. Every single granule of cocaine was neatly in its place as he offered me the plate and a tube. I put the tube to my nostril and snorted it up, allowing myself a moment to wallow in the high. It was the perfect antidote to the sluggishness from the drink. Not that I was feeling that sluggish. I was desperately curious. I wanted to know more about the Messiah.

'I told you it was good,' said Hargreaves. He seemed completely different to the broken man I had left earlier that morning.

'It's good,' I said. 'Thank you.'

I passed the equipment back to Atkins who took a line himself before handing it to Hargreaves.

'Who's the Messiah?' I asked out the blue. I feigned ignorance to test for his reactions but he gave nothing away, unlike Hargreaves who suddenly started spluttering half way through his line.

'You know full well who he is, Stirling!'

'Yes, I know who he is,' I said, shooting Hargreaves a look before turning back to Atkins. 'I just want to know who he is to you.'

'The Messiah,' he paused and looked into the middle distance. 'The Messiah is a nut,' he said finally. 'And the worst kind of nut.'

'What do you mean?'

'There are two kinds of nuts in my opinion: the harmless ones and the psychotic ones. I believe I am of the first kind and our robed and bearded friend is the latter.'

'Why do you think that?'

'Well surely it's obvious my dear boy.'

My dear boy. Isn't that what Callahan called me?

'It's not obvious to me,' I said, wanting him to carry on.

'He thinks he's the Son Of God,' said Atkins. 'Not only that he's convinced many deluded fools that he really is and that's what makes him dangerous. A nut is one thing. A nut with power is another. I'd stay well away from him. Well away.'

'What if he really is?' I said.

Atkins let out a guffaw of laughter which Hargreaves joined in with, snorting dustings of cocaine over the table.

'What's funny?' I said feeling myself going red.

'Anyone with half an iota of common sense knows that God doesn't exist. In the last few centuries these ridiculous superstitious notions have all but been eradicated, except amongst the desperate few.'

'Who are the desperate few?'

'People who have nothing left to cling to,' he said.

'The underclass?'

'Most definitely. Now my dear boy, this is not conducive to the tone of the evening. Do limber up and have another line.'

18

I stayed at Atkins' house. He seemed grateful for the company and I suspected the relationship between him and Hargreaves was perhaps a little more than platonic. The two of them would stay in the house all day whilst I roamed the streets. I would go in and out of bars and try and talk to people about the Messiah. What they knew about him, what they thought about him. Most had the same opinion as Atkins and were particularly scornful of the Messiah's repeated warnings of the apocalypse.

Often I would end up sitting on a bench in the middle of the street, gazing up at the holograms and hovercrafts whizzing overhead. I would think of Miranda and our daughter who never had the chance to be born. Rosie—what would she have looked like? Would she have been beautiful like her mother? Would she have been care free and brave like her namesake? It was ironic that both Rosie's were killed by the mentality of their respective town or city.

Often, after pondering these thoughts I would wander to the hotel and look up to where Miranda was staying. I would think about going in and asking for forgiveness. Ask to rebuild my life with her. Then I would think of her and Jackson in there and turn away. I would go back to Atkins and Hargreaves and lose myself in a haze of amphetamines.

Sometimes I would dream of my old life. I would remember the old town, my old house, my old school. I would think of the people that had gone; David, my parents, my wife, my unborn child, Killinger, Jackson and his mother. They were all either dead or had disappeared never to return, but I was used to loneliness. It was not the kind of loneliness that was to do with external circumstances; it was a deep life time affliction that could never be cured. Every now and then I would think that it had gone for good, but it would always return like a bad smell. I could sense it in others as well. I knew that people like my father had it and people like my mother and David did not. The trouble with the people that shared this emptiness is they were never any comfort. Even if you could share your feelings with them; once you've established that the world is ultimately cruel and pointless, where do you go from there? This is why people like my father have to find people like my mother; who regardless of her Cause believed it so sincerely that it gave out an anesthetising energy for weak minded people like him.

This is why I had always found comfort being around David and why I had ultimately found Miranda. Whilst she had had her lows I knew that she would always bounce back. She was my blanket, my energy source and what had I done? I had thrown it all away on another soul sapping, toxic drudge like Rachel.

Now my comfort was in narcotics and my energy source was finding out about the Messiah and about the underclass. I would see them shuffling along the streets as if trying to make themselves invisible. They were so apparent that they may as well have had signs around their necks. Everyone would give them a wide berth as they passed in the street and I was drawn into their isolation. I could relate to that a lot better than the self serving, hedonism of the mainstream crowds. The underclass were also on the outside, just like me. I would wander past their slums at night, on my way back from the bars and covertly glance into their shadowy lives. They lived in homemade shacks built from items collected from refuse dumping grounds. They had no source of running water or sanitation and the smell was nauseating especially in the heat. They would occasionally catch my eye and I would wait for them to run out and attack me, steal my clothes or my money. I half wished that they would sometimes, but they never did and I would slope back to Atkins house.

It was through one particular incident that the doors of their homes were opened to me.

I was on the way back from the bars when I heard muffled sounds coming from a side alley. For some reason I was drawn towards the noise, my feet unconsciously moving as if directed by fate. As I got closer I heard a woman's voice, groaning under what sounded like a barrage of slaps and punches. I turned the corner and I could see a man with his back to me, his right arm swaying to and fro like a pendulum. In front of him I could see the outline of a young woman, kneeling and another man behind her, grabbing onto her hair. The man doing the slapping began to talk, his voice high pitched and tense:

'I'm telling ya bitch—*[slap]*—you gotta suck it—*[slap]*—suck it—*[slap]*—suck it!' He curled his hand into a fist and drove it forward. The girl fell back, her nose spouting blood.

'Fuck this! Hold her down, Gary!'

Without realising it, I had a rock in my right hand and was creeping towards the gang. The man who was doing the beating was now trying to pull the girl's skirt off her flailing legs while "Gary" held down her arms.

'Keep her still, will you?' said the first man. 'You bitches just don't know what you want. Well now you're going to get it.'

The girl looked at me, her eyes blazing. I paused, thinking she was going to say something, but she remained frozen.

The first man continued cursing at her and tugging at her dress.

'You fucking bitches have got to learn your place. Dirty little whores, filthy little cracker whores—'

And that's all he got to say before the rock in my hand swung through the air and crashed into his temple. He rolled over onto his side, his genitals spread out to the open sky. I then flung the rock at the other man just as he looked up and it smashed him in the forehead bowling him to the ground. I reached down and pulled the woman to her feet. She screamed and fought against me, her skirt around her thighs, her top pulled off one breast. For a moment I was captivated and there was a moment of stillness before she kneed me in the groin and ran. I sank down to a crouching position, my vision blurred and my mind unable to focus. Somehow I realised I had to get out of there before the two guys I'd laid out came to. If that happened I'd be lucky to get out alive. Eventually I staggered out and got back to Atkins house where I collapsed and passed out on the bed.

A couple of days later I was staring at a naked woman on the screen who was advertising toothpaste. I had already drunk two potent green cocktails and was about to go home when I heard an all too familiar voice behind me:

'Hey hero, can I get you another?'

'Rachel . . .' I murmured. I wanted to say more, but the shock had taken my voice away.

She sat down next to me, elbow on the table propping up her head, her hair flowing down over her hand. I didn't know if I loved her or hated her.

'What are you doing here?' I groaned.

'I heard about your little skirmish. The woman you saved was a friend of mine.'

'What's her name?' I asked.

'Fran,' she replied. 'She's sorry about the way she reacted.'

She started running her hand up my thigh.

'I can always rub it for you,' she whispered in my ear.

I grabbed her hand away and got up to leave.

'Please Richard, don't go.' She followed me out onto the street.

'I need you,' she called out.

I turned round to look at her and she seemed to shrivel up, her eyes cast down to the pavement.

'Well, I don't need you,' I said. 'I don't ever want to see you again.'

'Please Richard, I have no one.'

'Who cares?' I turned to walk away.

'Miranda wants you back.'

I stopped and turned to face her.

'She's with Jackson.'

'No she's not,' said Rachel. 'That's based on nothing more than your own suspicious ego. I know you, Richard. Better than you know yourself, I think.'

'You don't know me at all.'

'I know you like to play the moral card whilst keeping your dick wet.'

She flinched away as I seized her by the shoulders and shook her. My whole body convulsed with rage.

'How could you tell her?' I said. 'How could you do that to me—to her!'

'Let go of me!' She wriggled from my grasp, her eyes shocked and hurt. I felt ashamed, but no less angry. 'How could you,' I said again.

'I didn't.'

'You're a liar!'

She looked down at my hands, curled into fists. 'You going to hit me are you?' she retorted. 'I thought you were too high and noble for that.'

'Don't fuck with me Rachel.'

She stepped up to me and put her hands on my shoulders. She leaned into my ear. 'I didn't tell her,' she whispered. 'Brad did.'

'Brad?' I remembered him telling me how Rachel had told everyone about it.

'I told him; he told Miranda.' She leaned back to look at me. 'You know you're kind of sexy when you're this roused.'

'Why would he do that?'

'Oh come on Richard, don't be naïve.' She leaned forward again, whispering into my ear. 'He was making a play; you know nothing is sacred round here.' She run a hand down my back and over my buttock.

'Cut it out!' I said, pushing her away.

'Sorry, I can't help but find you cute.'

'It's not happening again,' I said.

'I know,' she said. 'But I'll be upfront with you. I've been thrown out the hotel.'

'And—'

'And nothing. I just wanted to talk.'

I didn't know who I couldn't trust; me or her.

'Look, I know you love Miranda and that's fine. Just a few drinks. Nothing wrong in that is there?'

We went back inside the bar, ordered some drinks and sat down. Rachel sat opposite me, stirring her drink, eyes cast downwards. I couldn't help but lust after her. I despised myself for it. 'So this girl then?' I said. 'She's alright now?'

'Who Fran?' Rachel looked up to meet my eye. 'Yes she's fine.'

'How do you know her?' I asked. 'She seemed too poor to be a whore.'

Rachel looked back down at her drink. 'There's no need for that.'

'I'm sorry, there wasn't,' I said, taken aback by the crushed look on her face. It was as if her whole personality had been washed away. Then I realised: 'She's the underclass isn't she?'

Rachel nodded.

'And so were you—once upon a time?'

'Yes,' she whispered.

'Your whole family?'

Her hands clenched in front of her face and she sobbed. I resisted the urge to take them, but waited for her to finish. When she had, I handed her a tissue. She wiped her face and looked at me, her face softened, mascara smudged.

'My brother, Jacob, he never knew it,' she said. 'We left when he was very small. But I remember it. I swore I'd never go back to that life.'

'But you have now?'

'I've got no choice,' she said. 'They threw me out the hotel. I've got no where else to stay.'

'Why not just go home,' I said. 'They'd take you back.'

'And admit that I'd failed?' she laughed and took a drink. 'My parents don't have a clue about what I actually do. They think I'm actually working in a respectable trade.'

'What is it you want from me,' I said.

'The people that I'm staying with want to meet you, Richard. They've never know an outsider to stick up for one of them. As soon as they told me I knew it must be you.'

'I've got to find Miranda,' I said. 'I have to make things right.'

'Miranda's taken off for a bit, to get some space. Just come and meet the people I'm staying with, then go and find her. She won't go away for good.'

'Do you know where she is?'

'Yes.'

'But you won't tell me?'

'Just come and visit, Richard. Then I'll help you find her.'

19

As Rachel led me to her new home I was beginning to wonder if I was falling into some kind of trap. She led me in silence through the streets and down a back road—the one that Jake, on our first night out, had said never to use. There was only about three or four metres in between the buildings which towered either side. I half expected someone to jump out and attack me at any moment. The alley reached a dead end and we had to scramble over a pile of bricks; the other side of which lay a carcass of a big white dog. There were holes in the torso where rats and crows had pecked away at it. We scrambled under barbed wire and made our way across dry, rocky earth. A solitary flood light illuminated the terrain, leaving us completely exposed. It reminded me of the barriers to the town. It would be easy for someone to take a shot at us if they so wished, but I reminded myself that this was not the town and it was evidently a journey Rachel was accustomed to making.

'Quite a comedown from hotel life, then?'

Rachel just ignored me and carried on plodding forwards.

'I hope you actually know where she is,' I said thinking of Miranda.

'I'll help you find her,' said Rachel, her eyes straight ahead.

We carried on in silence; in the distance I saw a little red glow.

'Is that it?' I asked. 'That is the underclass den?'

'We call it a village.'

As we got closer I could see the red glow was a fire and there were people around it. As we got closer still, I could see it was two men, wearing nothing but torn and dirty slacks. One of them was middle aged, the other possibly my age. They could have been father and son. The older one was prodding the fire with a stick. They both stared at me, the whites of their eyes illuminating from their dirty, bearded faces. Rachel spoke to them:

'Matthew, Bartholomew, this is Richard; the man who rescued Fran.'

The older man stood up quickly and grasped me by the forearms. I tried to shrink away from him, partly out of alarm and partly because he stank. I could feel his eyes boring into me. Then, as if he suddenly recognised me, he let out a little guffaw and threw his arms around me. 'You are our brother,' he said. 'You must stay with us.'

Before I had a chance to make any excuses I was being led away, each man with an arm around me. We approached a number of makeshift homes made from corrugated iron and chipboard.

'Martha, Francesca!' called the first man. 'Come and meet your new son and brother.'

A tiny middle aged woman approached from one of the huts. She reached up and clasped my face with strong, rough hands. She beamed at me; her face wizened and wrinkled like a walnut. I was waiting for her to speak, but she just continued peering at me as if I was a miracle from outer space.

'This is my wife,' said the older man, leading me away. 'And this is Francesca, my daughter.'

In front of me stood the young woman I'd rescued. She was undoubtedly beautiful, despite the dirt and rags she was in. Her wild, untamed hair was in stark contrast to her face which was shy and gentle. She wore a skirt which revealed soft thighs and shapely hips. The man then stood in front of me, looking earnestly.

'You saved my daughter and for that, you have my gratitude.'

He took my hands and kissed them.

'You must eat with us, my friend. Tell us of your story.'

Dinner consisted of roasted rat, cooked in cloth on a metal sheet over the fire. I forced myself to eat it before finding it didn't taste too bad. Afterwards I told them of the town I had come from. I told them of meeting Rachel's family, of arriving at the city. Rachel, in fact had relatives there. A man who went by the name of Theodore was her uncle, Joseph's brother. She sat next to him, her arm propped up on his shoulder, his arm wrapped around her. They seemed so keen to be hospitable I felt bad saying I needed to go.

'You must come back,' said Matthew, Francesca's father. 'You can teach us you're fighting skills.'

'I have none to teach,' I laughed. 'It was blind luck.'

'All the same, we would like to see you again,' he said. 'You are a part of our family now,' he said, giving a little bow.

Rachel walked with me across the rocky earth. As we walked I felt the air was a little fresher than it had been. It had been a while since I had felt that level of warmth. It had been a while since I had felt good about myself.

'They're nice people,' I said to Rachel.

'They are,' she said. 'I was wrong, what I said about them.'

'Then why did you?'

'I didn't know any better,' she sighed.

I noticed the stars were out across the plain. They weren't often noticed; the combination of pollution, street lights and air traffic usually obliterated them. I also noticed for the first time that we were holding hands.

'Isn't it nice,' she said looking around. 'It's kind of romantic isn't it?'

She spun round in front of me and took my other hand, her brown eyes locked into mine. She leaned forward and I found myself leaning forward to, before I stopped myself and held her away.

'No,' I said. 'I'm not making the same mistake again.'

'You know I'm in love with you Richard,' she said. 'This isn't just some silly crush.'

'I'm with Miranda,' I said. 'I'm sorry.'

I turned away and walked before my will power gave way. I felt her eyes burn into my back. When I got to the pile of bricks I dared myself to turn around, and realised she had gone.

20

As I was walking back to Atkins house I realised I hadn't found out from Rachel where Miranda was, but I assumed that she didn't know anyway. It was clear that she had led me there so I could see a different side of her. I have to say, if it wasn't for Miranda, I probably would have fallen for it, but I'd vowed I'd never betray my wife again; not after all we had been through. Halfway back, I suddenly took it into my head to go back to the hotel. Maybe Miranda hadn't gone after all? In fact I felt sure that was just a ruse of Rachel to keep me tagging along. This could be my chance to reconcile with her. My visit to the underclass had invigorated me. My priorities were re-established and my hope restored. As I got closer to the hotel however, a sense that something was wrong kept gnawing at me. As I passed people I would sense them glancing at me out the corner of their eye. I quickened my pace as I got closer. Something was definitely wrong. I walked straight into the hotel and up to our old room. It was empty. I saw some of Miranda's clothes left lying on the floor as if she had packed in a hurry. I went to Jackson's room and that was empty as well, with the door left ajar.

Going back to Miranda's room I ransacked it, looking for some clue. Going into the bedroom I found it, scrawled in red lipstick on the mirror:

'GET OUT NOW'

All the breath was sucked out my lungs. It was Miranda's handwriting. Who could possibly be after us? I heard footsteps outside the door. I didn't hang around to find out. I stepped out onto the balcony and leaped off it. There was a chute which ran all the way down from each floor to the ground. I bounced down the red tube of hell at break neck speed. I had never exited the building this way before. Presumably the chute was put here as a fire exit but it wasn't a comfortable descent. Instinctively I put my hands out to try and brake myself and got nothing but friction burns for my trouble. I wondered for a moment if certain death awaited me at the bottom but mercifully the chute levelled out and I slid out onto the sidewalk below. I staggered to my feet, nauseous and dizzy, and somehow managed to fight through the encroaching spectators. When my senses were clear enough I ducked into an alley. I figured I had to keep off the main streets. I kept my head down as I passed the bars. I took comfort from the usual sounds of drug fuelled bawdiness and sex fuelled entertainment. Everything was normal here; I was safe to move around as long as no one saw my face. I still had no idea what was going on. Why were people giving me glances as I went to the hotel? What had happened to Miranda? The handwriting was definitely hers which at least meant she probably got out by her own volition rather than taken out. Jackson had gone as well so presumably he was with her. For once that was a good thing; I knew he'd look after her. As I passed an alleyway my heart froze. Out the corner of my eye I saw two cleaners who flashed a light on me as I passed. I heard one of them shout something. I quickly took a corner and darted over a fence, crashing into tins and bottles on the other side. I crawled away, my left knee in agony and hid in a huge concrete cylinder. I heard the cleaners pass by, saw the flash light sweep around. I tucked my head between my knees and suppressed my cry of fear and pain. The footsteps got louder. They couldn't have been more than a metre or two away. I forced myself to breathe slowly through my nose. A warm dampness spread from my knee and I resisted the urge to look. Eventually, after what seemed like a century the footsteps passed. I stayed frozen for another minute, before I dared to lift my head and inspect my knee. The squeal I had trapped in my lungs escaped. A shard of glass was wedged in my knee cap; the blood stain had already spread halfway up my leg. I put my sleeve in between my teeth and clamped down on it as I tugged the glass out. The flow of blood bubbled over my jeans. I took my shirt off and bound it around the wound. I leaned against the side of the cylinder and gave myself a moment to get focused. I had to get to Hargreaves. Presumably if there were people after Miranda, Jackson and I, they would be after Hargreaves as well. I couldn't let him down. I wondered if they were after Roberts, wherever he was.

I crawled out the tunnel and limped back to Atkins house through the dirt and the rubble that was the back streets of the city.

21

'Where's Hargreaves? What's going on?' I said, staggering through the door.

'My dear boy,' said Atkins, his face pale as he studied me from head to toe. 'Something awful has happened. It really is most dreadful. The Cleaners are after you.'

'After me?'

'All of you. I'm afraid—'Atkins gulped.

'What happened to Hargreaves?'

'They took him.'

I punched the wall with frustration. 'Why, why are they after us?'

'I'm afraid I have no idea. They burst in and demanded to know where the two of you were. I tried to hide the poor boy but they found him anyway.'

'Well I have to find him,' I said.

'No!' said Atkins firmly. 'No, no, no, that will never do. The best chance you have is to get away from here. Do you know a good hiding place?'

I thought of the underclass' camp. Was it right to impose myself on them? To put them at risk? I couldn't see how I had a choice. It would at least give me time. Maybe things would settle down and then I could work out how to search for the others. Besides, no one would think of looking for me there.

'Yes,' I said. 'I know of somewhere.'

'I'll take you straight there. I'm afraid it's not safe for you here any more my boy. Come quickly.'

I followed Atkins out into his back yard. 'I have a hover craft,' he said. 'If you keep your face hidden, hopefully no one will recognise you. You just direct me and I will take you there forthwith.'

I jumped into the vehicle. Atkins gave me a cloth which I put over my face. Atkins started the engine and we raced through the streets. Everything appeared to be as normal. Atkins kept muttering as I was directing him, his eyes darting about like a whippet.

'They really are beastly these Cleaners,' he said swerving round the traffic. 'No sense of fair play at all. They just burst in, guns poised. I tried my best, my dear boy, I really tried but they were relentless. I'm glad to say they didn't hurt him as they took him, but it is never pleasant, it never is.'

I peered under the cloth keeping an eye out for the turning to the encampment.

'Turn left down here.'

'I say, old boy are you sure,' said Atkins.

'I'm sure,' I said.

When we got to the end of the alley I told him to stop.

'Thank you, Atkins,' I said shaking his hand. 'You've saved me yet again. Just do one more thing, will you?'

'Of course,' said Atkins clasping my hands in his. 'Anything I can do will be pleasure.'

'Don't tell anyone you left me here,' I said. 'In fact, don't tell anyone I came back. As far as you know, I never came back.'

'My lips are sealed my dear boy.'

I got out the vehicle and was about to thank him once again when he sped away without a word. Getting over the rubble and under the barbed wire was more of a feat in my wounded condition. As I limped my way across the rocky lumps of earth I wondered what had happened to my wife and all my friends. Was this it? Would I never see them again? I couldn't allow myself to think that right now. I was no use to anyone if I was captured. Had to keep focused, had to keep my mind clear. As I got closer I could see the red glow and I heard voices; shouting, wailing, crying. I skirted around the parameter keeping low. I scrambled closer coming up to hide behind one of the huts.

'Where is he?' demanded a voice.

'We have told you, he is not here,' said another voice.

I heard the sound of a blow, probably with a stick followed by a groan.

'You shut your mouth, you insolent son of whore!' screamed the first voice. 'He is here somewhere! I demand to know where he is!'

I could hear what sounded like women and children crying as the first voice continued the tirade.

'You will tell me where he is, even if I have to beat it out of your filthy mouths. Even if we have to cut every finger off of every diseased hand, you will *talk*!'

At that moment I felt a hand on my shoulder. My heart nearly jumped into my mouth until I recognised who it was. It was one of the children; a little girl named Mya.

'Mya,' I whispered. 'What's going on?'

'They are looking for you,' she whispered. 'The Cleaners.'

I nodded, the horror of what was happening slowly dawning on me.

'You have to go,' said Mya. 'We won't tell.'

'Oh God,' I gasped. 'Oh God, what will I do now?'

Mya started stroking my hair and whispered in my ear.

'It's ok, you have to go. Go now, please.'

I could hear more blows from the sticks and more groans.

'You don't worry,' continued the girl. 'We can take it, you can't. You have to go.'

Suddenly out of nowhere came a nerve shattering scream from a woman, followed by a baby crying. I stood and walked forward to see one of the Cleaners dangling the baby upside down, by one leg over a camp fire. Another two were pinning down a woman who was screaming at the top of her voice. The Cleaner holding the baby dropped it a little lower over the flames. The infant's cries intensified under the added heat as did the woman's screams.

'Where—is he?' said the Cleaner in a growl. 'I won't ask again.'

'I'm here,' I found myself saying. I heard a collective gasp as all eyes turned on me. One of the men suddenly got up and took the baby from the Cleaners grasp, handing it back to the mother who by now had been released. The Cleaner didn't seem to notice or care. I could make out his features by the firelight; a head like a tank, eyes glimmering, moustache twitching.

'Are you Richard Stirling?' he asked.

'I am,' I said. I looked around the faces in the crowd, looking for the one I knew was responsible for this. She wasn't there. At least she had some shame.

'You're under arrest!' the Cleaner snapped, at which point I was surrounded and seized. I was forced to my knees, my arm twisted behind my back. The cleaner walked up to me and lifted my chin. I forced myself to stare into his eyes, refusing to be beaten entirely. They were practically overflowing with satisfaction. I must have been the find of his career.

'There's someone who'd like to meet you, Mr Stirling,' he said, a grin forming at the side of his thin lips. I felt a sharp pain in the back of the neck—then nothing.

22

When I came to I found myself in the dark. Pain flooded across my whole body, especially my arms which were pinned above my head. My hands were numb although there was a throbbing ache in my biceps, shoulders and sides. I realised my arms were taking my weight and tried to find my feet but they would not respond. As far as I knew, all that was left of me was a torso, chained to a wall. As my eyes focused I could see my legs collapsed uselessly beneath me. I tried to will them into action, to take my weight to alleviate the pain in my upper body but they refused to move. I could see a small, dim square of light coming from my left. I tried to call out but my throat felt like sandpaper. Then it was blackness again. Little sparks of light shot through my brain. I could see David, calling for me; I saw my parents', standing over me in judgement. What had I done wrong now? I saw Miranda's face; saw her tears, of disappointment, in me. Jackson was there, shaking his head in disappointment.

I felt a hand gripping my throat, a strong hand, cutting off my air. A voice whispered in my ear. It was a voice I recognised. It spoke in a whisper, I could feel the warm breath tickling the hairs in my ear:

'You have failed!'

Then I heard the chains rattling and felt myself falling to the floor. I felt cold wet stone on my cheek. I could see legs in front of me, silhouetted by the pale square of light. A boot made contact with my ribs, crushing the air out of me. Footsteps walked away, door closed, the square of light disappeared with a click. For a moment I thought I would die, right there and then. I couldn't breath and scarcely had the strength to try. The darkness spread over me, swallowing me whole.

The next thing I was aware of was a door opening and a light piercing my eyes. A bowl was placed in front of me. Bread and water. The door shut again. I sat up, cross legged and picked at the loaf. I could taste the salt which brought me to my senses a little, brought me to the pain coursing through my body. I looked down and could see my ribs; the skin stretched over them was virtually translucent. There was an ugly green bruise in my sternum. I put my hands to my face and could feel rough, hairy skin. I examined my hands; thick red lines encircled my wrists. I moved the fingers; at least they still functioned. As far as I could make out everything was still working as it should. I started to piece together what had happened. I had been taken by the Cleaners, put in this cell and chained to the wall. I had no idea why any of this had happened. I had no idea what had happened to Miranda, Jackson or Hargreaves. I had no idea if any of them were still alive. I took the water and drank it in one. It didn't satisfy my thirst. I hurled the cup at the door and lay back on the tiles, staring at the cobwebbed beams in the alcoves.

It could have been five minutes or five hours before the door opened again. Two men hauled me up and walked me backwards to the wall. They put my arms back in the shackles. I knew better than to argue. They left and I stood there staring at the rectangle of light, waiting for something else to happen. A figure came to occupy the space. A tall figure. As he walked forward my subconscious knew before my mind would allow myself to believe it.

'Callahan?'

There was a whistle and a thud and my left leg crumpled as I cried out in agony. I could sense the figure coming towards me, could feel a rough hand grab me by the chin and force me to gaze at the face which had been in my nightmares for years.

'Well boy,' he said. 'Now we're even.'

23

'I expect you're wondering what has been going on?' said Callahan. 'I expect you're wondering why you are here, where are your friends.'

I grimaced through the pain determined not to show weakness in front of him.

'I prayed you were dead, you asshole,' I grunted.

'I see you have learnt some colourful new language, boy. Unfortunately that kind of talk will not get you very far.'

'You want to kill me, fine,' I said. 'Just spare me the bullshit.'

'And then you will never know,' said Callahan. 'My oh my, how the tables have turned. You were so pleased with yourselves, weren't you? The only ones to break out of the town. And I have to hand it to you. Not many get out alive.'

I concentrated my pain into the cracks of the floor. 'What do you want with me Callahan?'

'Ah now, we're getting to it,' said Callahan. 'What did I want with any of you?

I looked up into his eyes and saw them sparkling with glee.

'What do you mean?'

'My boy, you have to understand something. In my town, I am in charge. I decide who stays and who goes, who lives and who dies. In my town I am God. Do you understand now?'

'So this is revenge,' I said.

'This is restoring the mess you made when you stormed into my office like a pack of wild animals. This is restoring order. Without order there is nothing. Nothing!' he snapped.

'You think you can control people like robots,' I said. 'You can't. Your empire was all in your head, you sick deluded old man.'

'I am in charge!' he bellowed. 'I had a plan! You ruined the plan.'

'So kill me,' I muttered. 'Kill me like you killed my brother, you coward.'

Callahan laughed. 'My boy, there is a lot you need to learn.'

'Learn about what?' I was beginning to feel as if he was just enjoying sending me round in circles.

'About your brother.'

'You're playing with me, Callahan. I'm not playing this game any more.' As I looked into his face a surge jolted though my body. My hands went for his throat, stopped dead by the chains.

'Get me out of here!' I screamed. 'Get me out these chains; I'm going to kill you, you bastard! I'll wring your fucking neck!'

Callahan walked out and left me shouting up into the air, thrashing around at the chains before I passed out.

When I came to I was horizontal and staring up at the ceiling. I couldn't move at all, not even my head. Moving my eyes from side to side I couldn't see anyone else in the room. Then I heard Callahan's voice:

'I have an old friend to see you, boy.'

A face moved into my eye line. Another one I'd never wished again.

'Hello Stirling.'

'Frampton.'

Since I had seen him last he had acquired a moustache. His hair was a little longer and plastered with some kind of wax. His little eyes had a glint in them. 'I thought you'd like to know, Stirling. I killed your little friend Roberts.'

I lay there frozen to the spot. I didn't want to say anything to fuel his lust.

'I found him and he tried to run. I shot him in the lower back, then I shot him in the shoulder, then I shot him in the belly. I shot him seven times before I finally shot him through the head. He was a useless fat idiot. Begging for his life, at least in the beginning. By the time I'd finished with him he was begging to be put out his misery.'

I concentrated on my breathing. I tried not to give anything away.

'I fucked your wife as well, Stirling,' he hissed. 'Truth be told, I think she liked it in the end.'

'You're a liar,' I said, a tear escaping and rolling down my cheek.

'Am I now,' he said. 'Well we'll see about that.'

He disappeared and I heard Callahan saying something. I think it was 'only two.' I heard a swishing noise and felt something resting across my abdomen. Then there was another whoosh and a fearsome crack and a horrific burning sting across my belly. I screamed, but I was bound tight. I was helpless.

'You think I'm a liar, do you Stirling!'

Another one landed almost on the same spot. He must be practised.

'Is that all you've got!' I screamed through the pain. 'Come on, you coward. Again!'

'Enough!' called out Callahan's voice. Then his face hovered over me.

'Your defiance will not last for long, boy. I have questions and I want them answered. I also have a selection of thorns. When I don't get an answer I like, I will push one up underneath your finger nail. Do you think you will last until I have gone through all ten fingers?'

'You can go and fuck yourself, Callahan.'

'Then I will start cutting things off,' continued Callahan. 'Starting with the fingers and ending with your testicles.'

His face was so dead set and impassionate it was almost calming. It demanded obedience, but obedience did not come without a price.

'I have questions too,' I said.

'Of course. I will tell you what you want to know.

24

'For years you will have been familiar with an individual known as the Messiah,' said Callahan. 'You will have seen him making his appearances on television network; proselytising for his ridiculous cult who believe him to be the true second coming of Christ.'

'I have heard of him,' I said.

'And your brother showed an interest in this individual, did he not?' said Callahan.

'I don't know,' I murmured.

'Oh come on boy,' snapped Callahan. 'You don't need to pretend now.'

'I never knew,' I said.

'Well I can tell you he did,' said Callahan. 'There were many not satisfied with our culture of science and fact. There were many who considered practising all kinds of perverted practices in direct contravention of our laws and culture. You were one and so was your brother and so were your pathetic little friends.'

'What happened to the people that disappeared?' I asked.

'Ah the golden question. I admire your direct approach.'

'Were they killed?' I asked.

'This is the question that's been torturing you for so long hasn't it Richard?'

'What happened to my brother,' I said, holding the tears in.

'David is alive,' said Callahan.

To hear those words, even from a monster like Callahan caused me to lose my control, the tears releasing all the pain I had held for so long.

'You said you killed him,' I choked.

'I was wrong Richard,' said Callahan; his voice seeming to convey some kind of compassion I hadn't heard before. 'I was being spiteful. I hold no apologies for this. Like I said, you humiliated me. I bit back in the only way I could.'

'How do I know you're not playing with me now?'

'You don't,' said Callahan. 'But when you hear the whole story you will see how it all fits into place.'

'Where is he?' I asked.

'He is at the Messiah's commune, along with your parents, along with Vincent, along with all the people that disappeared.'

'Why?'

'Simple business my boy,' he said. 'This man who calls himself the Messiah; he and I have an agreement. I provide potential members for his cult and he provides me with money.'

'What about Vincent and his father?' I said. 'Is that where they went? Was it part of your scheme to take over the town?'

'Alfred Vincent was a weak man,' said Callahan. 'It was a mutual decision to leave. Remember the time when he rescued you and your brother? That was the day his whole family left. I was happy to take over the leadership of the town.'

I did remember. I remembered I would have killed Vincent if his father hadn't showed up.

'You were one of us, until that moment,' I heard Frampton say. 'You could have really been someone. You and your brother made some bad decisions that day.'

'We were bullies,' I said. 'Vincent was a psychotic and so are you.'

'Enough!' snapped Callahan. I sensed that Frampton had reached for his cane again and was glad that Callahan seemed to be some kind of restraining influence; a little like an owner of a rabid pit-bull.

'And part of your plan was to send me to this cult?' I asked. 'And all the others?'

'Of course,' soothed Callahan. 'But we need to know where Jackson and your wife are.'

'Where's Hargreaves?'

'He is there also. I'm afraid your new found friend Atkins informed on you. You see your pictures have been up for a while. A huge reward on each of your heads. Two thousand credits—each.'

'And Rachel?'

'Yes. I'm afraid that little whore you picked up led the Cleaners to the underclass. Nearly got them all killed in the process; just to spite you. You shouldn't have turned her down, boy. You really can't trust anyone around here, especially a woman scorned.'

'And Roberts is dead?' I asked.

Callahan scoffed in disgust. 'Enough of this tedious questioning. It is time for you to do the telling. Where is Jackson and where is your wife?'

'I don't know,' I said.

'Don't play games with me you stupid boy. You will tell me in the end. Jackson didn't take long to tell me about you and your brother. Do we need to see who lasts the longest?'

'I'm telling you, I don't know.'

'If you think you're protecting them you're deluding yourself. They will be found and they will be shot on sight without my protection. Tell me where to find them and I will see they make it safely to the commune.'

'I'm telling you, I don't know,' I said through gritted teeth.

There was a swish and a crack as the cane landed over my abdomen again, this time with even more venom than before. I guessed Frampton had taken exception to being called a psychotic.

'You'd take care to mind your tone!' snapped Callahan. 'You forget who's in charge.'

'I can't tell you what I don't know,' I said, my face contorted.

'You know!' snapped Callahan. The stick came down again causing me to scream at the top of my voice. 'I don't know. I don't know!'

'You are trying my patience boy. Again!'

'Stop!' I called out. 'I'll tell you, I'll tell you.'

The horrific burning had all but taken away my ability to speak. It flooded my whole mind like a siren getting louder and louder. All I could see in my mind was bright red torn skin across my belly. I imagined if he could thrash all the skin away and get right to my intestines. How anyone can withstand torture I have no idea to this day, and this was only mild. Probably milder than what Jackson had gone through.

'I still have the thorns to go yet,' said Callahan in my ear. 'Make sure you tell me the truth.'

'They're in the hotel where we were staying.'

'That's a lie!' roared Callahan. 'You take me for an idiot boy. Don't you think that's the first place we looked?'

A terrifying sharp pain registered in the tip of my finger. I screamed out in agony. I could feel Callahan manoeuvring it, prising the nail off with cold blooded calculation.

'Stop! Please stop!'

'That was one, do we need to go through the other nine.'

'They're not in the hotel,' I screamed. 'They're in the bar; they're staying in the bar across the road.'

'They are not there either!' roared Callahan.

'I mean they are staying in the one on the other side of the street. The one with the little old man, the one with the old artefacts in.'

'He doesn't know, kill him,' said Callahan.

At that moment I heard two shots.

25

I wondered if I was dead. Miranda's face hovered over me. Was she an angel? Was this heaven? If it was, why was I still in excruciating pain?

'It's ok, it's over now,' she said, stroking the tears and sweat off my face.

'Miranda?' I said softly.

'Yes it's me. Me and Jackson are here.'

'It's ok man,' I heard Jackson's voice and felt his hand on my arm. 'We'll get you out of here.'

'You can't,' I said. 'They'll kill you, they'll kill us all.'

'Some people are easily bought,' said Jackson. 'We'll be ok.'

'You bribed your way in?'

'The Cleaners are for hire,' said Miranda. 'They'll serve whoever pays the most.'

'Oh God, I wish I was dead,' I sobbed. 'They made me say it.'

'You didn't say anything,' said Miranda.

'But I would have,' I said. 'If I had known.'

'You wouldn't, trust me,' said Miranda kissing my forehead. 'There's plenty of time for this later Richard, but we have to get you out of here.'

'He's loose,' said Jackson. 'Come on buddy.'

Jackson slid his arm under my back. I screamed in pain as I leaned forward.

'It's ok, nearly there, can you stand?' said Jackson.

I put my feet on the floor, raising my arms for balance as I let them take my weight. Callahan and Frampton were lying dead on the ground. Callahan had a bullet through his head; Frampton had taken one in the chest. It would seem that Jackson had finally got justice for his mother. I slowly hobbled out the room with Miranda and Jackson supporting me on each side.

'David's alive,' I said suddenly finding my purpose again. 'They're all alive! All the ones that were taken.'

'We know,' said Miranda as we walked down a long corridor.

'How do you know?'

'We saw Vincent in one of the Messiah's broadcasts,' said Jackson.

'Really?'

'Really,' said Jackson. 'Standing there right next to him. He must have some high rank there.'

'We have to go there.'

'There's a hovercraft out the front,' said Miranda. 'We'll go straight there.'

'Who's driving?' I asked.

'You'll never guess,' said Miranda.

We exited a door into the sunshine. I felt strong arms pick me up and put me in the back of the hovercraft. I had seen that face before, the kindly expression, the huge beard.

'Joseph?'

'You're alright now,' he said. 'No one is after you.'

'Joseph put up part of the money for our release,' said Miranda.

'What? How did you know?'

'Rachel came to me,' said Joseph. 'After the cleaners came to find you, she was so ashamed. She came straight home. Told me what had happened.'

We had already started moving through the busy streets. I drank the scenery in, my light-starved eyes couldn't get enough.

'Luckily for us by the time we had been picked up, Joseph had already put up five thousand credits,' said Miranda. 'We were able to cover the other four and then come and get you.'

'Callahan thought he owned the Cleaners,' said Jackson. 'But we out priced him, simple as that. He was paying two thousand credits for each of us and we offered three.'

'Too late for Hargreaves and Roberts,' I said.

'Frampton was with the cleaners when they found Roberts,' said Miranda.

I saw Jackson fix his gaze in the distance. Frampton's blood lust had superseded his business sense for the second time. The first time it had cost Rosie Jackson her life.

'He was selling people to the Messiah,' I said. 'Although I think he planned to kill me anyway. The pleasure of it would have been worth more to him than the money. I'm just glad I didn't know where you were.'

I reached out and put my hand on Jackson's arm. He took my hand. It was all that was required. I wondered if it was dawning on him that he'd just killed two people. If he felt bad about it he didn't let it show; he was lost in his own thoughts.

'How did you get the money together,' I asked Joseph. I winced as I tugged the thorn out of my fingernail with my teeth. It didn't look as bad as I imagined it would, but it still hurt like hell along with my leg which had a bullet in it and my stomach which had been lashed raw.

'Rachel came back to me and told me. I went straight to the village, the place where you met my family. They told me of how you rescued Francesca, of how you gave yourself up rather than allow a child to be harmed. Between us we raised the cash which I took to the cleaners.'

I realised that I was crying again. I couldn't be sure if it was through the pain or the fact that I was among true friends. I lay back in Miranda's arms and allowed her to stroke my head.

'We never turn a back on our family,' said Joseph. 'You are family now to us.'

'You're a good man,' I said. 'Please tell Rachel—no hard feelings.'

I put my arms around Miranda; felt her body melt into mine.

'Will you forgive me?' I whispered.

Miranda smiled and kissed me and I lay back and watched the passing clouds.

PART THREE

The Commune
2996-2999AD

The path will not be easy. Many of you shall perish. But he who believes shall live eternal. This world is but a stepping stone to a higher place. Take faith my friends. We shall meet in Paradise.

I

I couldn't believe it was actually happening. As we left the bustle of the city behind, it was reminiscent of when we escaped the town. Now effectively, we had to escape the town again. Even from a distance of hundreds of kilometres the town still had us in its clutches and presumably it would continue to do so if, as Callahan had said, it had links with the commune. At least that link, if it existed had ensured the survival of my brother. I couldn't allow myself to believe that that wasn't true. After believing for so long that he was dead, I couldn't face losing him a second time. As for my parents, I felt ambivalent. I felt that even now they would be disappointed in me, if indeed they were there as well.

The sun bore down on us as we sped through the desert, travelling towards seemingly nowhere.

'You know where you're going, Joseph,' I murmured.

'Oh yes,' said Joseph turning round and beaming at us. 'I have internal navigation.'

I remembered how Roberts had driven us through the barricades and led us to Joseph and his family. I felt a twinge of sadness, thinking of his demise at the hands of Frampton. It wondered why it was the fundamentally innocent who seemed to suffer the most. I thought also of Killinger, who had confided in me the story of Jackson considering suicide not long before a stray bullet had taken his own life. I looked at Jackson who was staring into the horizon, his eyes expressionless. Had I driven him to consider taking his life? Now I owed him my life. I tried to speak but my mouth was too dry. Miranda held a bottle of water to my lips and I guzzled it like a baby as she stroked my head.

'I don't deserve you,' I said in a hoarse whisper.

'I love you,' she whispered. 'It's ok.'

She wiped a stray tear from my cheek. I hadn't even noticed it.

'Do you think he's there?' I croaked.

'Of course,' said Miranda. 'Why don't you get some sleep?'

It seemed like only a minute later when I realised we had stopped and Joseph was talking to someone. Then I drifted off to sleep again.

The second time I awoke, I was in bed and shards of light were hitting me in the eyes. A figure stepped into my eye line, blocking the light.

'Brother Richard?' a voice enquired.

As my vision adjusted I could see it was a man, in a robe. His hood was down, revealing a balding head and a kind face.

'Brother Richard, my name is Brother Francis. Do you feel any pain?'

I felt sore and stiff but was generally too comfortable to be in pain. I shook my head and tried to sit up when my abdomen cried out in protest.

'Please rest,' said Francis. 'You have been through much turmoil, but you are safe here. Everyone is safe here.'

'Francis is my mother's name,' I said. 'Is she here?'

'We have no regard for biological relations here,' said Francis smiling. 'We are all brothers and sisters in Christ.'

'Who's Christ?'

'The one true King. The Son of God,' said Francis, as if it were a ridiculous question.

'The Messiah?' I asked. 'He's here?'

'Undoubtedly,' said the man.

'In flesh?'

'We are truly blessed Brother,' he said, a broad smile on his face. 'Three thousand years have elapsed. For Him to come a second time, to save us yet again . . .'

'Is it Jesus?' I interrupted.

'No. He comes under a different name. It is too sacred to be spoken.'

'Brother Francis,' I said. 'May I see my family?'

'We are all family . . .'

'I know,' I said. 'It's just my brother—my biological brother, I thought he was dead and now he's here. Could you find him?'

'I'm afraid I have no idea my son.'

'What about my wife?' I asked. 'May I see her?'

'I'm afraid you have no wife,' said Francis, shaking his head.

'What do you mean?'

'You did not marry in this institute?'

'No—' I stuttered.

'Then I'm afraid your marriage is not valid and you will not be permitted to see her.'

'I must!'

'Women and men are housed in different sections of the Church. You see chastity and the sanctity of marriage are imperative here. The Lord has insisted.'

'What? This is ridiculous! How does anyone get married?'

'They are arranged,' said Francis. 'Now please—'

'Arranged!' I blurted out. 'By who?'

'By the Lord of course; through his trusted senate who act on His behalf.'

'I'm sorry Brother Francis,' I said. 'I don't mean to be disrespectful but I cannot agree to marry anyone else. Miranda is my wife and I must see her.'

'Calm yourself my child,' said Francis. 'The Lord will direct you in His own time.'

'What about my friend Jackson. Is he here?'

Francis looked confused for a moment and then seemed to suddenly recollect.

'Oh Brother Frederick,' he said. 'He is at work. Yes he will visit you, my son. All in good time. First you must rest and recover.'

'Will I get to see the Messiah,' I asked.

'All in good time my son.'

2

It was a few days later that Jackson came to see me. 'Hey Stirling, how are you? Or should I call you Brother Richard.'

The sight of Jackson wearing a long white robe with a basket under his arm made me crack up.

'I'm better thanks, Brother Frederick,' I laughed. 'You've been reaping in the celestial harvest I see.'

'Oh, you should see it out there,' he said his eyes wide with amazement as he sat on the bed.

'They've got fruit trees, galore. I thought I was well off having a lemon tree in my old house. They've got apples, plums, tomatoes, mangoes. It's like a paradise.'

'How do they manage to grow all that?' I said. 'Is it a miracle?'

'I expect the Messiah does his little conjuring trick,' said Jackson. 'If he can come back after three thousand years he shouldn't have too much trouble with a few apples.'

Jackson passed me a bright red apple from the basket.

'Should I say grace?' I said, biting into the apple. It was sweet and juicy. 'That's really good!'

'There's more where that came from,' said Jackson. 'Though I'm afraid it's the only kind of flesh we're gonna get our hands on for a while.'

'No women at all,' I said. 'Not even old and ugly ones.'

'Not a single female in sight,' said Jackson. 'I think our bearded friend keeps them for himself.'

'Oh don't,' I winced, thinking of Miranda.

'Only kidding,' said Jackson. 'We'll have to arrange some visits. I'm sure we can arrange a private little rendezvous.'

'Have you seen anyone else? Hargreaves, my father—David?'

Jackson shook his head. 'Sorry, not as yet. The trouble is that this place is huge Richard. I mean really huge. There must be thousands of people here. They don't use last names and it seems just about every other man is a David or a John. Can't expect they'll be many Ruperts around though.'

'What do you make of this place, Jackson?' I asked. I realised I hadn't looked out the window yet and slowly got out of bed and peered out.

'Prepare yourself for a shock, Stirling,' he said. 'It's quite a sight.'

The window looked out onto a massive garden. I couldn't see any walls or barriers in sight. There was a wood sealing off the garden probably about half a kilometre away. White robed men filled the garden, tilling the soil or tending the plants, like a colony of worker ants.

'This is Paradise?' I muttered. 'Are we really still alive?'

We stood for a moment and I felt awkward, standing next to a man who I had invested so much hatred in.

'I've missed you,' I said. 'I'm sorry—'

'Don't—' said Jackson. 'You had every right to feel the way you did.'

'You did nothing wrong.'

'Well I did sleep with your wife,' said Jackson. His blank tone took me back for a minute until I realised what he was doing and punched him on the arm. He collapsed into laughter. 'You're such a sucker,' he said.

'I'll get you for that.'

'Yeah yeah,' said Jackson. 'Anyway, seriously I think we'll be alright.'

'You said Vincent was here,' I said.

'Looks like he may be but I don't think he'll bother us.'

'Really?'

'Nah!' he said. 'This is a place of sanctity, Stirling. No one does anything except pray and pick plants.'

'And David's here—somewhere. I can't believe it Jackson. After all this time wondering where he is and he's right here, not more than a kilometre away and I still can't find him.'

'It won't be long now,' said Jackson. 'I'm just glad it all turned out ok.'

As I looked across the scene I felt inclined to believe him. This was the first time perhaps in my life, that I felt there was no threat from anyone. Perhaps here, as well as finding my family, I could find some peace. Perhaps I would even find God.

3

I spent a few days recuperating and being tended to by Francis. I missed Miranda and was worrying if I would get to see her at all. I knew that this wasn't a full time solution but I was desperate to see my family again. I would sit at the window and try and search for their faces amongst the hordes of white robed workers in the garden. I wondered if they would look a lot older; then I realised that it had only been two years since we had escaped the town. It had felt like an eternity.

Francis was the only person I saw in those few days. I grew to be quite fond of him and his slightly paternal manner.

'Are you feeling stronger, Brother Richard?' he asked as I devoured a meal of bread and fruit.

'Much,' I said with my mouth full. 'You are very kind Brother Francis.'

'You are most welcome,' said Francis. 'I also tend your friend, Brother Rupert. He has a broken leg, but it is healing well. You also have a lot of scars. Pray, from where do you come?'

'It's a long story,' I said with a smile. 'Let's just say I won't be hurrying back there.'

'Of course not,' said Francis. 'This is your home now.'

The man seemed so intent on this idea that I couldn't bring myself to tell him I didn't think we would be staying that long.

'I must meet my family,' I told him. 'And my wife—'

Francis was about to speak but I cut him off.

'I know, about your laws but we have been through so much together.'

'I cannot bring women here,' said Francis.

'What about my brother?'

'Brother David.' Francis pursed his lips and furrowed his brow. 'I think I know of a Brother by the name of David.'

'What does he look like?'

'I'm afraid I can't recall my son. But he does important work for the Lord.'

'The Messiah?'

'Yes, but now you must rest. Tomorrow you will join us for a meal.'

'Can I not join you tonight?' I was desperate to get away from that room and see more of the building and the area. Maybe then I could find a way to get to Miranda if nothing else. I wondered if they had armed guards here like they had in the town.

'No tomorrow,' said Francis. 'You must get your rest Brother Richard.'

I hardly got any that night. Lying there in the dark I had repeated flashbacks to being chained to the wall or tied to the bench. Callahan's face would emerge from the gloom like some phantom judge. I could remember every line that ran down those cheeks, every nuance in his chiselled features. I could remember that better than the faces of my family. I watched the room coming into focus as the sun rose and the images in my mind subsided and gave way to exhaustion. The next thing I was aware of was someone shaking my shoulder. Francis stood over me, beaming. 'It is a very fine morning,' he said. 'There are many people wanting to meet you.'

I followed him through endless corridors lined with stained glass pictures of saints. My whole body was throbbing and my head was numb. I wasn't in any fit state to deal with what Francis presented me with next. He led me into a room with a huge table, seated around which were thirty men, dressed in white. They all looked up at me, their faces blank.

'Brother Richard,' said Francis. 'Please will you take a seat?'

Francis showed me to an empty chair and the men either side moved away. I couldn't be sure if this was out of politeness or distaste.

'Brothers, please welcome Brother Richard,' said Francis. I observed a few heads nodding in acknowledgement before returning to their food.

'Please eat,' beamed Francis. 'I will be back shortly to explain to you your duties.'

I sat there in silence as I forced down the carrot and tomato soup and a husk of bread. When Francis left the room a man on my left turned to me.

'Where did you come from Brother?' he asked in a quiet voice.

'A long way away,' I said.

There was a stagnant pause as the man stared at me. I didn't know what to say but was determined to make the most of the opportunity to find out more. 'Do you like it here?' I asked.

The man seemed to choke on his soup for a moment and I felt eyes turn and stare at me.

'This is my home, Brother,' he said. 'This is all I ever wanted.'

'And where do you come from?' I asked.

'A dark place, Brother, a dark place,' he muttered. 'We don't talk about it.'

'Really?'

The man leaned forward as if he wanted to share something that was highly embarrassing.

'For fifteen years I was an agent of the Devil, Brother,' he said. 'My soul was twisted and broken. Then I found the Lord and He healed me and cleansed me of my sins.'

'You mean the Messiah,' I asked.

'The One and only,' the man said, his eyes now bulging out their sockets. 'The one true King of Kings, eternally begotten of the Father.'

'So you've met him?'

'Oh no Brother!' the man said, astounded. 'No one meets him.'

'No one?' I was beginning to find this hard to believe. 'Then who are the men with him on the videos?'

'Why, his Disciples. They are the only ones allowed to see him.'

'And who are the Disciples? What are their names?'

The bald man was just drawing breath to speak when a younger man interrupted him.

'Brother Patrick,' he said. 'Why don't you let Brother Richard gain his strength? There is plenty of time for questions later.'

We ate the rest of the meal in silence, my head buzzing with questions. There were two facts I was sure of though, stuck in my mind like anchors. The first was that Vincent must definitely be one of these Disciples. Jackson had said he had seen Vincent in one of the broadcasts although I could hardly think of someone less likely to be a prophet of God.

And then there was David. Francis had said that there was a Brother David working closely with the 'Lord'. It could be another David but somehow I felt that it must be my brother. It somehow felt like fate, as surely as the sun would always end up in the west; David was always going to end up here. I remembered all those times when I had walked with him to school. When I had felt that there was something going on in his head that I couldn't access. I remembered when he had come to the defence of Hargreaves, who had been lying helplessly in the dust waiting to be crucified. Vincent had then turned on him. Now Vincent was with him again, in the inner circle. It made me shudder to think of it. I knew for certain I had to get into that inner circle—somehow or other. I had to reach David.

4

After eating I was ushered into the garden. I was faced with row after row of tomatoes and given a basket. As I started plucking the fruit from the vine I was looking around to see where I might sneak out and explore. The men around me all worked in silence and I felt an air of conspiracy amongst them. I was certain they were all very conscious of me, although they all pretended to ignore me. Scanning across the red brick wall I caught sight of an oval wooden gate, ajar. I tried not to make it obvious as I inched my way across the row, towards that gate. It seemed impossibly far away but I kept imagining Miranda behind that gate. I had got to perhaps about thirty metres from it when I heard an ear-shattering fog horn blast come out of nowhere and was jostled with the crowd into the building.

We were all packed together into a big open space. The walls were white stone and the main focus of the room was a pair of purple cloth curtains covering almost the whole wall.

Was this one of the Messiah's speeches? Was I about to see him for the first time in the flesh? There was a low murmur of excitement as the curtains opened, but I felt slightly disappointed that it only revealed a huge blank screen. The murmur became a little more animated as the screen flashed on before a respectful silence fell among the crowd. The Messiah's face penetrated the screen, surveying the crowd through his motionless blue eyes. For a moment I wondered if this was just a still picture. Then he began to speak:-

'The promised time is nearly upon us!' he bellowed and a round of applause rose up from the crowd.

'Did I not tell you that I would lead you to the Kingdom of Heaven?'

'Yes!' called back the crowd in unison.

'Did I not tell you that you were my chosen people?'

'Yes!'

'Did I not tell you I would deliver you from the enemy?'

'Yes!'

'And the enemy has been working hard,' he continued. 'Throughout the lands we have been vilified, lied about, accused of all sorts of terrible things. The Devil has been hard at work, my people, but we will not be defeated!'

There was another round of applause.

'In just two years time, we will have our moment of glory. In the year three thousand, the world will sit up and take notice! They don't believe us when we talk of the Day of Judgement. They don't believe us when we talk of the choice between Heaven and Hell, salvation and damnation. They sit idly by; too consumed with worldly passion to realise the world is falling around them and the eternal fire of Hell is about to consume them!'

Another round of applause.

'But when the time comes, we will be triumphant, we will be saved. While they ridicule us and demonise us in this world, they will be begging for mercy in the next—but will we listen?'

'No!' the crowd chorused back.

'My people, God is merciful and God is just. He will look favourably on you and be forgiving of your trespasses, for you—you have accepted his only Son. Before, they who did not accept me, crucified me. I came to save the world with my blood, my pain, my sacrifice. But the people were not grateful; they were not appreciative of the wondrous gift that they had been freely given. Yet again they rejected me, they spat in the face of God and became in union with Satan. Now I am back, but this time, the pain will not be mine, the sacrifice will not be mine and there are no second chances.'

The screen then went blank and there was a round of applause. I found myself applauding too without realising. Then everyone shuffled out without a word and carried on picking tomatoes. In a daze I did just the same.

5

Each day at the commune was much the same. At six in the morning we would rise and shamble into the hall. There we would kneel on the stone floor and bow our heads. During these sessions someone would start humming. I have no idea if it was the same person each time or if it started at random but before too long the hum would spread around the room until everyone was joining in. I would join in with the humming, I was never told to, but it was infectious. For a brief moment I would feel a moment of unity with the other Brothers. After a while the hum would pilfer out and at times I would feel an overwhelming desolation; a terrible loneliness that would engulf me, only to leave me with my demons. At other times however, in this silence I would feel I was being touched. I almost reached out to reciprocate the touch but something would always stop me. I knew what it was. I couldn't be at peace until I'd seen Miranda, until I'd seen David and my parents. It was unfinished business. And sometimes I did pray. I would pray I would be reunited with my family again, that somehow all would be forgiven and we could live in harmony. I prayed that I could hold my wife again and tell her I loved her.

After breakfast we would work in the garden, tilling the soil, picking vegetables, pulling weeds. I continued to keep an eye out for the gate, but it was never ajar anymore. It was firmly shut so I could only imagine what lay beyond it. After lunch we would gather into the hall again and sing. One of the Brothers would lead the chants and the rest of us would join in. We'd have a communal supper and then we were largely left to ourselves. I scarcely spoke to anyone; in fact no one spoke much to each other. I would sometimes use this time to write poems, although I was guarded about the content of them. I would sometimes sense a figure peering over my shoulder before sliding away. It seemed ironic that in a place which appeared to be the polar opposite of the town, there were some things which were just the same. My poems would usually be haikus and to do with God or nature:

> 'The bumble bee flies
> Collecting pollen and seeds
> It has all it needs'

Or this one which Brother Francis took a liking to, muttering it to himself to commit it to memory:

> 'God provides the bread
> Ensures we are well and fed
> In his hands we are led'

After a while I began to stir up some interest with my poems. Francis would gather people around who would listen in apparent appreciation. In truth I never thought much of them myself, but I was eager to impress and earn my place in the upper circle.

During one of my 'recitals' I thought I saw a familiar face. Then after I had finished the man approached me and shook my hand. I recognised him immediately.

'Hargreaves?'

'It's good to see you Brother Richard.'

There was something unmistakably different about him. With his leg now fixed up, he walked straight and tall and moved with a new found authority. His eyes sparkled with enthusiasm. It was as if all his internal nervous energy had been transformed into a radiant joy.

'It's good to see you too,' I smiled. 'How are you?'

'Fantastic!' he said with quiet reverence. 'I can't believe it's taken me so long to find this place. Isn't it amazing?'

I couldn't bring myself to pour cold water on his enthusiasm by telling him my own concerns, so I agreed as wholeheartedly as I could.

'It's all changed for me now, Brother,' he said. 'No more depravity or baseness. Just purity and love and living for God.'

'You think the Messiah is the true son of God?'

'Of course!' said Hargreaves with that same incredulous look upon his face that I had become used to seeing. 'He is the one that can save us all Richard. Think back to when we were in the town. That was Hell—or purgatory at least. But now we've been given a second chance. We've been delivered. Don't you agree?'

'Of course,' I said managing a smile. 'It's great.'

I wasn't always putting up pretence. I really wanted to believe that there was something genuine at the core of this group. There were times, however that I felt I was immersed in some conspiracy which I was not privy to. I often wondered of the true thoughts and intentions of the men around me. I was a long way from trusting anyone. Even that meeting with Hargreaves had made me uncomfortable. It was as if he was now unreachable; there was no point discussing anything any more as his mind was made up. The same was true in part with Jackson. Every now and then we would talk but it wasn't the same as it used to be. Even he had adopted their language and tone, although having said that, I found myself using it as well. I began to feel more and more of a separation between my inner thoughts and feelings and my outer behaviour—but then I suppose I was well trained in that.

At night I would sleep in a dormitory, my eyes fixed up at the ceiling. I was desperate to go outside and explore, maybe even to try and find where the women's wing was, but I didn't dare. There was a strict rule that no one should leave the dormitory after lights out and I didn't want to jeopardise my chances of being promoted to the sacred 'upper circle'.

However, one night my curiosity got the better of me and I sneaked out.

6

It reminded me of the time when I had sneaked out the house to escape the town. I half expected someone to grab my wrist at any moment as David had done. The moon cast a dim light over the rows of tomatoes in the garden as I searched for the gate I had seen before. I found it. It stood about two metres tall, locked and bolted. As I scrambled over the top I could feel eyes burning into my back and in my haste to get over the over side, I fell straight into a gorse bush. The thorns scratched my hands as I fought my way out and I hoped that it wouldn't give me away the next day.

There was a slope in front of me, running parallel to the wall, forming a kind of moat around the enclosure. I scrambled up the slope and looked around. It was pitch black and I couldn't see a thing, but as if on autopilot my feet slid down the embankment.

I heard a noise, not far away and looking around I saw a dim light in the distance. As I got a little closer I saw it was a woman. She was perhaps in her fifties and hunched over a pump washing a pan. I could hear her muttering something under her breath as she scrubbed at the pan.

The light was coming from a hut nearby. As I walked around the back of the hut so she wouldn't see me, I saw several other yellow glows and realised I was in some kind of village. Was this where all the women were?

The water stopped running behind me and I heard the woman grunt and wheeze her way into the hut and the door close.

I suddenly felt very exposed and so ducked behind the bushes surrounding the encampment. As I crouched there in the dark I began to feel the acute need to urinate. I held it off for as long as I could before I seized the opportunity to relieve myself. When I was done, I turned to see a little girl staring at me.

'Who are you?' I hissed.

'Antoinette,' she replied.

'What are you doing up?' I said in an attempt to justify my presence there. She didn't seem to realise *I* was the one who didn't belong.

'Are you one of the disciples?' she said.

One of the *disciples*? Had I heard right? I had to pursue this one.

'Yes,' I responded. 'Have you seen the others?'

'They're in the hall,' she said. 'They must be waiting for you.'

'Antoinette,' I said, considering my options. 'Could you take me to them?'

'Don't you know where they are?' she asked.

I shrugged. 'I can't remember.'

'My mother doesn't know I'm out,' she said. 'I should tell her.'

Antoinette turned to go back in.

'Wait!' I hissed. 'Don't tell her Antoinette. I mean—no need to disturb her. Just show me and then get home.'

Antoinette turned to look back at me.

'I shouldn't be up,' she whispered.

A female voice barked out her name and the little girl turned and ran.

'Who were you talking to?' the voice demanded.

'It was one of the disciples—' Antoinette started but I didn't hear any more as I had run back the way I had come.

I half ran, half slid down the moat and scrambled over the gate. I carefully made my way through the gardens and had just got to the entrance when I heard a voice call my name. I spun round to see one of the senior pastors, Father Neil, standing in the shadows.

'What are you doing up, Brother Richard?'

'I'm sorry Father,' I stumbled. 'I needed some air.'

The pastor walked up to me and took my hands in his, inspected them and looked at me with a furrowed brow. My hands were dirty and scratched from the gorse bushes. There wasn't much I could offer in terms of explanation. Having said that, I had always thought of Father Neil as a kind old man and was hopeful I could appeal to his better nature.

'You have left the grounds?'

'No Father, I tripped outside and fell in a rose bush.'

The pastor let go of my hands and looked me in the eye. 'Brother Richard it is only natural for a young man to seek the pleasures of the flesh—'

'Oh no, Father, it wasn't that—'

'Please Brother, let me continue,' said Father Neil.

'Sorry Father,' I said. Maybe it was best to keep quiet and let him pontificate for a while; maybe he would consider that enough.

'There have been young men before you who have attempted to find the women's encampment, so intoxicated by the allure of sensual delight. Our path, however is a spiritual one. One which leads directly to the Kingdom of Heaven. Do you understand me, Brother Richard.'

'Yes Father.'

'The path of the flesh, of easy pleasure only leads in one direction. There is no future in it.'

'I understand Father.'

'Well, get to bed, there are prayers early in the morning.'

7

I was hopeful that nothing else would be mentioned about my little escapade. The next day passed without incident and the day after. The day after that I met up with Jackson whilst we were digging weeds.

'I heard you went over the wall, Brother Richard.'

'What do you mean?' I said, stunned.

'I heard you went over the wall,' he repeated. He stopped digging and looked at me, leaning on the shovel. 'What was all that about?'

I turned away from him and started digging again, not wanting to meet his gaze. He had a very captivating stare. It seemed to look right through you.

'You heard wrong,' I said. 'I was going for air.'

'Brother Richard,' he said putting a hand on my arm.

'Don't call me that!' I snapped, shaking him off. 'Don't you realise what this is, Jackson. It's a brain washing camp. It's all fake, phony just like we always knew it was back in the town.'

'You'd want to go back there?' he asked. 'Don't you remember what it was like? Don't you remember how unhappy we all were?'

'Are we really any better here?' I replied. 'Every day we do what they tell us to do. We have someone looking over our shoulders every minute. That's not happiness for me.'

Jackson put his hands on my arms again, to stop me digging. I continued to avoid his eyes.

'I know you want to see your family, to see David and Miranda. We are that close,' he said. 'You've just got to hang in there.'

'So what's in it for you?' I asked looking up to meet his gaze for the first time.

'I'm just in it for the apples,' he said with a smile. 'Don't worry, Richard. Things will work out, trust me.'

I knew it wouldn't be long before things came to a head. If Jackson knew about it, then it must be common knowledge and it would only be so long before I reaped the consequences. I could feel the whispers and suspicion around me wherever I went. Even Brother Francis treated me with a mild disdain, as if he had been let down by his favourite son. Then after prayers one morning I felt a hand on my shoulder.

'Brother Richard,' an anonymous voice said in my ear. 'One of the disciples would like to see you. Apparently he is known to you.'

'Where should I go, Brother?' I said without looking around.

'Go directly to the pastor's office after lunch,' the voice said before leaving.

All through the morning I was trembling with anticipation. For some reason I was convinced that it was David who wanted to see me. He was after all, one of the disciples, or at least I thought he was—and it was someone known to me. I braced myself as I knocked on the door. The sight of the person who answered almost made me pass out.

'Ah Brother Richard,' he said.

'Vincent.'

'Well don't be so surprised,' he said. 'I've known about you for ages. I knew we'd meet again some time. I could feel it in my waters somehow. You could call it fate.'

'I knew you were here too,' I said. 'Although I couldn't quite believe it.'

'Why don't you sit down Richard,' Vincent said. 'You're looking a little pale.'

Vincent sat down behind the desk and I lowered myself into the chair the other side. He leaned back, strumming his fingers on the desk and grinning at me. I noticed the gap he still had in his teeth.

'Where's David?' I said.

'David's fine,' said Vincent. 'He's doing well for himself.'

'Where is he,' I repeated.

'He's around,' said Vincent, his eyes dancing with amusement. There was a silence for a moment as he continued to weigh me up.

'Your mother's here too,' said Vincent. 'And your father. Your mother's doing well; your father's not so good I'm afraid.'

'What have you done to him?'

I saw Vincent's face change, as if a dark cloud had passed over it. I began to feel the same nauseous tingling that I felt all those years ago.

'I'm not sure I like your tone—Richard,' he said, his eyes boring into mine. I wanted to bury myself in the ground but was determined to hold my ground. 'We're not fifteen any more Vincent. You can't scare me any more.'

I could feel the hairs on the back of my neck rising. Vincent's stare was relentless, it drove you down

'So you're the big hard man now are you?' he said with a characteristic cock of the head. 'Do you know who I am?'

'I know you're a bully Vincent,' I continued. 'Do the people here know what you did to people like them?'

Vincent laughed and shook his head back.

'It doesn't matter Richard. None of it matters—don't you get that. Besides you're in no position to be high and mighty are you? You were a part of it.'

I had to concede that that was true. I wondered what he meant when he said none of it mattered.

'So are you changed?' I said, meeting his eyes again. 'Have you seen the light?'

'I am one of the Lord's disciples,' he came straight back. 'A prophet you could say.'

I raised an eyebrow, to which Vincent glowered in return. He stood up and looked out the window.

'The thing you don't get is loyalty Richard,' he said with his back to me. 'I was selected as one of the chosen few because I have that quality. Your mother has that quality and so does your brother. You don't and neither does your father.'

He spun around and gestured with a knife towards me. I wondered if it was the same one he had commanded me to cut my brother with, the same one I had contemplated ramming into his ribs.

'What is it you want,' I asked.

Vincent laughed again and returned to the window.

'I've heard about your little adventure,' he said. 'Did you actually manage to get any action then?'

'I was getting some air.'

'You were getting a bit more than that,' he said. 'Come, come Richard. It's not the crime of the century to want to get your hands on some firm young flesh. It's only natural.'

'It wasn't that—' I began before Vincent cut me off with a wave of the hand.

'Unfortunately—for you, the elders don't see it that way,' he said. 'A crime such as this would normally warrant a term of incarceration in the cells—my cells I might add.'

'You run the prison?' Why was I not surprised?

Vincent nodded. 'Law and order, Brother. It can't all be prayers and apple picking. Without law and order you have nothing.'

'So you want to put me in your cell and torture me is that it?'

'I wouldn't be so cocky if I were you,' he glowered at me. I realised I had better start playing his game. Once again, he was in charge and I had no wish to go through again what I had gone through under the hands of Callahan and Frampton.

'What do you want?'

Vincent turned back to the window and put the tip of the knife between his teeth, biting on it. 'I do have a deal for you,' he said. 'I remember you as someone with talent. It would be a shame to let those talents go to waste.'

'You want me to work in the prison with you.'

'You got it.'

'And can I get to see my family?' I asked.

'You'll see one of them straight away,' he said with a grin. 'The rest—well all in due course.' He peered over the desk at me and held out his hand,

'Do we have a deal?' he asked.

I took his hand. 'We have a deal.'

8

The tightness in my guts was intensifying the further we spiralled down the staircase. Vincent was in his element as he explained the procedures of the jail.

'The prisoners are here for all sorts of crimes, Richard. Stealing, insubordination, sexual deviancy. Some will stay here for just a while, some for longer.'

'I've never heard of anyone who's been in here,' I said.

'Oh it's never talked about,' replied Vincent. 'And of course there are some who will never leave. Some whose very presence infects the colony. They must be kept in permanent confinement.'

'And what do you do with them,' I asked.

'You mean *to* them,' said Vincent. His eyes flashed as he turned to look at me; his lip curled up into a sneer. 'I don't do anything to them,' he said. 'This isn't a torture chamber, Richard. They play fair with me and I play fair with them.'

We had reached a bolted door which Vincent unlocked with a huge iron key.

The first thing to hit me was the stench. A musty, putrid combination of damp stone, leather, sweat and excrement. As my eyes adjusted to the gloom I could see bars along the sides of the walls and could hear a groan and jangle of chains. I could feel the bile rising to my mouth and my head spin. For a moment I felt like I wouldn't be able to go any further but I knew I had to; not just to avoid becoming a prisoner in one these hell holes but because I knew I had to find out more.

'Come and meet the prisoners, Richard,' said Vincent. 'I'm sure you'll get on.'

Vincent turned to a cell on the right and slammed his hands against the bars. 'Stand up!' he barked into the cell. 'Come forward!'

I looked into the cell to see an old man. He was wearing torn trousers but was bare from the waist up. His ribs protruded from yellowing skin, his beard was in clumps. He looked like he might dismantle into a pile of bones at any moment.

'This is Brother Richard,' Vincent snapped at the man. 'But you will address him as Sir, just as you would with me. Do you understand?'

The old man nodded, his eyes forlorn.

'Speak when you're spoken to, you imbecile!' shrieked Vincent. 'Do you understand?'

'Yes sir,' mumbled the man.

'Good!' Vincent turned to me and smiled. 'This is one who'll never leave Richard. God alone will forgive him when the day comes.'

'What did he do?' My mouth was as dry as a bone, the words stuck in my throat.

'What did he *do?*' Vincent turned to me and shook his head before turning back to the pathetic skeleton behind the bars. 'What *did* you do?' he snapped 'Tell Brother Richard your crime.'

The old man looked away.

'Tell him what you did!' ordered Vincent.

'I tried to lead a revolution in 2979,' he said.

'You tried to overthrow the Messiah in 2979,' corrected Vincent. 'Blasphemy no less! Well what do you think now?'

'I am a sinner sir,' sighed the man.

Vincent nodded in approval before walking on.

'Twenty years have passed and the insolence is still there,' he muttered. 'Have no sympathy for these vermin Richard. They are nothing but villainess scum; it greaves me to have to show you what I am showing you now.'

'What are you showing me?'

Vincent turned and gestured towards a cell. I didn't recognise the figure in there immediately.

'I will allow you some time,' said Vincent. 'It is bound to be a shock.'

I walked up to the bars.

'Stand up and walk forward!' snapped Vincent. 'Come and face your son.'

I couldn't comprehend the hollow faced man in the cell as being my father. His chains rattled as he shuffled forward, his eyes were like craters.

'Father?'

I didn't want to believe what was before my eyes.

'Richard.'

I put my hand through the bars and he reached out to take it. His skin was like leather.

'He doesn't have long,' said Vincent. 'He has cancer.'

'What have you done to him,' I muttered without taking my eyes of my father.

Vincent walked around me and unlocked the cell.

'Five minutes,' was all he said, before leaving.

I let go of my father's hand for a moment to open the cell door and wrap my arms around him. He almost recoiled from the embrace and I flinched, afraid I had hurt him. He placed his hands on my arms and smiled. 'Come and sit with me Richard,' he said. 'It's good to see you.'

He grimaced as he lowered himself onto the bunk. I sat next to him and took his hand.

'You've grown strong,' he said with a smile.

I took a breath, tried to compose myself.

'Why are you here, Father? What happened?'

'They came for us, all of us, the Enforcers. They said we were all traitors and bundled us into a van. I haven't seen your mother or David since then. I was sent straight to this place. Have you seen them?' he said, his eyes shimmering in the pale light that escaped through the bars.

I shook my head and my father looked down at the floor.

'Is it true what he said?' I asked. 'Are you—'. I gulped down the word and looked at the floor.

'It's true,' he said. 'My only wish was to see you and David once more.' He took a breath. 'Well at least I've seen one of you.'

'You can't give up hope,' I said taking both his hands. 'I can get you out, Father. I can get you well again.'

'No Richard,' he said softly. 'We both know that won't happen.'

'You can't say that.' My eyes welled up and I turned away, ashamed.

'You have to be strong now,' my father said. 'You have to think of David and your mother.'

'I can't just leave you down here.'

'Please Richard,' he said, patting me on the shoulder. 'Don't make it worse.'

'I'm sorry Father,' I said, wiping my eyes.

'Tell me about you,' he said. 'I want to hear what you've been doing.'

'Time's up!' snapped Vincent.

I clenched my fists and glared at him. 'Another five minutes, please.'

'No Richard, that's it.'

'It's ok, go,' my father whispered. 'Take care of yourself.'

'We can arrange another meeting,' said Vincent. 'But not now.'

I looked at my father who nodded in agreement. I held out my hand but he just patted it in encouragement. With eyes and nose streaming I followed Vincent out.

'Must be hard, seeing him like this,' said Vincent as I picked up a chair. Vincent ducked and punched me in the gut as the chair landed on his back. I collapsed back winded as Vincent clambered on top of me, his hands gripped round my throat, pinning me. 'You're just going to have to get used to this Stirling,' he spoke in a low hiss. 'I'm in charge here.'

'Not for much longer.' I choked. 'Because I'm going to kill you Vincent, I swear it.'

'No you're not,' he said, his eyes flashing. 'Because I have all the keys to what you want. Your brother, your mother—I could decide whether you see them again or whether I have them both killed. I have all the power around here.'

'You don't have shit!'

'You wanna bank on that,' he said. 'I control the Messiah did you know that? I control everything!'

Then suddenly he was up and standing over me. He flung a wet flannel at me.

'I was once in your shoes, Richard,' he said. 'My father was once in here and he was just as pathetic as yours. He thought he was something, you see. I thought he was everything, but then I saw him for what he was Richard. He thought he could buy his way into an easy life.'

'The deal with the Messiah?'

'That's right,' said Vincent. 'You catch on quick Richard. It didn't take long before he was in these cells. I could barely stand the sight of him, wallowing in self pity. He sold out and for that he paid the price.'

'You killed him,' I said.

'I cast him out,' said Vincent. 'But as far as I'm concerned, he's dead. Now sort yourself out, there's work to be done.'

9

The "work" as it turned out, turned out to be not much at all. I spent a few hours a day doing petty errands for Vincent and the rest of the time I continued with my usual duties above ground. Vincent treated the prisoners with a cold indifference but I didn't witness any acts of violence on them. It was almost as if they were non existent—*non humans* in a sense.

Vincent didn't allow me to see my father again. I was put to work in other wings of the prison, handing out meals to prisoners, sweeping floors, sorting out paperwork. I think my main purpose of being there was to be Vincent's plaything. He would remind me constantly of the power he had over me, the commune and even over the Messiah. I wondered how much that was true. I wondered how much influence he could have, or if this was some kind of egocentric fantasy; a bluff to keep me in line. Whatever status he had in the commune as a whole, down here, in this little dungeon, he was king. This was his world and I had to tow the line. Just as I had done in Callahan's office I kept my head down and my mouth shut in the hope that I would regain his trust. Maybe he would throw me a crumb here or there. In the end my time came. One morning as I was cleaning the floors Vincent invited me into his office.

'You've done well here Richard. I trust you're repentant for your little episode on your first visit.'

'I apologise Brother Trevor,' I said. 'It was rude of me.'

'Apology accepted,' he said. 'As a reward I have a treat for you. We're men of the world, with manly appetites. A man needs a woman, wouldn't you agree?'

'Absolutely.'

'Some of the pastors say we should rise above the desires of the flesh, but I never saw it myself. It's not natural. Don't you feel the need Richard?'

I thought for a moment and nodded.

'I knew you did,' said Vincent. 'Well it can be arranged.'

'How?'

'I can arrange anything,' he said with a cock of the head. 'I'll collect you from your dormitory tonight.'

I didn't like the sound of this at all, but I had to admit he was right. After several months of male company my body tingled with the prospect of seeing women again.

That night I lay in bed staring at the ceiling when someone shook my shoulder. Vincent was standing over me. 'Keep very quiet,' he said. 'Don't want to disturb the others.'

I followed him out into the night where a truck was waiting. As I approached I saw four men sitting inside who looked round at me as Vincent opened the door.

'This is Brother Richard,' said Vincent. 'He will be joining us tonight. I trust no one has any objections to this?'

The four men sat quietly.

'Good,' said Vincent. 'Richard, this is Brothers Peter, Luke, John and Paul.'

'They are the Disciples?' I asked.

'Some of them, yes. You realise this is top secret don't you Stirling? Don't tell anyone about this or there will be trouble. You know what I mean, don't you?'

'I won't tell anyone.'

'Well enough talk. Let's be off,' he said as he gestured me in.

We sat in silence as we drove, except for Vincent who looked out the window, whispering to himself.

We entered a thicket of huts and I recognised it as being the place I had ended up when I had escaped. I could see a lot of lights dotted around, but no people. We approached a building which sat square amongst all the huts. The truck stopped outside and the men shuffled out.

'Just remember I get first pick,' said Vincent as we made our way to the door. A middle aged woman stood in the entrance and bowed as we filed past into a hall, filled with row upon row of women.

The men strolled down each aisle, studying the women. For a while the only sound was their boots treading the floorboards and the breath of the women they passed. I caught a young woman's eye and her eyes widened. I could see her forcing her lip to stop quivering before she looked down at the floor, her hands shaking. Every woman I passed I could sense her shrinking away from me.

'Ah this one's for me,' said Vincent. I glanced over at him to see him undoing the front of a woman's dress and cupping her breast in his hand.

'And what's your name?'

The woman whispered something, her eyes closed as she looked to the floor.

'Speak up!'

'Philomena,' the girl said, head down.

'Such a pretty name,' said Vincent. 'Brother Peter, have you chosen?'

'Not yet,' a voice replied.

'So picky,' said Vincent.

Then it occurred to me—Miranda. I picked up the pace as I tried to pick out her face among the rows.

'Brother Richard, calm yourself, we are in no hurry,' said Vincent with a laugh.

As I made my way, sideways down the line I walked straight into a man. His hands enveloped a woman's face—Miranda's.

She glanced up at me, tears in her eyes. I turned to the man. 'Brother, please may I have this young woman?'

The man sneered at me, his hand cupping Miranda's chin. Miranda kept her jaw clenched, her eyes half closed. I prayed she would have enough sense not to acknowledge me.

'Please Brother, it would mean a lot to me,' I continued.

'Let him have her, Brother Luke,' said Vincent. 'It's his first time let's be gracious. Next time the girl is yours.'

The man glared at me before shuffling off like a wounded gorilla. I took Miranda by the arm.

'Brother Richard, you can take her to one of the rooms at the back,' said Vincent. 'Fifteen minutes only.'

Holding onto her arm I walked quickly through the maze of women to the back of the hall and into a cubicle.

It must have been at least five minutes before either of us could speak.

We lay there on a single bunk, sobbing into each others arms. I consoled her, trying to keep the sobs down, reminding myself that we were supposed to be having sex. Around us I could hear the sounds of doors being closed, followed not long after by the sounds of male grunts.

'I love you,' I managed to whisper as she clung to me, her body melting into mine. If the situation wasn't so sickening, I could almost have made love to her there and then. She continued sobbing her body convulsing.

'Shhhhh, shhhhh, stop crying, stop crying,' I whispered. I held her face away and looked into her eyes, she met my gaze and I could sense her body relaxing.

'It's ok, I'm here, I'm here,' I said.

I held her again, her head on my chest as I stroked her hair.

'They come once a month, sometimes more,' said Miranda.

'I'm going to take you away from this,' I said.

'You can't Richard. No one can.'

'I will, I'll find a way.'

'Next time that fat oaf will have me. Maybe he'll make me pregnant.'

'No he won't' I said.

'How do you know?'

'I won't let it happen.' There was a pause for a moment as I tried to find some words of comfort, some glimmer of hope. 'Vincent doesn't know about us,' I said. 'He'd disappeared before we got together.'

'So?'

'So he'll see no reason why I shouldn't pick a favourite.'

'Please,' said Miranda.

'Don't worry, I'll sort it. I'll ask him to let me have you to myself. I work for him-'

'You work for him—'

'Not by choice.'

Miranda sighed.

'I'm sorry, I'm just trying to think of a way—I'll sort it don't worry. No one else will have you.'

'Have you seen David?'

'No,' I said. 'I've seen my father.'

'I've seen your mother,' Miranda said.

'Have you?'

'She's a high ranking member here. Sometimes she makes us all pretty for when the men arrive.'

'I'm sorry.'

'No, I'm sorry,' she said, cupping my face. 'I shouldn't have said it like that. How's your father?'

'Dying.'

Miranda put her hands around my neck and kissed me.

'Don't worry about me I'll be fine,' she said.

'I'm going to get you out of here, somehow.' I whispered as there was a bang on the door.

'Your time's up,' she said.

'I mean it.'

'I know.'

There was another bang on the door.

'Go now,' she said. 'Wipe your face now.'

She wiped the tears from my cheeks and kissed me again.

'See you soon,' I whispered.

10

Vincent found it quite amusing that I had taken a shine to one particular girl at the women's camp.

'I'm sorry, Richard. You can't have favourites. After all Brother Luke is next in line.'

'I would appreciate it, Brother. I will take no other woman.'

'There's a lot of flesh for the tasting,' said Vincent. 'You don't want to sample any other?'

'It's my peculiarity,' I said. 'She indulged me.'

'She indulged you?' Vincent said, shaking his head. 'Well I will think about it, Brother Richard. There is something about it I do not like.'

'I understand your concerns,' I said. 'But I assure you this is purely physical.'

'I would hope so,' said Vincent. 'It is best to keep feelings out of it, in my experience. Women are here to serve us, Richard. To satisfy our basic needs. Anything more—and it gets complicated.'

'I agree with you Brother Trevor. But I have never had it better from any other.'

Vincent slapped me on the arm, leering at me, showing the gap in his teeth. 'Like I said, I will think about it,' he said.

I carried on working in the cells doing my best to win Vincent's favour, smiling at him through gritted teeth and doing his every bidding. I was determined to make sure that it was me that got Miranda this time and

232

in truth I wasn't just thinking of her. Vincent was right when he said that a man needed a woman. I longed to make love to her again, to smell her hair in my face.

What is more I couldn't face the thought of somebody else having her; of that other man placing his hands on her body. Spoiling her, contaminating her.

I imagined his face in the throes of ecstasy; red, contorted, flecks of saliva shooting from clenched teeth.

I would rip out the throat of any other man who touched her; I was sure of that. I didn't feel proud of these feelings but they were there, they were real and I began to wonder if they were on the surface, if Vincent had become aware of them. I had thought I was good at concealing my emotions but maybe I wasn't.

I was always convinced that Vincent had a sixth sense that he could see into people; and what is more, that he would use it to his advantage. Around a week later, something happened which made me wonder how much he knew or suspected.

Vincent took me into one of the cells where there was a man facing the wall, bare above the waist. His arms were suspended and bolted to the wall. I recognised it as the old man who Vincent had shown me on my first visit, just as emaciated as before.

'This piece of filth has been slandering the Messiah, yet again,' said Vincent. 'My ears ring with his treacherous lies and conspiracies. He has had his warning.'

Vincent handed me a leather strap, the length of a belt. 'Six lashes.'

I looked at him, imploring not to make me do this. He shot me a look back, it was the same one he had given me when we were twelve years old, the one which had made me hit my brother.

The skin on the old man's back stretched over his bones like paper. I flicked the strap at it, merely a slap.

'Is that all you've got, you son of a whore!' shrieked the old man. I sensed Vincent's eyes burning into me. I remembered what he said to me: *I have all the keys!*

I hit the old man a little harder. 'Oh please spare me,' he cackled. 'I can't take it any more.'

Vincent leaned into me, his hot breath in my ear. 'Do it properly or I will see your little favourite is defiled in every way conceivable.'

I swung at the back again, this time causing a grimace—it was genuine.

'Good!' said Vincent. 'Break the skin, teach him a lesson!'

A surge of adrenaline and another crack of the whip, this time causing a louder grimace.

'You bastards!'

I hit him again, as hard as I could, causing the old man to wail and slump on his shackles.

'It's enough,' I said to Vincent.

'More!'

'It's enough!'

'Again!'

I raised the strap again.

'Please forgive my insolence, Brother!' sobbed the old man. 'I swear I will never again—'

'Silence you old fool!' shrieked Vincent. 'Richard, hit him again or I will fuck that whore from every orifice until she bleeds. Again!'

'I can't,' I said.

Vincent took the lash off me, his eyes burning with contempt.

'Brother, please!' I begged.

Ignoring me, Vincent flogged the old man over and over, with an intensity that terrified me. Dark red blood oozed from the yellow skin as the old man screamed out, sobbing. As the strap continued taking the skin off his back, the old man eventually gave up and collapsed, hanging off the wall like dead rotting meat. Vincent threw down the whip in front of me and flashed me a look of disgust as he walked out the room.

It was on that very night my father died.

Vincent took me to the cell where my father was laid out, his hands resting across his chest, his eyes sunken, his whole body gaunt. Nonetheless there was a peaceful expression on his face. The fight was over; the one he had never wanted to fight. I knelt beside him and placed my hands over his. They were already cold and stiff. Vincent had decided I wasn't to see my father at the end; a punishment for my cowardice, no doubt. It wasn't until I was alone with my father's body that I allowed myself to cry.

I begged Vincent to allow me to bury my father and pay my respects, but he wouldn't have any of it.

'Criminals don't have *services* Stirling,' he said. 'His body will be burnt without ceremony. If you wish you can have the ashes to do with as you wish.'

The next day when I went to the office, Vincent was sitting with his feet up on the desk. He gestured towards a cardboard box. 'Try not to make a mess with them Stirling,' he said. 'And be inconspicuous if you can. I don't make a habit of this, you know.'

I took the box and walked outside, trying to find a suitable place within the barren section of grounds which Vincent had allocated to me. In the end I found a dead sapling, shrivelled up against the boundary wall. I dug a hole the best I could with bare hands and rocks. The earth was cold and hard, it took a while but finally with my hands bleeding, I placed the box inside. I covered it over with the dirt and stones and knelt there for a while. And then I found myself praying. Praying that there was a heaven. Praying that my father would find himself there and that one day I would be allowed to see him one more time.

11

After that I wasn't invited down to work with Vincent anymore. It was a relief not to have to go down there anymore. Not to have to see Vincent in his little kingdom of suffering. Above ground, with the sun in my face, I could feel myself beginning to heal. I set about aiming to be the best worker, digging more vegetables and tilling more soil than any other man. I prayed routinely and genuinely. I had not a bad word to say about anyone or anything. Maybe this was an attempt to forget. If it was, it didn't work. At nights I would lie awake wondering what was happening to Miranda. I imagined my mother getting her ready for the Disciples; the thought made my stomach turn.

Now that my contact with her was completely severed I had to find another way in and definitely had to get her removed from the selection list. I worried that Vincent would carry out his promised threat and 'defile' her. All I could do was bide my time and hope for the best.

It was a lonely experience at the commune. I got on well with the other workers but there was always something that got in the way of forming any true friendships. Everything was coded, with layers of subtext behind every conversation. The experience of working with Vincent had shown that there were pitfalls within this Garden of Eden, not to mention the odd snake in the grass. Hargreaves and Jackson didn't seem to be aware of this and I wondered if this would be their downfall.

One morning I was taking a break under a tree and eating an apple when Hargreaves approached. He greeted me with a smile and sat beside me looking out over the crops. Beads of sweat rolled off his brow; he wiped them off with his sleeve. 'Hard work isn't it?' he said.

I smiled in return. 'You like it here, Hargreaves?'

'This is the best place I've ever been to, Richard. Where else could we just sit and talk in such peace.'

I looked out over the white robed workers, plucking apples and tilling the soil. 'My father passed away,' I said.

Hargreaves looked round at me; his eyes concerned. 'I'm sorry, I never knew. I haven't seen him around.'

'I didn't until recently,' I said. 'But at least I got to see him in the end.'

'He'll be in a better place, now. An even better one, that is.'

'Hargreaves, there's been something I've been meaning to ask.'

'What's that?' he said, picking an apple from a basket for himself.

'Do you still—?'

Hargreaves looked across at me and exploded in laughter. 'Like men? Is that what you're trying to say Richard?'

'Yes, I suppose so.'

'Sure.' He took a bite from the apple. 'Why do you ask?'

'You know that it's a sin in the Bible?'

'Oh I don't think anyone cares about that.'

'You've talked about it with people?'

'Not really,' he said. 'It's not something that comes up in conversation.'

'Well how do you know they wouldn't mind?'

Hargreaves lay back on the grass. He looked up at the clouds and sighed through his teeth.

'It's not like I do anything about it.' He propped himself up on his elbow. 'No one does it with women either. We're all celibate, so what does it matter?'

'Well—'I started, and then stopped myself.

'This is the land of peace—of love Richard,' he said. 'You fret too much.'

'You know that Vincent's here?'

'Yes.'

'And that doesn't bother you?'

'Why should it?' Hargreaves picked a blade of grass, pulled the seeds off and watched them drop through his fingers. 'We've all moved on since then, Richard. We're all different people.'

'Well maybe you should carry on keeping quiet about it,' I said, looking into the distance. 'Just in case.'

'I used to worry like you,' said Hargreaves, looking me straight in the eye. 'But I gave it all up. I leave it all to God now.'

It would seem Hargreaves was a convert. I had half considered telling him what I knew about Vincent and the Disciples, but it wouldn't do any good. The vast majority wouldn't believe it and the few that did would end up in Vincent's little torture chamber.

I didn't tell Jackson for the same reason. I had to go higher. I had to go to the top. It was only by becoming one of the Disciples myself, that I could have any influence over their activities. I had to try—for Miranda.

12

That evening I approached Father Neil, the older pastor who had caught me on my return from the women's camp. He was at his desk, glasses at the end of his nose, scribbling on a piece of parchment.

'Father Neil, might I have a word?'

'Of course my son,' he gestured towards a chair opposite, his face softened as he recognised me. 'You have done some good work here since your misadventure,' he said. 'I'm sure your sins are forgiven.'

'Thank you, Father,' I said. 'I have paid my penance.'

'To err is human, to forgive is divine.'

'I wanted to talk to you about that,' I said. 'I have a confession to make.'

Father Neil took his glasses off and leaned over the desk.

'I am listening.'

'That night, I was not looking for women, Father.'

'Oh come, come,' tutted Father Neil. 'Please don't try to tell me you were just taking the air.'

'No Father, I am guilty and my punishment was just. I was looking for someone, but it was not a woman—it was a man.'

I saw Father Neil's eyebrows raised.

'It was my brother. David.'

'Who is David?'

I took a deep breath.

'He is one of the Disciples, Father.'

Father Neil looked at me motionless for a while, before picking up a cloth and polishing his spectacles.

'I do not have to tell you how family relations are irrelevant in this place,' he muttered.

'That is true—'

'And that the Disciples are strictly off limits.' He looked up, holding my gaze. 'Strictly, you hear me.'

'Yes Father.'

I swallowed and looked down at the desk as the pastor continued polishing his spectacles.

'And you are asking me to arrange a meeting. That is what you are asking is it not?'

'Yes Father.'

'And you realise this is tantamount to blasphemy!'

'Forgive me Father. My circumstances are unique.'

'Unique, you say?' Suddenly Father Neil didn't seem the kind old man he was before. This wasn't going as well as I'd hoped.

'It is you, who think *you* are unique,' he continued, jabbing his spectacles at me. 'I have seen it before. Plenty of young men who think they are above the rules.'

'I do not think that Father. I merely wish to tell him our father—our biological father is dead.'

For a moment everything stood still as the old man stared at me, his head tilted back, mouth slightly open.

'I will pass the information on, through the appropriate channels,' he said in the end.

'Please Father.'

'You may leave now, Brother Richard. Please close the door on your way out.'

So that was that. I had blown it. To think I was so hopeful that not only I could rescue Miranda, but that I could meet David again. Now all I had succeeded in doing was blacklisting myself further. I just gave up.

For the next few days I refused to leave my bunk, I refused to talk to anyone, I refused to eat. I lay there as the others would mill around me, talking in hushed tones: 'Brother Richard has lost all will.' 'He has lost his soul.' 'A demon has taken him.'

On the second day, Jackson came, kneeling down beside me, whilst I gazed at the ceiling.

'You can't give up hope,' he said. 'Think of the future. You can't go on like this.'

I sighed and turned away from him, waiting for him to go. When I heard his footsteps walk away I turned back to the ceiling, gazing at the cracks. I watched a bug crawl across the ceiling and disappear. I wanted to disappear. I wanted the world to be swallowed into a crack of the Universe, like water down the drain.

That night I began to get stomach cramps and wished I would die. I could see no point any more.

I was awoken early by a man shaking me.

'Brother Richard?' he asked.

'What?'

My first word in three days, it felt like a razor stuck in my throat. The man put his hand under my head and a canister to my lips. The cold water made me gag but I managed to swallow some. The man let my head fall back on the pillow

'You must restore your strength.'

'Why?'

'There is someone who wants to see you.'

'I don't care.'

'You requested to see him,' said the man. 'It is your brother, David.'

13

Twelve hours later, we were bouncing along the road which led to the Disciples commune. I had managed to eat some soup, earlier in the day, although I felt weak and feverish. As we approached the marble pillared mansion I felt my stomach turn and I vomited the soup back up, over the side of the truck.

'It is alright, Brother Richard,' the man said rubbing my back. 'He is keen to see you.'

I managed to smile and the man helped me out and to my feet. I stood up tall and took a deep breath.

'Are you ready?' the man asked.

I nodded.

'Well come this way.'

I followed him through two stone pillars which seemed to lead into some kind of church. Looking across the sea of marble there was a huge stained glass window, depicting the Messiah. He looked just like he had done in the videos but all the more imposing, as he gazed over his empire. My eyes were diverted to a few metres in front of me, where a man stood, dressed in a brown robe, his hands folded in front of him. 'Brother Richard,' he said with a smile.

I gave a little nod and the man nodded back.

'We have waited for your arrival,' he said. 'Brother David is anxious to meet you.'

I nodded again and followed him down a stone corridor lined with hanging gas lamps. There were more stained glass windows on the left and big oak doors on the right. I kept waiting to see which one he'd stop by. Suddenly he turned to face me.

'We are pleased to meet you,' he smiled before thumping on the door.

'Please go on in,' he said. 'Brother David requested.'

With that the man was gone and I was left staring at the brass handle on the door. I felt my legs shaking and my heart racing and leant against the door to steady myself. Before I lost my nerve, I opened the door.

David looked much the same as he had before; a little bigger, hair a little longer, beginnings of a beard. He was kneeling on the stone floor, when his eyes looked up and engaged me. He rose and embraced me, his arms were strong. After a while I noticed he was crying. 'I've waited so long for you Richard.'

He held me away and then I saw his eyes turn to concern. 'You're sick,' he said.

'I'm ok,' I said, tears streaming my face. 'How are you?'

'I'm well,' he said. 'Very well; although I worried about you every night.'

'Well I'm here,' I said.

'It's great to see you,' said David. 'Come and sit down. I want to hear everything.'

'I want to hear from you first,' I said as David guided me over to a seat by the window. 'How did you end up here?'

'Oh Richard, this is where I was meant to be. I've always known it.'

'We broke out the town,' I said. 'We looked for you but you had gone; you and our parents. For years I thought you were dead.'

David reached over and touched my knee. 'I'm sorry Richard. It happened so quickly.'

'What happened?'

'They came with guns, the Enforcers. I thought we were all going to die.'

'They knew you were going to Jackson's house,' I told him. 'The secret meetings.'

David shrugged. 'I've no regrets. It was Hell in that town. I'm so glad to be here. That we're both here, now.'

'But how did you get to be in the Disciples?' I said. 'I don't understand.'

'When we arrived I was brought straight here to meet the Messiah. He came out to meet me, just one to one; can you believe it Richard.' David's eyes were as wide as his smile. It disturbed me.

'Do you think he's the saviour of mankind?' I asked.

'Absolutely, don't you?'

'I don't know,' I said. 'Sometimes I'd like to believe it.'

'You should meet him. I'm sure he'd like to meet you.'

'David, there's some things you should know—'

He sat cross legged, resting his chin on his hands. It was as if he was waiting for me to tell him another story. Despite the fact that he was now bigger than me, he looked so naïve, so vulnerable. Could I bear to break his spirit?

'You know why you got here, don't you?'

'The Messiah arranged it,' he said. 'He delivered us.'

'And Vincent?'

'Isn't it amazing?'

'You think he's changed?'

'He's transformed!' said David. 'That's the power of this place, the power of the Messiah. He's one of the kindest people you could meet.'

It was no good; I couldn't bring myself to tell him that Vincent had been our father's jailor.

'What's the matter?' said David, putting a hand on my arm. 'You look troubled.'

'You can tell?' I said, forcing a laugh.

'You used to look like that a lot of the time,' he smiled.

'Do you know what happened to our parents, after you came here?'

'They've got other business to attend to. I haven't seen them since.'

'Our father died, David.'

The words tumbled out my mouth almost accidentally. I watched the momentary flash of sadness cross David's face, followed by a philosophical acceptance. 'I'm sad to hear that. Did you see him?'

'I saw him—just before. He had cancer.'

I saw David pause for thought before he looked at me. 'He's in a better place now,' he said.

I nodded in return, not knowing what else to say.

'Who broke out with you?'

'Miranda, Jackson, Roberts, Killinger, Hargreaves . . .'

'Can I meet them?' he said, his face looking more hopeful. I could hardly bring myself to tell him.

'Killinger's dead.'

My heart dropped when I saw the reaction in David's face, but what else could I say?

'Roberts is too probably. We went to a bad place, a rough place, they were both killed and Miranda lost the baby.'

'The baby?'

'Yes—' I couldn't say any more.

'I'm so sorry, Richard.'

'At least you're well,' I said with a smile.

David returned the smile, placing a hand on my arm. 'And you're well?'

'I'm well,' I replied. 'But I want you to do something for me.'

'I'd do anything for you Richard, you know that.'

'I haven't seen Miranda for a while,' I said. 'She's in the women's camp and I'm in the men's.'

I heard David sigh: 'Richard—'

'The thing is—I want you to ask the Messiah if we can marry.'

'Marry?' he said, trying the word out as if to taste its flavour. 'Marry,' he repeated, a smile broadening on his face. 'Why not?'

'You think that will be acceptable?'

'There's no reason why not,' he said. 'Of course it will be—it will be more than acceptable—that's perfect!'

'Tell him how much we love each other and how we could benefit the community so much better together—'

'Yes, yes, yes,' said David. He was already sold on the idea. I could see him planning it all out in his head. 'Leave it to me,' he said. 'It will be fine.'

'You really think so?'

'Of course! You and Miranda were meant to be, anyone can see that.'

'Well, that would be great!'

'Consider it done,' said David, looking up behind me. The brown robed man was standing there. David got up and hugged me goodbye. 'I'll see you again soon,' he said.

'You'd better! And don't forget about—'

'I won't forget Richard. You should go now. I'll talk to the Messiah.'

'Take care,' I said. 'I've missed you David.'

'I've missed you too,' he said as I walked out the door.

When I got back to the men's camp it was after lights out. I got straight into my bunk and cried my eyes out.

14

It was two days later, whilst lost in my own thoughts that I was collected and taken to the Disciples again. It was the same man who came to collect me and the same brown robed man who greeted me at the door.

'There is much excitement here, Brother,' he said, bouncing on his toes. 'Please come with me.'

This time I wasn't taken down the corridor but towards the back of the church, towards the big stained glass picture of the Messiah.

To the right of the window was another oak door. The monk was about to knock when a voice called out:

'One moment, please.'

I recognised the voice immediately and my suspicion was confirmed by the monk's reaction. He wrung his hands together and hopped about like an excited little girl.

'Come in,' said the voice. 'Jacob, please leave us.'

The monk scuttled away and the door opened.

The Messiah didn't look as impressive as he did in the videos. He had aged considerably, his beard showing signs of whitening and lines running down his face. He stood a little shorter than me and looked worn and weary. Despite this, I felt a certain sense of awe. This was the man, verified and vilified in equal measures, who had charted the course of my life.

'Richard, my son, won't you come in?' He gestured with his hand behind him and stood to one side. I walked past him into a little bare room. There was a wooden table with a chair either side. A statue of a naked woman stood in the fireplace.

'Sit, please,' the Messiah said.

I sat down in one of chairs, feeling a little vulnerable with him standing behind me. He came and sat down in the chair opposite. One of his eyes was looking out to the side and the other fixed on me. I'd never noticed that before in the videos.

'I've heard so much about you,' he said with a smile.

I managed a smile back, but didn't know what to say.

'How do you like it here at our commune?'

'It's great.'

'Your brother loves you very much,' said the Messiah. 'He's often told me about you.'

I wanted to get to asking about Miranda but floundered, not knowing how to address him.

'Your request at marriage is under consideration,' he said as if reading my mind. 'Do you ever feel you are lost, Richard. In some kind of void?'

'Sometimes.'

'I do too and I've sensed that in you. What is it you most desire?'

'I want to be with my wife and family,' I said.

'You want to claw your brother back from me, don't you? You want control back.'

Despite the accusatory tone of his words, his face and voice remained friendly and open. My mind went back to my first conversation with David about the Messiah: *'You do know the Messiah is phony, don't you?'*

'He seems happy,' I replied.

'But you don't trust me do you,' he said. 'You suspect my motives.'

'I'd like to trust you,' I said.

The Messiah laughed. 'Good answer,' he replied. 'Do you believe me when I say that the world is headed for destruction?'

'Do you mean in a literal sense or a spiritual sense?'

'Aren't they one and the same thing?'

'What do you want from me?'

'I want followers, Richard. True men, believers. Your brother is one and I sense you could be one if you were to just unlock your heart.'

'How do you plan to save the world?'

'You misunderstand me Richard. The world is headed for Apocalypse, Judgement day; of that there is no escape. It is what comes after we must prepare for.'

'Everyone will die?'

'What is life, as you call it? You think it is about the heart beating and the lungs breathing. I am offering eternal life. Above and beyond anything that this shallow, material world can offer.'

He continued looking at me. 'You have lived a bit more than your brother,' he continued. 'He has had a somewhat sheltered life, whereas you—you have witnessed terrible things haven't you? I can see that in your eyes.'

I felt there was no point in saying anything. He seemed to know everything about me anyway.

'You lost a child.'

'In the womb.'

'And you feel responsible.'

'No—'

'Don't lie to me, Richard. The burden of guilt is heavy on you. You feel responsible for deserting your true love in her hour of need.'

'How do you know all this?'

'I see men's souls,' he said. 'That is what I do. Would it offer you comfort if I said your child is safe.'

'No it wouldn't!' I snapped. 'She's dead and there's nothing anyone can do.'

'Your tone surprises me, Richard. Do you know who I am?'

In a brief wave of nervous energy I burst out laughing, the statement seemed ridiculous. I stopped myself, crushed by his stare.

'I apologise,' I said. 'Like you said I feel responsible. I feel responsible for a lot.'

'You feel responsible for David being here, where he is happier than he has ever been. If he had not been rescued by me, where would he be? What might have happened to him?'

I supposed he had a point. If everything had gone according to plan David would have ended up in the city with the rest of us—and ended up the same way as Killinger or Roberts.

'I saved his life,' the Messiah added.

'What is life?' I said.

The Messiah laughed. 'Don't play games with me, Richard; that's my job. Come with me.'

The Messiah stood and pulled back a big red curtain at the back of the room revealing another door, which he opened. Despite the fact that we appeared to be on ground level we walked out onto a balcony overlooking fields and woods.

'You weren't accustomed to this beauty were you Richard, where you grew up? Every tree, every flower, every blade of grass, created with infinite care, infinite love. But soon it will all be gone. Nothing but fire, ash and brimstone.'

He looked at me and put his hand on my arm. 'I need to know Richard. Will you be there with me at the end, or will you forsake me.'

'The whole world is on the cross, this time?'

The Messiah nodded. 'It is the way it has to be. You know it and I know it. The world is broken, beyond repair. It needs to be ripped down, remoulded.'

'Like the Flood?'

'You know your Bible?'

'I studied it at school.'

'Where it was derided.'

'As fantasy, yes. It was studied as an antithesis to science. Something which should be avoided.'

'All your scientists, Richard, what has become of them?'

'They are all dead.'

'And their work has done nothing to further mankind. It has destroyed it. In the quest for advancement, man has destroyed itself.'

'Not everyone,' I said.

'That is true,' he said. 'I sense there is something different in you, Richard. There is hope in you.'

'Let me marry Miranda,' I said. 'Let me be with her.'

'I'll consider it.'

15

Being at the men's encampment was getting tedious. I became obsessed with getting into the Disciples commune, where David was, where I could try and figure out the Messiah and get him to let me see Miranda again. I could tell people were curious about what I was up to, but it was only Jackson who asked me about it outright one afternoon in the apple orchard.

'You saw him? The actual one?'

'I believe so,' I said.

'Did he seem real?'

'I don't know. I only know I need to get Miranda out of there.'

'Out of where?'

Reluctantly I told Jackson of the "selection process" at the women's camp. Jackson listened wide eyed and whistled through his teeth.

'This could be dangerous, Richard you know that?'

'I know that,' I said. 'That is why I have to get her out of there.'

'But David will never leave,' said Jackson.

'I don't think so and I won't leave without him. I won't let that happen again.'

We sat in silence for a bit before I said what needed to be said. 'You have to take her.'

'We've been through that one before,' said Jackson. 'You were convinced we were having an affair.'

'I was stupid,' I admitted. 'I trust you Jackson. You're the only one I can think of who can do it.'

'What about Hargreaves?'

'He won't leave either. Christ, I've got a bad feeling about all of this.'

'There is a way out,' said Jackson. 'We just need to tread carefully.'

'Her way out is with you,' I said.

'What about this marriage thing? That would get her out; out of that encampment anyway. You could live together.'

'And live happily ever after?' I said. 'No. As soon as Vincent and the others see me with her, she'll be in for it.'

Jackson whistled through his teeth.

'Can you get her out tonight?' I said.

'Tonight?' Jackson spluttered. 'You've got to be kidding!'

'It can't be left any longer.'

'Does she even know about this?' said Jackson. 'Have you even discussed it?'

'I haven't seen her, have I?' I snapped. 'Come on Jackson, do this for me.'

'Look this is just a big deal,' said Jackson. 'It's not that easy.'

'Do you want to leave?' I asked.

'I don't know really,' said Jackson. 'It's not really what I had in mind.'

'Oh forget it then!' I said standing up. 'I thought more of you Jackson.'

I turned to go and Jackson caught my arm. 'Look, ok, I'll do it. You're crazy for asking this of me, but if it means that much to you.'

'Do you know somewhere where you could go?'

'There's a settlement somewhere. We passed it on the way.'

I nodded. 'What's the matter?'

'I don't know Stirling, it's just—'

'Just what?'

Jackson looked around at the ground and sighed. 'How long is this going to go on for?'

'Not long hopefully.'

'No, I mean—we can't keep running for ever Richard. You know it.' Jackson stared at me with pensive, tired eyes.

'I know,' I said. 'But what choice do we have?'

As it turned out, that very night I was called to go to the Disciples commune again. It was David who met me this time, greeting me with a hug.

'It's good news, Richard,' he said. 'You get to see everyone today.'

'Everyone?'

'The Messiah said he has something special planned.'

I followed him into a hall and grimaced when I saw who was there.

Ten men were there, besides David and me; for some reason I made a mental count of them all. One of these was Vincent and at least three or four others I recognised from the selection process at the women's encampment. I began hoping in earnest that Jackson had succeeded in getting Miranda out.

'These are all the disciples?' I asked David. 'I thought there was supposed to be twelve.'

'Not after last time,' said David.

I could feel Vincent's eyes burning into me and I sat down trying to avoid him. Out the corner of my eye I noticed him whispering with some of the other men around him. In stark contrast I could sense David brimming with excitement next to me.

The doors opened and the Messiah walked through. Everyone stood and bowed. Being used to protocol, I followed suit.

'My brothers, please be seated,' said the Messiah. Everyone obediently sat and watched in earnest.

'We have a newcomer in our midst, Brother Richard would you come and join me.'

I could feel a wave of hostility coming from Vincent's corner and a solitary flow of warmth coming from David's. I wondered if he really knew what was going on around him. I wondered if the Messiah did.

'This is the natural brother of David,' said the Messiah. 'I ask you to honour him and respectfully listen to his proposal.'

I had no idea what was going on, but my awkward silence was broken by the doors opening behind me. Miranda was standing there, hair cut to shoulder length, wearing a white dress. Her face was cast down to the ground, her hands hanging loosely by her side. What was this?

The Messiah walked up to Miranda and kissed her on the forehead. Then he took both of our hands and put them together. She was shaking, her eyes didn't meet mine.

'Brother Richard has approached me and spoken of his love for this woman and Brother David has confirmed this. Does anyone see any reason why these two people may not marry?'

I glanced around the room to see everyone but two people avoiding eye contact.

'Then I pronounce you man and wife.'

The Messiah kissed us both on the forehead and left the room. David came bounding up to me and hugged us both. 'Married again!' he said. 'Two marriages must be twice as good.'

Myself and Miranda gave each other a look of resignation, our hands still interlocked when Vincent barged in, grabbing my wrist and placing my hand in his. He squeezed it to the point where it became uncomfortable and fixed me a hard stare and something which could have been a smile.

'Congratulations, Brother Richard,' he said between his teeth as he walked past me and out the room.

16

Being married meant that we could live together and we were given a hut near the Disciples commune. It wasn't the luxury we were used to in the city hotel, but the chance just to be together, unconditionally was priceless. The Messiah never visited us, in fact we hardly ever saw him. David visited us from time to time and I continued my work at the men's commune where I regularly saw Jackson and Hargreaves. They seemed happy enough and for a while so was I, but I always had the unsettling feeling in the back of my mind that it wouldn't last. There were people who I knew wouldn't let it last.

Eventually my suspicions came crashing to a head when Jackson sidled up to me as we were washing dishes after breakfast.

'Hargreaves has been arrested,' he whispered.

'What?' I nearly dropped the plate I was holding. 'Why?'

'I think it's because he likes men.'

I remembered the conversation I had with Hargreaves, several months earlier. To have looked at him then, in the commune, you wouldn't have thought he was a homosexual. He wasn't as limp and effeminate as he was at school, in fact he was becoming quite the opposite, he stood tall, talked with a deep voice and walked with a new found manly stride. I was certain that he wouldn't have made advances on anyone in the commune. It was clear what had happened. After failing to crucify Hargreaves ten years ago, Vincent had now decided to finish the job.

I was determined not to let him and so the next time David visited me in the hut, I asked if I could come again to the Disciples commune. David readily agreed and arranged for me to come to supper one evening.

Vincent wasn't there and neither was the Messiah. I had no idea what I would say anyway. Vincent wasn't going to listen to any pleas for mercy and as for talking to the Messiah . . .

I sat there at the table, with David and the Disciples, feeling progressively awkward. I got the impression they were planning another trip to the women's commune that night. I could almost smell the testosterone in the room as they shuffled around glancing at each other.

Halfway through the meal, Vincent walked in, wiping his hands on a little white towel. He cast me a grin as he sat down.

'How nice of you to join us Brother Richard,' he said, his eye glinting. 'A social call?'

I smiled in return, my nerves shot to pieces. This wasn't going to be easy but it had to be done. After the meal I managed to get him on one side and came straight to the point: 'What have you done with Hargreaves?'

Vincent smirked and cast his eyes to the ceiling.

'You disappoint me Richard. I think you know full well.'

'He hasn't done anything.'

'Homosexuality is a crime. You should check your Bible.'

'What harm does it do?'

'Don't be treacherous, Richard!' hissed Vincent. 'It harms us—as a community. It infects our very core. Don't you understand?'

'What about tolerance—and forgiveness and love. Doesn't that count for anything?'

'Don't be naïve!' scoffed Vincent. 'That's just an excuse for the weak. If we don't make a stand the perverts will take over.'

'I think they already have.'

Vincent shot me a look which made my insides coil. 'What have I told you about your tone, Stirling?' he said. 'You should watch it.'

'I'm not afraid of you.'

'You're a coward,' Vincent retorted. 'You're afraid of everything. Don't think I can't see into you and your pathetic little brother. You're both finished.'

As he slid away, I saw his face change to amicable banter as he melted into the crowd. He was a law unto himself. He seemed unstoppable and as I had predicted, my pleas were rendered redundant. This had left me with only one conceivable option. I had no idea however, the pain my actions would cause.

17

As I crept through the door I felt a breeze waft gently in my face. The Messiah was standing on the balcony. He didn't acknowledge me as I approached.

'Lord?'

The Messiah turned to me, a smile spread across his face.

'Come here Richard. Enjoy the sunset with me.'

The sky was painted crimson red over the line of trees. Flocks of birds pirouetted in the sky as they looked for places to roost.

'Isn't it wonderful?' he said, continuing to look into the distance.

I didn't answer but watched in silence as a hawk swooped in and snatched a small bird.

'All in balance, in harmony,' he continued. 'How can I help you Richard?'

'Do you think you can?'

The Messiah laughed. 'That's why you came, isn't it? Something is troubling you.'

'I'm lost and desperate, Lord. I don't know what else to do.'

The Messiah turned and leant against the balcony. He inhaled through his nose.

'Tell me, my son.'

'How much do you trust your Disciples?'

The Messiah looked at me sideways. 'What do you mean by that?'

'It's not beyond possibility that one could betray you?'

'Because it's happened before?'

'Yes.'

'What is it you're trying to tell me?' the Messiah asked.

'Vincent—'

The Messiah shot me a look.

'Brother Trevor,' I corrected myself. 'He has captured one of my friends and imprisoned him.'

I don't know what I expected, but it certainly wasn't the question that came next:

'And what's that got to do with me?'

I fumbled around, trying to find an answer. 'He is not a good man. I have known him for years.'

'You knew him as a child.'

'And he is still the same.'

'What precisely do you want me to do Richard? You want me to overrule his judgement? The one who I have appointed to keep law and order in this commune?'

'I want you to use your authority. Take some action.'

'I think our conversation has come to an end Brother Richard,' he said, turning his attention back to the skyline. 'Please never speak to me about this again.'

'But Lord—'

The Messiah raised a hand without looking at me.

'You can't just dismiss this!' I continued.

'I can and I will!'

'You don't know what's been going on.'

The Messiah glared at me; his eyes black and hollow in the paling light.

'I am unconcerned with details, Brother Richard.'

'Lord, there really is something you should know.'

It was then that I told the Messiah all I knew about the Disciples illicit trips to women's encampment. I don't know what possessed me; I suppose

I was just trying to get across what Vincent was truly like. The Messiah listened, giving nothing away in his face, before sending me away.

As I lay in bed with Miranda that night, my thoughts were of her and whether she would bear the brunt of Vincent's inevitable retaliation.

'It was the right thing to do,' she said. 'Think of all those other women.'

'We don't know what will happen to them,' I said. 'It might not have done any good at all. It was stupid.'

'It was noble,' she said, kissing me.

'I want you to just go,' I said. 'You can go with Jackson. It's too dangerous here.'

'It's dangerous everywhere,' she said. 'When have you known anywhere that was safe?'

'We will find somewhere,' I said. 'Somewhere where we can just live in peace, without looking over our shoulders for the rest of our lives.'

'If I left without you, I'd always be looking over my shoulder.'

'I can't go without David,' I said. 'I'm not letting him down again.'

'He's happy here,' she whispered.

'He doesn't know what he's dealing with.'

'He's a grown man now. Are you going to look after him your whole life?'

I shook my head. 'I can't explain it. I just can't go without him. Not after all this time.'

And so we stayed, keeping a low profile. Besides the fact that I never saw Hargreaves, life continued as normal. It seemed to be the calm before the storm.

Then one morning, several weeks later, there was a knock at the door. I told Miranda to stay out of sight as I crept up to the window to peer out. I could only see a dress and long hair; her face was out of sight. I assumed she had come to either thank or rebuke me for my actions. In a way I was right, although it still wasn't what I was expecting. I called out to Miranda that it was alright and opened the door. It took a few seconds to acknowledge the woman in front of me.

'Mother?'

18

She strode through the door and sat down on one of the wooden chairs. 'Some water would be nice,' she said to Miranda. 'It's a hot day out there.'

Miranda shot me a look and went into the kitchen.

'What are you doing here?' I said.

'Richard, don't be difficult,' she said. 'I came to see you—and Miranda. It's been a long time.'

'I heard you've already seen Miranda.'

My mother sighed and diverted her eyes to the table. 'We all have our duty.'

'Is that what you call it?' I said.

'It's something you've never understood,' she said, shaking her head.

'I've fulfilled my "duty".' I said. 'I've had it up to here with "duty". I'm sick of it.'

'I know you've tried to be a good son; and I have tried to be a good mother.'

Miranda returned with a glass of water which she placed in front of my mother. Neither of them looked at each other and Miranda left the room.

'She can't bear to be around you,' I said. 'Can you tell me why that is?'

'It was my job to look after the girls,' she said. 'I treated them well.'

"You prostituted them,' I said. 'You prostituted my wife.'

She fumbled with her fingers and turned her gaze back to the table. 'Your words hurt me,' she said.

'Because they're true.'

'Because they're cruel,' she said, tears in her eyes. 'I have only done what I have had to do. You think everything is about choice and it's not. You have never understood this.'

'It is about choice,' I said. 'And your choice is to be as high up in any society as you can. What is it you really think, what is it you really believe? Does the Messiah know how you used to corrupt his broadcasts, how you used to do everything in your power to bring him down—and now look at you.'

'Well why don't you tell him,' my mother retorted. 'You've told him everything else.'

'So that's what this is about,' I said, laughing with the realisation of it. 'I've taken away your little role. I've destroyed your little empire.'

'It was a rash move, Richard. You've no idea the trouble you've caused.'

'You came here to express your displeasure—'

'I came here to warn you. Despite everything, you're my son and I love you—'

'Please!'

'Just get out,' my mother said, standing and taking my hands in hers. 'Take David, take Miranda and leave. There will only be trouble if you stay.'

'I'd like you to leave,' I said, refusing to look at her. 'And never return.'

I stood there, frozen, jaw clenched, my eyes focused on a spot on the floor. My mother stood and stroked my chin and I felt a lump form in my throat.

'I've only ever wanted the best for you,' she whispered.

Then she was gone; just like that.

Miranda came and put a hand on my shoulder but I shrugged it off and went outside to cut some wood.

19

A few weeks later David came to visit. The three of us had lunch together and then David and I went walking through the woods.

'It's just like the old days isn't it?' said David. 'When the two of us used to walk to school.'

'It is,' I said. 'Except now it would be easier to play hide and seek.'

The thought of the two of us, as grown men in white robes, playing hide and seek suddenly struck me as amusing. David nudged me.

'I suppose there's more places to hide now,' he said. 'More trees.'

'Yes I guess so.'

'I'm glad we could meet again,' said David. 'I missed you.'

'Were you always praying when we were in the town?' I asked.

'Sometimes I was. Do you think that's bad?'

'Not bad, no. Although it used to worry me.'

'But we don't have to worry now do we?' he said.

'I wish that was the case.'

We walked on in silence for a while, our feet so used to walking together they felt in tune. I could sense his mind trying to figure out mine just as mine tried to figure out his. That was how our relationship had often been; more telepathic than verbal. In the end I just had to say it: 'David, let's get out of here. There's bad things happening here.'

'I've sensed something is wrong,' he said.

'You have?' I put my hand on his shoulder to stop him, taken aback by his agreement. He looked at me with his sad blue eyes. 'I can feel tension among the disciples,' he said. 'I can feel it like a knife.'

'Then let's just go.' I felt a wave of excitement at the prospect. 'We can move on. Find somewhere else.'

David shook his head. 'I can't.'

'Why not?'

David sighed. 'The Messiah is my Father, Richard—my spiritual father. I have always known it. I have known it since the first time I saw him on the screen. I won't leave him.'

'What about me,' I said. 'I'm your brother, or doesn't that count? I have spent a lifetime looking after you, searching for you.'

David shook his head, averting his gaze. 'Don't be like this,' he said. 'You know I've always looked up to you.'

'Have you really?' I asked. 'Sometimes I felt you were ashamed of me, sometimes I felt I deserved it as well.'

'How could you ever think that?' David said.

'I've been a coward,' I muttered. 'I've been stupid. I failed you at every time you needed me most.'

'It's not true,' he said. 'Everything that's happened has been part of a purpose, a destiny. This has been mine. It was my destiny to end up here, Richard. That's why I can't leave.'

'Well this is my destiny too,' I said. 'I won't leave you again.'

David turned and embraced me. 'You never have,' he whispered.

20

Rough hands grabbed me, a gag was put in my mouth and a sack put over my head. My hands and feet were tied together and another rope went around my neck, securing the sack in place. The fabric burned against my skin, the rope around my neck was tightened to the point that I begun to gag. Was this the end? Was this how I was supposed to end? I was carried and thrown against something metallic. A shock of pain shot through my elbow and up my arm. There were two more bangs—hollow and metallic. As I tried to get up, the floor came out from under me and threw me back down. I was in a vehicle, a van and it was moving, launching me across the floor from one side to another. My mind couldn't think, couldn't comprehend what was happening; all I could think of was air. I began to feel sick and feared vomiting in the sack and choking to death. The movement stopped and I slid backward until my head came into contact with a hard surface and I began to black out. I could vaguely feel myself been pulled out, feet first and propped up against a wooden pole. My hands were untied behind me and retied behind the pole which dug into my spine. The pressure around my neck eased and the sack thrust from my head. I was still in semi darkness when someone slapped me across the face.

'Come on, wake up, Richard,' said a voice.

'You shouldn't have pulled the rope so hard,' said another.

'He's alive, isn't he?' said the first.

A cold liquid was thrown in my face and some put down my throat. I began to gag as it went down my windpipe.

'Breathe, Stirling breathe,' said the voice. I recognised who it was now. My vision cleared to see Vincent leering into me. I could feel his hot breath against my face.

'I bet you think you are quite clever,' he said.

I shook my head.

'What game are you trying to play?'

'No game,' I said. 'I only wanted to save my friend.'

'You mean your little homosexual friend?'

'What have you done with him?'

'Oh he's right here,' said Vincent, standing aside.

Hargreaves stood on an upturned log; a rope was around his neck, the other end was tied to a tree branch above. 'It's ok,' he said. 'Don't worry about me Richard.'

'What are you doing?'

'Justice!' hissed Vincent, his eyes glinting.

I looked around but couldn't see anyone else. 'Where are the rest of you, you animals!' I screamed. 'Show yourself you cowards!'

'Brother Rupert has repented of his crimes and will now pay the ultimate price,' said Vincent. He walked up to Hargreaves, towering over everyone on the log. 'Isn't that true, Brother Hargreaves?'

Hargreaves whimpered in response and Vincent laughed.

'Don't do this!' I begged. 'I'll say I made it up. I'll do anything you want.'

Vincent slapped me round the face. 'Silence, you whore! Judgement is about to take place.'

He turned to Hargreaves who was looking into the middle distance, muttering.

'Brother Rupert Hargreaves, you have been found guilty of perverse and unnatural acts. Acts which have no place in our society. Acts which have no place in the sight of God. Acts described by the Holy Book as an "*abomination*".'

Vincent seemed to roll the word in his mouth as if he liked the flavour and I heard a few sniggers behind me.

'The penalty for this crime is death,' Vincent continued. 'Do you have anything to say before sentence is carried out?'

'I'm sorry,' said Hargreaves, his voice distant.

'Brother Rupert, you will now be hanged by the neck until dead and may God have mercy on your soul.'

Vincent nodded to someone behind me who emerged with a sledge hammer.

'No, don't do this!' I screamed and strained against the ropes binding my hands. 'You murderers! Stop!'

The man holding the hammer swung it back and knocked the log from under Hargreaves. I saw the brief flash of horror cross Rupert's face as he dropped. The rope snapped tight and Hargreaves' whole body flapped around like a fish on a hook. I gazed up at the sky, trying to blank out the gagging sounds. As I heard the rope creaking, I imagined blood vessels, exploding one by one in his head. I prayed up to the night sky, begged God to make this ordeal end soon. Eventually, after what seemed like ages, it did. The sudden silence brought both relief and desolation.

'Alright, that will do,' said a voice. 'Cut away the ropes from his hands and feet.'

I thought that they meant me, but I saw someone cut them from Hargreaves' lifeless body. It was obvious; they wanted it to look like suicide. There was now a crowd surrounding him. They were all wearing hoods apart from Vincent, who walked up to me.

'Now you know not to underestimate me,' he said.

'Why don't you kill me now?' I said. 'Because I swear, the next chance I get I will kill you.'

Vincent smiled and took a knife from his robes, holding it up to my chin. Then he lowered it and walked behind me. I could feel the ropes binding my feet loosen, followed by the ones on my hands. Someone threw a knife into the dirt in front of me. 'Why don't you cut him loose?'

There was the sound of an engine, tyres skidding against gravel, and then nothing. I bent down and picked up the knife. I walked up to Hargreaves until I was under him. I touched his feet and looked up into his twisted face, his eyes rolled back into their sockets, mouth half open. I climbed up the tree and cut the rope, letting his body fall to the ground. I couldn't bury him, but I dragged his body to a peaceful spot and left him there.

21

For the next few days I couldn't eat much and barely slept. The image of Hargreaves' face stayed with me. It haunted my days and nights. Several times when I did sleep I would wake with a start to find Miranda holding me, explaining that I'd been muttering or crying in my sleep. I had now seen three people who were close to me die violent deaths. The first had been Jackson's mother by the hands of Frampton; then there was Killinger and now Hargreaves. Each time it took something from me that I never recovered.

It was on the third day that Jackson came to see me. I didn't even have to tell him what had happened—he knew already.

'It's been put down as suicide,' he said.

'He took me to watch,' I said.

'What?' said Jackson. 'Why?'

'As some kind of warning, I suppose.'

'And you couldn't do anything?'

'Of course not!' I snapped. 'I was tied up. Don't you think I would have tried?'

'I'm sorry, Richard,' he said. 'I know you would. Have you told anyone else?'

'Only Miranda,' I said. 'She took it pretty hard.'

'What are we going to do?'

'I don't know.'

'We have to get out of here,' Miranda said entering the room behind me. 'All three of us.'

She sat next to me and took my hand. 'Please Richard.'

Jackson and I exchanged glances. It was of course always our plan for Miranda to leave with Jackson but I couldn't bear the thought of her leaving.

'I have to stay,' I said in the end.

'Richard!'

'I'll meet up with you. You should go with Jackson.'

'You have done your bit,' she said. 'David is fine.'

'How is he fine?' I said. 'He's still here, thinking he's in some kind of paradise whilst living with a homicidal maniac.'

'What if the prophesy is true,' she whispered.

'What?' I exclaimed.

'What if we are headed for Armageddon?'

'It won't happen,' said Jackson. 'I'm convinced it won't.'

'How do you know?' she said to Jackson and then turned to me. 'I won't ever see you again.'

I kissed her on the head. 'You will,' I whispered. 'I promise.'

Miranda left the room quickly and I was left looking at Jackson.

'Same plan as before,' I said.

Jackson nodded. 'If this "revelation" is true, we haven't got long.'

'Eight months,' I confirmed.

'I reckon something will happen then,' he said. 'Not the end of the world—but something. Try and get out before then.'

'I'll do my best.'

It was around midnight a week later that Jackson returned to my door. Miranda had packed a bag in sullen silence. She had been very cold and distant over the past seven days—but resigned. She was going with Jackson to this town that lay around thirty kilometres away in the east. I would leave when I could—with David.

We walked past the Disciples commune which towered over us in the dark. It looked completely different at night, casting its shadow over the valley like Death itself. We walked in complete silence as we cut through the women's encampment. I could sense Miranda shudder and I took her hand.

All three of us were in silent communion as we walked to the east gate. We all realised that this was the only option, although none of us were happy with it.

Finally we reached the exit. It lay unguarded and open. Theoretically anyone could leave whenever they wanted—it wasn't like it was in the town, but somehow it felt so similar.

I hugged Miranda and she put her arms around me. I felt her tears on my cheek, and her breath on my neck.

'I love you,' she said. 'I'll always wait for you.'

'I love you too,' I whispered. 'I promise I will come. I swear it.'

I kissed her and she wandered away near the jaws of the gate. I patted Jackson on the arm. 'Look after her, won't you?'

'You know I will,' he said. 'Look after yourself.'

I gave a wry smile and before I lost my nerve, walked away.

22

Things felt strange for a while as I realised that now I was the only one left who had broke out the town. Five down, one to go. I carried on living alone in the hut and going to work in the encampment. The story I told everyone was that Jackson and Miranda had run away together. It was ironic, seeing that I had once believed they had done it for real. I also had to answer questions about Hargreaves. I had to explain that it was me who had had found him and cut him down. I would admit that I had no idea of why he had committed suicide and that I had been too distraught to tell anyone about it; that is why I had left him to be found by a group of children on their way to morning prayers. No doubt by my omission, I had caused untold disturbances to impressionable minds. No doubt the sight of Hargreaves tortured body, his fingers gnawed by rats, his cheeks pecked by crows, would haunt them for the rest of their lives. I had probably caused a series of nightmares, wet beds, monsters in the closet. At least these kids could believe in a heaven though—if indeed God allowed homosexuals in.

There was a new atmosphere in the encampment, a quiet solemnity as men contemplated their fate; calculated their karma. How much did it take to get into Heaven? How many sins were allowable? Was the odd curse let go? How about an unkind thought? You could almost hear the mental calculations: *well yesterday I took more than my fair share of porridge at breakfast but the day before I had given an apple to a fellow brother, so surely the two cancel each other out?'*

I barely spoke to any of them. I would go about my business at the encampment and then return alone to my hut. If I needed a distraction I would go outside and chop wood. Sometimes I would write poetry.

Whereas before my poems had been quite wistful and dreamlike, they were now dark, unforgiving, relentless—a nightmare with fiery demons and nothing but your own tortured soul for company.

Sometimes I would pray. I would really try and feel something—anything. I can't tell you how desperate I was to feel some connection but I felt nothing. It was just me—talking to myself—alone in a room—with no one to hear me. I tried to comfort myself with logic. If there was no God, how could there be an apocalypse? The Messiah would be a phoney—as we had always believed he was and we would all be safe—to live another few decades in this brain washed, plastic coated illusion—planting trees and spouting drivel until we were all toothless old men.

However, I knew it would never be as simple as that. No doubt the Messiah could come up with a good reason why the apocalypse hadn't happened as planned. Maybe God had changed His mind, maybe it was postponed? That must surely be God's prerogative. Maybe He was planning on surprising us all one day? *Ha! You thought you were safe and now here comes the hell-fire. That will teach you for letting your guard down—**you do not know the day or the hour!***

I felt sure however that the Messiah **had** to have his apocalypse. This had been building up for decades—since before we first heard about it in his broadcasts. It had been at the back of everyone's minds for so long—the Apocalypse, Judgement day—Damnation—the end of the world in the year 3000. For nothing to happen would be a disaster. He might be able to explain it away but it would cast doubt, maybe even amongst his most loyal disciples. This led me to the most chilling conclusion of them all:

If mass destruction wasn't coming from above, he would have to **orchestrate** it

This is why I had to stay. I had to get on the inside even more to find out what was happening. My chance came sooner than I thought.

23

A few months passed before I was invited round to the Disciples. Out of the eleven, I recognised the four who had been at the women's encampment with Vincent; Peter, Luke, John and Paul. Luke had been the man who had chosen Miranda. He had a scar down the back of his left hand. I remembered it caressing Miranda's face. I remembered it holding the hammer at Hargreaves' execution. I caught his eye and he glared at me until I diverted it to Peter, a tall and wiry man with a black beard. He was sitting with Vincent, talking quietly. They glanced over at me and then back to each other, Vincent laughed.

Paul was looking out the window and John, who I took to be in his fifties and with a kind face was sprawled out on the cushions, sleeping.

The Messiah walked in with David and everyone stood up and bowed.

'I trust you are well, Lord,' said Vincent.

'I am feeling well, thank you Brother Trevor. I have been talking with Brother David. He is a man of infinite wisdom. I would urge you to listen to his council on all matters.'

'Your Highness,' said Vincent giving a little bow. 'Your judgement is as sound as ever. Brother David is a true man of God.'

'We are all facing Judgement Day soon,' said the Messiah wandering over to the window. 'We must make preparations.'

'We are all prepared my Lord,' said Vincent. 'We will stand by your side when the time comes.'

'I have faith in you Brother Vincent,' said the Messiah, putting a hand on his shoulder. 'I trust there has been no further adultery.'

There was a silence as Vincent and the others exchanged glances.

Luke bowed as low as he could.

'My Lord we are all repentant sinners. We beg for your forgiveness.'

'It is not my job to forgive, Brother Luke,' said the Messiah. 'You will all answer for your sins when the Day arrives.'

There was a further pause as the men shuffled their feet and the Messiah continued to gaze out the window.

'Sinners we are my Lord,' said Vincent. 'I can assure you that we have purged and repented of our sins. It will not be repeated.'

'I hope it to be true,' said the Messiah. 'If I find it has, the culprit shall be sent from my sight forever. Is that clear?'

'It is clear my Lord,' said Vincent.

'You should be grateful to Brother Richard for bringing these crimes to my attention. If it weren't for him you would surely be damned for eternity.'

I looked down at the ground. I couldn't bring myself to face the burning hatred directed towards me.

'We are grateful my Lord,' said Peter. 'Brother Richard is a man of integrity and honour.'

'He has caused us to see the error of our ways,' said John. 'We were blinded by lust, our eyes shuttered from the True Light. To have this further chance of Salvation is a blessing beyond any earthly delight.'

'Do you think I can't see through your weasel words, Brother John?' said the Messiah.

I stole a glance at John to see the stunned look on his face. 'Your Highness, please.'

'You pontificate and flatter but your words are hollow. You take me for a fool, Brother John. You all do.'

The Messiah looked into the distance. I could sense the Disciples considering their next move.

'It is my curse to be surrounded by cretins and fools,' said the Messiah. 'Not one of you is fit to enter the Kingdom of Heaven with me.'

'My Lord,' said one man called Simon. 'We have devoted our lives to you. How can you say this?'

The Messiah walked to Simon, an old man nearly blind from cataracts. I could see tears forming in his blank eyes as the Messiah put a hand on him. I wondered why the Messiah couldn't have restored his vision as he had done with others in the Bible.

'Brother Simon, you are a good man but you are not ready,' he said before turning to everyone. 'Out of every thousand souls there is unlikely to be one who is. Billions and billions of men, women and children, tossed into the Lake of Fire.'

'How can we save ourselves Lord?' said another man. 'How can we avoid this awful fate?'

'You are all so egocentric,' said the Messiah. 'All you are concerned about is your *own* fate. How to save your*self*. You are all so pitiful. Grasping at your own salvation like spoilt children. Not one of you has true love. This is what I am talking about. Selfless, pure love that comes direct from within, direct from God—except for this man.' The Messiah clapped a hand on David's shoulder. 'If one of you had a tenth of this man's love, you would join me in the Kingdom of Heaven.'

The Messiah looked at David who didn't meet his gaze but looked away. I had seen that look before—he was trying not to cry. I felt a wave of compassion for my brother. I longed to go and comfort him but the Messiah was already there, an arm round him, stroking his face.

'You feel this man's love,' said the Messiah. 'The only man here who would sacrifice his own salvation for another human soul. That is the only reason why he has it. If you remember one thing, remember this. Whatever you cling to will fall from your fingers like grains of sand. It is only what you are prepared to sacrifice, that you are entitled to keep.'

The Messiah then swooped out the room, leaving us all in awkward silence.

That evening myself, David and the other Disciples were in the dining room eating. Sitting across from me was David. The two people either side of him; Peter and John were slightly turned away from him. Simon, the blind man was sitting next to me.

'You know we all must take heed of what our Lord tells us,' he said. 'Brother David is a true Disciple, a true man of God.'

Vincent cast him a steely look over his soup bowl. 'That is true, Brother Simon.'

'We are all miserable sinners,' Simon continued. 'As it says in the Creed, we are not worthy to gather up the crumbs under his table.'

I noticed a few hostile glares from the other men, a few nodded in agreement.

'Brother David, you must teach us, you must show us the way,' said Simon.

David looked up, his expression was that of a cornered deer. 'I'm not worthy.'

Peter turned to him. 'Surely, Brother, you cannot be saying that the Messiah is wrong.'

David, penned in by all the stares sat looking down into his bowl.

'My brother is modest—' I began.

'You will hold your tongue!' a sharp voice said. I looked to see it belonged to Luke, his eyes burning into me.

'Brother Luke—' said Vincent.

'I will not take this any more. He is not even a Disciple, he has no voice here.'

'Brother Luke!' Vincent stood and glared at the man. 'Brother Richard is a guest at our table, invited by the Lord. You will have some more respect.'

Luke looked around him and shuffled to his feet. 'I apologise Brother Richard,' he said. 'My words were unkind and untrue.'

Luke sat down and Vincent gestured towards David. 'As Brother Richard was trying to say, Brother David is a modest man. It is this which gives him his virtue. Brother Peter, you will not put Brother David on the spot like that again.'

Peter nodded while narrowing his eyes at me.

'We are all honoured to have you in our presence,' Vincent said to David. 'I suggest we all finish our meal in silent contemplation and consider carefully, the words the Messiah has said to us today.'

As we sat there in silence I caught a glance at Vincent, his eyes were on me and the side of his mouth twitched ever so slightly into a sneer.

After the meal we washed up without saying a word. I noticed David had disappeared and I found him sitting outside, looking at the night sky.

'It's big isn't it?' I said.

'It's not true what they said,' said David. 'I'm no better than anyone else.'

'Maybe it's not a case of better or worse,' I said. 'But you've always been different.'

'How have I been different?' he asked.

I had to think for a while. 'You've always had faith,' I said. 'That's what's different.'

'Why did Miranda and Frederick leave,' he asked.

'They didn't have faith,' I said. 'I don't either really.'

'Are you going to leave as well?'

'No, I won't leave.'

'If you have to leave, I'll understand,' he said. 'You're place is with Miranda.'

'My place is with you.'

'You want me to leave as well,' he said. 'But you know I can't.'

'I know,' I said. 'And that's fine.'

'It's funny when you look at it,' said David, crossing his hands behind his head and lying back.

'What's funny,' I said.

'When you look up at the stars and feel so free, that everything will be fine.'

'I know what you mean.'

'I saw your story you know,' he said.

'My story?'

'You know the one you wrote about us all escaping, the whole family.'

'You read it?'

'I'm sorry Richard. I couldn't *not* read it and I loved it. I remember hearing Father shouting at you.'

'I'm sorry you heard that,' I said.

'But it made me realise, Richard. This was our destiny. We escaped and now we're here.'

'But what about our parents? Our father is dead and our mother is—I don't know.'

'This is our family here,' said David.

'How can you say that?' I asked. 'How can you believe that the likes of Vincent are family?'

'You know another thing about the stars,' said David.

'What?'

'The light from them takes years, sometimes even thousands of years to reach us.'

'I know that, I was taught that in school as well.'

'So we're not seeing them as they *are*, but how they *were*.'

'Oh don't start on this,' I sighed. 'You can't use that analogy on people.'

'That's what you are doing, Richard. You can't see that people have changed, times have changed.'

'Why don't you trust me?' I said. 'I'm your big brother, why don't you trust me.'

'And why don't you tell me anything,' said David. 'I'm not a child anymore and you're still holding back from me.'

It was true, but I couldn't tell him about Vincent and his gang murdering Hargreaves. He would believe me, but it wouldn't make him leave and would cause untold consequences. I realised this whole conversation was a waste of time.

'There's nothing to tell,' I said. 'Maybe you're right. Maybe I should be more trusting like you.'

'Brothers,' a voice said behind us. 'May I join you?'

It was Simon, his eyes directed into the distance as he leaned on his stick.

'Of course you can Brother Simon,' said David, leaping up to his feet to help the old man sit down.

'Thank you, my son,' said Simon as he adjusted himself into a comfortable position.

'The stars are beautiful tonight, no doubt,' he said. 'Alas, I can only guess.'

'Are you well tonight, Brother?' said David.

'I feel a little vexed,' he said. 'I feel there are dark forces at work.'

Myself and David exchanged looks.

'What do you mean, Brother?' I asked.

'When you are blind, people think you are a fool,' he said. 'When you are *old* and blind, well—no one even gives you any notice. It is like you don't exist. They let their guard down, you know what I mean?'

'Brother Simon,' said David looking around. 'Take a care with what you say.'

'When you get to my age, my son, you stop caring,' said Simon.

'What do you mean by "dark forces"?' I said

'I can't say anything for sure,' he said. 'It's not like I have heard anything but I can feel it.'

'What can you feel brother?' said David.

'Hostility,' said Simon. 'That's all I can feel—and a lust for power, I can feel it in my bones.'

At that point Simon choked on his words and put his hand to his face. David put a consoling hand on his back. 'Brother Simon, please don't upset yourself.'

'I'm sorry my son. I love the Messiah. He has been my redemption.'

'You are a true servant, a loyal disciple,' said David.

Simon put a hand up to David's face. 'You're a good boy,' he said.

David smiled and took Simon's hand in his.

'Can you not say more, Brother?' I asked. 'Who has the hostility, the lust for power?'

Simon looked at me, his white eyes bleary with tears. 'You know who I mean, Brother Richard,' he said. 'Don't make me say it.'

'Brother Simon is upset, Richard,' said David. 'Please leave it.'

I stood up and walked back inside. I heard a laugh and looking to my left I saw Vincent and Luke together. They caught my eye briefly and sneered before carrying on with their mumbled conversation. I carried on walking and went home.

24

A few more months passed without incident; with only three to go until the promised apocalypse there was a renewed vigour at the men's encampment. The apples were picked faster, the grounds were raked more thoroughly, prayers were said more fervently. There was little time for small talk. Everyone was in preparation for the beast with seven heads, the final plagues, the division between the righteous and the wicked. I could feel myself, an impending sense of doom, although I had no idea what would happen and therefore no idea of how to stop it. I only knew I had to stay around. All the time I thought of Miranda and what she was doing. I wondered if I would ever see her again; I longed to be with her but I knew that that wasn't an option. Not with the apocalypse headed our way.

Every day we would be drafted into the prayer hall and reminded of how the destruction of the world was imminent, how we were all miserable sinners and how the Messiah was the only route to Salvation. At the end of the day I would go home alone to my hut and continue trying to pray. That was my routine.

It was during one of my prayer moments that I was interrupted by a knock at the window. Looking out I noticed a man with blond hair and beard.

'Who are you?' I shouted as I scoured the room for anything that might be used as a weapon. I was feeling particularly vulnerable being stuck there alone and wasn't taking chances.

'My name's Elijah. I am one of the Disciples.'

Casting my mind back I didn't recall him being at the women's commune. I didn't know if he was at Hargreaves' execution or not.

'What do you want?' I called back.

'You're wanted. The Messiah asked for you.'

I looked around outside and couldn't see anyone else there.

'Wait a moment.'

I went to the kitchen and took a knife, concealing it up my sleeve.

'Please Brother Richard. I mean you no harm.'

'Come to the door,' I said.

I went to the door and slowly opened it keeping a grip on the knife handle.

'People usually come for me at the encampment,' I said.

'This is a matter of some urgency,' said Elijah.

'What's this about?'

'Please Brother Richard, come quickly and leave your knife behind.'

'Don't take me for a fool!'

'Your testimony is required, Brother.'

'Testimony?'

'A most grievous matter. Please, delay no further.'

'Has someone been accused of something?'

'I can't say, Brother Richard.'

'Is it David?'

'I can't say Brother Richard.'

I gripped on the knife handle. 'Please—' I whispered.

'I don't know Brother. There's not much time.'

I closed the door and walked back to the kitchen. I put the knife back on the counter and breathed through my nose, trying to steady myself. I would have to do this, I reasoned. I had come this far, keep going. I returned to the door to see Elijah still waiting.

'There is nothing to fear,' he said. 'We only seek the Truth.'

I stepped out, closing the door behind me. As we approached the Disciples lair I began to feel that this was the beginning of something bad, something that would forever shape the way our lives would turn out. I turned to Elijah.

'I know the Truth,' I whispered as I stepped through the door.

As we arrived in the main hall the other Disciples were sat there, stony faced. I saw David, his face ashen white.

'What's going on?' I said.

At that point the doors opened and the Messiah walked in, with Vincent by his side. Everyone stood to bow but the Messiah gestured for them to sit; his eyes cold and hard.

'Brother Trevor has told me some disturbing truths.'

I looked at Vincent who seemed to have a look of immense satisfaction on his face. 'Would you care to elaborate?' the Messiah said, turning to him.

'My Lord,' said Vincent as he feigned a cough. 'It grieves me to say this, but one of your Disciples has been untrue. He has been defaming your good name and trying to undermine your work.'

'This person has been blaspheming?' asked the Messiah.

Vincent hung his head. 'Yes my Lord.'

'Which one of you would betray me?' asked the Messiah, pacing around the room. 'I give you the chance now to redeem yourself.'

There was a silence through the room.

'Brother Trevor?'

Vincent coughed again and looked away. 'My Lord—'

'I have no time for this!' snapped the Messiah. 'Tell me the whole truth.'

'My Lord, myself and several other Disciples have heard a fellow Brother claim that you are not the true Messiah. That you are a false prophet.'

'Who has said this?' demanded the Messiah. 'Tell me now; my patience is at an end.'

Vincent mumbled something.

'What is it!' exploded the Messiah, flecks of saliva shooting from his mouth. Suddenly, the Christ had become the Antichrist. 'You will tell me now!'

'Brother Simon, my Lord. It was Brother Simon,' stammered Vincent. As the Messiah turned away I saw Vincent's face twitch.

Simon staggered to his feet, his face panic-ridden. 'My Lord?'

'You?' the Messiah roared. 'You would say such things about me?'

'I swear it no, my Lord. I live only to serve you.'

Simon sunk down to his knees and fumbled about on the floor, sobbing.

'Please my Lord, forgive me.'

'Forgive you for what, you worthless cripple. Don't you know that it is I who has saved you? Who set you free?'

'I would never say such things,' said Simon. 'I ask for your forgiveness for my conduct at this moment. I swear Lord. I would never say such things.'

The Messiah scoured the room. 'Who else has heard this man defame me?'

There was a silence for a moment before Peter stood up.

'Forgive me, my Lord, but I must speak.'

'You have heard this too?' said the Messiah.

'It pains me to say it, Lord; but my duty to you has to prevail. Brother Simon said to me that he believed you to be a good man, even a great man, but not the true Son of God.'

'Who else?' said the Messiah, strutting around the room like an impatient schoolteacher. 'Who else has heard Brother Simon say such things?'

'I heard it too my Lord.'

I looked round to see Luke raising his hand.

'What did he say?' the Messiah said, raising his eyebrows.

'Please my Lord.'

'Come on man! What did he say?'

'He said you were the Devil incarnate.'

There was a collective gasp around the room. I saw the Messiah's face turn as black as thunder.

'Please believe me my Lord,' wailed Simon. 'These are lies. Vicious, malicious lies. These people don't love you, like me. There are dark forces my Lord.'

Suddenly I found myself standing up.

'It is true my Lord. This man is innocent.'

'Silence!' exploded the Messiah. 'I will have no more slander in my house.'

It felt like the scene of a bombsite. This was the Messiah's empire, crumbling around him. He turned to Simon, still on the floor.

'Get up, you worthless fool!' he commanded.

Simon stood up, his eyes bleary, tears streaked down his face, but he stood tall.

'Brother Simon, you will leave my house immediately and never return. Do you understand?'

Simon nodded. 'If it is your will my Lord.'

'Brother Vincent, see him out.'

I looked up to see Vincent's face flash with triumph.

'I beg you my Lord,' I said.

'Come with me Brother Richard.'

I watched Vincent haul Simon off out the door whilst seeing the Messiah glaring at me out the corner of my eye.

'Come with me, my son,' he repeated, his voice softer than his eyes.

I followed him out through the door and into his private office. He sat in the chair and studied me, his hands crossed behind his head.

'You don't trust my judgement, Brother Richard?'

'My Lord, forgive me but this is a grievous mistake. Brother Simon is a good man.'

'Has he said to you about dark forces?'

I swallowed. 'My Lord, I am convinced Brother Simon meant nothing but to serve you. What he has felt, I have felt also.'

The Messiah looked up to the ceiling and took a deep breath.

'Brother Richard. You have told me your concerns about Brother Trevor and I know about the visits to the women's encampment—'

'I'm not talking about that, my Lord.'

The Messiah looked at me with his one eye, the other trawling off into the distance as he waited for me to finish.

'He has committed murder my Lord.'

I could feel the reaction in the Messiah, even though he didn't show it on his face. I waited for a response but he gave me none.

'Brother's Trevor, Luke, Peter, John and Paul all took a man and hanged him in the woods. I saw it with my own eyes.'

The Messiah carried on looking at me for what felt like an eternity. Keeping his face completely still he rose and turned towards the balcony. I saw his shoulder blades rise and a shudder run through his body.

'You are saying Brother Richard, that nearly half of my Disciples—half—committed such an act.'

'It grieves me but yes my Lord.'

'And what does that make me then?' said the Messiah whirling back to me.

'I'm sorry—' I stammered.

'A bloody fool that's what!' he roared. 'All these years. Three thousand years and when I return half of my Disciples are murderers.'

'I can only state what I have seen, my Lord.'

'Get out!' he exploded, his face turning red, his eyes bloodshot.

'You are the Devil,' I whispered.

'Get out of my sight and never return!'

I took a breath to say something and then just turned and walked away.

PART FOUR

The End
3000AD

Just one month to go until the promised day and I feel like a lamb being led to slaughter along with all the other men I am with. We have all just turned into machines; eating, drinking, sleeping, praying. Despite everything the work continues; soil is tilled, tomatoes plucked; seeds are planted; but there is little hope left. No one speaks of it but you can feel it like a wet blanket, smothering everything. I long for the time when we could be free, at least in mind if not in body, but those days are long gone. It is a constant tumour in the soul, a paralysis that stops any flight of fancy, any passing moment of pleasure, any glimpse into the eternal. I walk with an iron weight, as if my clothes are soaked through, with the knowledge that I have failed. All that struggle, all that sacrifice, all that pain, all for this. Whenever I catch a glimpse of myself in the mirror I shudder. I am rake thin, my beard is ragged. I am the hollow man—I always was. I only ever wanted something else other than the status quo. Isn't that what we all want? To be a little bit special? To be something and achieve something? To feel as if you may be the one person in history whose existence might stand for something? Now I realise I am nothing. An empty shuttle heading towards a black hole—to eternal nothingness. If there is a God, how could He be so modest as to take glory in us? We are all damned.

*

I staggered into the hall with everyone else to await my inevitable destruction. I had barely eaten or slept but I was swept along with the others like cattle. I heard the doors close; we all gazed up at the screen. The image of the Messiah loomed out over all of us. Before too long the Disciples filed out in front of the screen. I caught a glimpse of David although I couldn't see much of him. I imagined he would be afraid.

The Messiah himself walked out and everyone bowed. He walked up to the microphone and raised his hand for everyone's attention. In front of me I saw a small child cling to his mother's leg. She comforted him quietly, stroking his face.

'My friends!' the Messiah began. 'This is what we have been waiting for. The Day of Judgement is amongst us. Many of you will be wondering what will become of you, what will become of your children? I ask you, what *has* become of you in these past three millennia? I came before—and I died for you, for the sins of Mankind. I paid for *your* transgressions with *my* blood with *my* sacrifice and how have you—the human race treated my great gift?'

There was a pause as I heard the child in front of me cry.

'With contempt!' the Messiah continued. 'With scorn!

'You think you do not need religion, you do not need God. The Holy Father despises your arrogance. You build weapons of mass destruction to destroy yourselves and you think you are advanced? You leave your children to run wild in the streets and you think you are compassionate? Let me tell you even ants provide for their young. You—the human race—are no better than ants and like ants you will be washed away, like the vermin that you are.'

I started edging through the crowd towards the front.

'A lot of you may be thinking that my words are unfair. That you have followed me, given your lives to me and in some cases—this has been so.

'However, think of the sacrifice *I* made. Not *one* of you is pure, is sinless as I was—yet I died a criminal's death upon the cross. Now the debt is upon you—for the whole of the human race.'

I continued making my way through the crowd. The stale smell of sweat and urine hung in the air. I was focused on David. I had to get to David.

'My friends, your reward will be in Heaven. For your sacrifice, you will sit at the right hand of the Father for all eternity. I ask you all to kneel in prayer and beg forgiveness for your sins. The end is near for your physical lives but be assured. This life is but a shadow cast by the greater light of eternity.'

I had almost got to the front. I pushed past a couple clinging to another. I called out David's name.

'What I am doing is an honour. I offer you the chance of martyrs' deaths. The greatest honour of any human being. The noblest sacrifice. My gift to you. Farewell my friends.'

'David!' I called out through the fog of bodies. I saw David look up and jump off the stage. I pushed past the last few people and clung onto him.

'If we are going to die I want to die with you,' I shouted. 'I love you David.'

There was a hissing noise near to me, the sound of our end. Screams, moans, platitudes bounced off every wall. I buried my face in his chest. Just a moment I thought and then one deep breath to get it over with.

'I guess this is it,' I said.

He forced my face away to look at him. 'It's alright,' he said.

I composed myself. 'I know,' I said, resigned. 'It's fine.'

'No Richard, I switched canisters.'

'What?'

David was leading me through the crowd finding little alleyways to drag me through. 'He wanted to gas everyone but I switched it to oxygen. We're not going to die, not yet.'

'What, so we can leave?'

'We're going Richard, the two of us. I'm sorry I didn't believe you earlier.'

'Come on then let's go,' I said. Suddenly, the nightmare had become the dream. We could go, meet up with Miranda and live in peace forever.

The hissing sound suddenly stopped. There was a huge bang and we were pushed forward by the crowd. We weren't going anywhere.

'Stop!' called a voice through the microphone. I looked up to see Vincent there. What was he up to?

'Where are you going you fools?' he bellowed.

'We're getting out of here!' called a male voice. 'This is insanity.'

'And don't you want to know who led you into this insanity?'

There was a pause. I looked over at the Messiah who was being held by Luke and another Disciple.

'It was him!' called out another voice.

'Exactly!' said Vincent. 'He led you all here to die in a self created apocalypse. This is what he has been waiting for all these years—to watch you die.'

'What are you talking about?' called another voice. 'That is the Messiah! Unhand him, Judas!'

There were a few other calls of 'Judas' across the crowd.

'You call me Judas?' said Vincent. 'He is the Judas. He is the False Prophet don't you see?'

'He was sacrificing us for the good of mankind,' said a woman's voice.

'You foolish cretins! Would the real son of God have to orchestrate a mass execution with gas canisters? Look at these!'

Vincent held up a gas mask. I noticed that there were enough scattered across the stage for all the disciples.

'He didn't even want to sacrifice himself. He's a coward! He promised a global apocalypse and all he could manage was a mass murder of innocents. All for his own glorification!'

'Well what happened, why are we alive?'

'My friends,' said Vincent. 'I am a compassionate man of God. I saw what he was planning and I couldn't let it go ahead. I switched the tanks to oxygen. I saved you all.'

There was a murmur throughout the crowd. 'I say *he* is the Saviour,' a voice cut through.

'Here, here,' said another voice.

'Wait a minute!' a man said. 'Are you all willing to throw away everything we have believed in all these years?'

'And what have we believed in?' another man spoke. 'He's a fake, a phony, look at him!'

I looked at the Messiah, standing there, restrained with his head bowed. He barely looked the same man who cast so much awe and mystery throughout my life.

'I say kill him!' shrieked a female voice. The crowd roared in agreement.

'Wait a minute,' said a male voice. 'What kind of people does that make us?'

'What kind of people are we now?' said another. 'We've been taken for idiots and led to slaughter like helpless cattle. I say we slaughter *him*!'

I could hear David gasp next to me. 'I can't let this happen,' he choked.

'David—' I tried to reason.

'Well what do you say?' said Vincent. As your new Saviour, your new leader, I give you the choice. Do I set him free or do I kill him.'

'KILL HIM!' roared the crowd.

'Do I let him walk to continue his perverted lies, to exercise his evil machinations on another group of hapless followers?'

'NO!'

'Is he not the Devil Incarnate?'

'YES!'

'Did he not lead you all here to die—needlessly?'

'YES!'

'Did he show you any mercy or compassion?'

'NO!'

'So should we show him mercy or compassion?'

'NO!'

'Should I set him free or should I crucify him?'

'CRUCIFY HIM!'

I noticed David had collapsed into tears next to me. 'It's ok,' I said. 'It's ok.'

'Let me hear that again. Should I set him free or should I crucify him.'

'CRUCIFY HIM!'

A woman behind me was snarling, the crowd were shuffling forward, they wanted blood. The disciples pinned the Messiah, spread eagled across the back wall.

'Hand me the nails, Elijah,' said Vincent.

'I'm sorry Richard,' said David.

'No!' I called but David was already up on the stage. I ran up after him as he shoved Vincent away. David stood there, tears in his eyes, hands up.

'Please brothers,' he entreated.

'Get out of my way!' said Vincent marching towards him. I saw the flash of steel. David staggered back. I overtook him, grabbed Vincent's hand with the knife and rammed it backwards. Vincent staggered, his eyes disbelieving, his hand still on the knife wedged into his own chest. I grabbed hold of my brother and swept past them all out the side door on the stage.

'It's ok, it's ok,' I kept saying. I heard shouts and screams from the hall, sounds of stampedes. We went down a winding staircase, David slipped a few times. I had to hold him up.

'Just hang on in there, little brother,' I said. 'Almost there.'

Eventually I saw a door, it was ajar. I eased David through it. We should be safe from the crowds here. Not many people knew about this exit. Everyone else would be trying to get out the doors in the hall. I could hear them the other side of the building though. A few ran past us but they were a distance away.

'It's not too much longer now,' I said. 'We have to get out of here.'

We staggered on towards the gate, now only around a few hundred metres away.

'Stop!' said David, his voice faint and weak.

'We can't stop now,' I said. 'We're almost out, can't you see?'

'Richard, look at me,' he said. He moved his hand away from the side of stomach. It was gushing blood, a dark crimson in the moonlight.

'Let me lie down, Richard,' he said.

'It's ok,' I said. 'We'll just rest here for a bit and then we'll go, eh. We'll get out of here.'

David smiled and nodded. 'Richard please,' he said. I saw him start to waver and I caught hold of him, taking his weight as he sank to the ground. He grimaced as his upper body unfolded onto the cold earth.

'It's ok,' I said again. 'I'll help you. I can help you.'

'Could you put some pressure on this?'

'Oh that will be fine, it's just a scratch.'

I took off my outer robe and held it against the wound.

'I was always good at being a doctor wasn't I?' I said. 'Remember when you gashed your leg. I helped you then.'

'That's right,' said David. 'I'm lucky to have you.'

'Is that feeling better now?' I said. 'We have to be getting going in a bit.'

'Richard,' said David.

'We can't lie around all day, we have to get home.'

'I'm home,' said David. 'I'm not going anywhere.'

'We just need to stop this bleeding.'

I carried on pressing down. The blood soaked through and I doubled it up as I'd been taught to do and continued the pressure. You had to stop the stem of blood until the blood clotted. That was the rule; we had been taught that in school.

'Richard, wrap it around.'

'What do you mean?'

'Wrap the robe around me and tie it.'

'Ok,' I said. 'This shouldn't hurt too much.'

I threaded the robe under his lower back and wrapped it around tying it together.

'Does that feel comfortable?' I asked. 'Is it ok?'

'It's perfect,' said David. 'Can you come up here now so I can talk to you?'

I shimmied up and lay next to him.

'How are you?' I said managing a smile. 'You're not too bad are you?'

'Richard can you hold me?' he asked.

'I'm not sure I can,' I said. 'You can't move.'

'Just slide an arm under my head,' he said. 'And put the other on my shoulder.'

I did as he said and he winced.

'I'm sorry,' I said. 'Was that me?'

'No that's fine.'

I felt his tears against my cheek, maybe my own too.

'Don't cry Richard.'

'I'm sorry,' I said, pulling myself together. Big brothers had to be strong.

'Tell me a story.'

'A story?'

'Yes a story. You were always good at stories.'

'I'm not sure I want to tell a scary story now.'

'Not a scary one,' he said. 'The one you wrote before—about the river.'

'What river was that?'

'You know.'

'The one we could see from our window.'

'That's right,' he said with a smile. 'I really wanted to go there too Richard.'

'Maybe some day we will,' I choked through tears.

'I think so,' he said and then he sighed and closed his eyes.

I lay there next to him as I felt his heart beat slow down.

'Wait for me there,' I whispered. 'I don't want to lose you again.'

I stayed there for a while after his heart had finally stopped. I kissed him on the forehead and stood up. He looked peaceful there, sleeping like he did as a child; his hand curled up next to him. I could almost think there was a slight smile there, though I couldn't be sure. Either way I didn't want to move him, so I left him there and started walking.

*

I was wandering through the night. I'm not sure which direction I was going in but I saw nothing and no one, just desert for as far as the eye could see. It was when the sun came up that I remembered I was supposed to be going east. By the time I saw the shape of buildings the sun was high in the sky and beating down on my bare shoulders. I don't know what had possessed me to keep walking all through the night and most of the day, but eventually I collapsed outside the town gates. I can recall being lifted and carried before I passed out.

When I came to I was in a bed, I saw a face looking down at me.

'Hush now, you'll be alright,' a voice said.

I recognised the voice, it was a woman's voice, but it wasn't Miranda.

'Are you an angel?' I croaked.

'No, my love,' she smiled. 'It's me, don't you remember?'

I looked up and saw a broad smile revealing pearly white teeth. The eyes danced with compassion.

'Rosie?' I asked.

'That's right,' she said. 'It's nice to have you back.'

'Back? You mean I'm back—in'

'Yes that's right.'

'We came round in a circle,' said Jackson suddenly appearing at his mother's side with the same broad smile. 'But its ok now, Richard. It's not like it was. The bad times are gone.'

'There's good management now,' said Rosie. 'The old laws have been done away with—it's a free town.'

'What happened,' I muttered. 'I thought—'

'I thought it too for a moment,' said Rosie. 'They beat me, they beat me bad but I lived.'

Jackson put his arms around his mother and kissed her. Without warning a sob escaped from me. Rosie stroked my face, brushing the tears away.

'I know. You don't have to explain.'

'He saved everyone, you know,' I said. 'He sacrificed himself.'

Jackson came round the other side of me and gripped my hand.

'It's over now, Richard,' he whispered. 'He's at peace.'

'Richard, there's a few more people to see you,' said Rosie.

Miranda suddenly appeared over me like an apparition. She leaned over and kissed me.

'I've missed you,' I said.

'I've missed you too,' she said. 'And someone else has as well.'

'Who?'

She placed a weight down on my stomach. I looked down to see big blue eyes staring up at me, tiny little hands and feet clawing at thin air.

'It's your son,' said Miranda.

'You mean—?'

Miranda nodded. 'I didn't want to tell you before I left, but that's the only reason why I left.'

I sat up and cradled the baby boy, who gurgled and shook his hands at me.

'When?'

'Just two days ago.'

I leaned over and kissed him on the forehead. He still had the fuzzy shock of hair on his scalp that newborns often have. 'He's beautiful.'

'What are we going to call him?' said Miranda. 'Do you want to name him after David? He looks like him.'

PART FIVE

Postscript
3005AD

Five years on and Matthew David Stirling is a happy, healthy little boy. It gives me no end of pleasure watching him play and use his imagination in a way that myself and David never could as children. I have taught him how to play baseball, the game I learnt from Joseph and Maria's family—the first I had met in the free world. I play hide and seek with him as I used to with David, I talk with him often and I tell him stories every night—although I leave out the scary ones.

Rosie was right; the town is different, but not drastically different. There is still a stigma about anything which strays from the mechanical, although things are changing as people are stretching their wings and discovering what they can do, how free they really can be.

Two years ago my mother returned to the town. She was a broken, empty woman who had been wandering aimlessly since the dissolution of the commune. I think she had been cared for in an asylum for a while before returning back to what she knew—as we all did. I remember the first time she came round and Matthew was playing with a cardboard box, lifting it up and hiding in it before peering out and laughing at us. She just sat there rigid, clinging onto the arms of the chair as I picked him up and swung him round. I think she sniffed and not long after left. I took Matthew round to see her a few times but she didn't know how to react to him, how to talk or play with him and in the end I decided it was too painful for all involved, so I gave up.

Miranda and I are now both teachers at the school, the same school that we all went to; the same school that Matthew attends now. The lessons are much the same, but at least the children are allowed to play at break times.

Recently, the house David and I grew up in went up for sale and I went to have a look. I saw the room where David would sit and do his homework, where our parents would watch the screen, eager for the next propaganda video. I remember my mother calling from the kitchen about her meetings and how the Messiah was sure to go down. In the end he did—or did he? Recently I caught a glimpse of him back on the screens. Somehow he managed to escape and start afresh somewhere else. It gave me a start when I saw those pale, earnest eyes once again. His beard is now almost totally grey and he sounds more deranged than ever. No one really sees him as a threat anymore; he has nothing to threaten these days. People deride him as lunatic, although I wonder what hold he has on his new found followers. It astonishes me how willing people are to throw themselves blindly into a cause and hope for the best.

Anyway, back to where I was, I was talking about looking round our old house.

I remember going upstairs to the room which David and I had shared and looking out the window at the stretch of water in the horizon. I still had not gone there and I probably never will, but I see no need now. That stretch of water is in all our minds and in all our hearts. It is the magic that can never be stolen from you unless you let it. David never let it and that is where I meet him every day and that is what I hold onto.